FATES AND FORTUNES IN LITTLE WOODFORD

CATHERINE JONES

An Aria Book

First published in the United Kingdom in 2021 by Head of Zeus Ltd
This paperback edition first published in 2021 by Head of Zeus Ltd
An Aria book

9 7 5 3 1 2 4 6 8

A CIP catalogue record for this book is available from the British Library.

ISBN (E) 9781838938109
ISBN (PB) 9781800246119

Head of Zeus
5–8 Hardwick Street
London EC1R 4RG
www.ariafiction.com

Print editions of this book are printed and bound by CPI Group (UK)
Ltd,Croydon, CR0 4YY

MIX
Paper from
responsible sources
FSC® C171272

ALSO BY CATHERINE JONES

ONE

Heather Simmonds, the vicar's wife, and Jacqui Connolly, the wife of Little Woodford's doctor, sat either side of the big table in the community centre listening to the distant bongs of the church clock die away. In the subsequent silence, Heather gazed out of the windows and across the cricket pitch to the ancient oak trees that surrounded the outfield. The leaves were starting to fade and a chill wind made the branches wave and dance. There was a little gang of hardy teenagers, off school because it was the autumn half-term, gathered beneath one of old trees and she was sure she could see the odd puff of smoke rising from the group. She hoped it was just tobacco.

'I've got a horrid feeling,' said Heather, bringing herself back to the reason why she was there, 'that you and I might be the entire fête committee.' She tugged back the sleeve of her ancient black cardi to check her watch, also practically an antique. No one could accuse Heather of being a victim of fast fashion or designer clothes, as most of her stuff was recycled from the Oxfam shop on the high street.

'Let's give it another five minutes,' suggested Jacqui who, in contrast, wore a pair of beautifully cut slacks and cashmere sweater and which, most certainly, hadn't been purchased from the same outlet. 'It's only *just* gone eleven.'

'I really don't think it's going to make any difference. Olivia said she was working today, although she will help at the fête on the day, and I've had a number of apologies from people saying they feel it's someone else's turn to do the heavy lifting, and absolutely nothing from several others. I'd hoped that meant they were coming and I suppose they may yet turn up but…' She gazed bleakly at Jacqui. 'It's understandable. It *is* a lot of work—'

'Even more if it's only you and me doing it.'

'But it's very rewarding.'

'I don't think a warm fuzzy glow after the event quite makes up for the blood, toil, tears and sweat leading up to it.'

'I don't recall any blood,' said Heather with a faint smile.

'Ooh, I don't know – there was that incident about who should run the PA system…'

'Oh, yes. I'd forgotten. Anyway, I've got the accounts here and we need a list of people we might try and co-opt.'

'Like?'

'Like Miranda.' Miranda Osborne was a relative newcomer to the community and, apart from being wealthy, was quite a mover and shaker.

'Good shout.'

'And Maxine.' Maxine was a local artist and retired schoolteacher.

'Isn't she busy running those residential painting courses for wannabe artists at Woodford Priors?'

'I think they're only about once a month. I heard the hotel has a whole programme of courses and Maxine's art one takes its turn with creative writing, quilting, yoga and a long list of other things for people with a lot of spare time and even more money.' There was a pause for a second then Heather said, 'Sorry.'

'Why on earth…?'

'I sounded resentful – very unchristian.'

'No… human.'

'Moving on… I think we should each take half the list and try a serious bit of arm-twisting and I also think we need a poster to display all around the town. A *"Your Fête Needs You!"* campaign.' Heather pointed a finger dramatically at Jacqui. 'I'll see if Maxine will do the judging if we run a competition for the school kids to produce one.'

'Good idea. And if the poster doesn't produce a result and no one volunteers?'

'We can't run it with only two of us, so we'd have to pull the plug on the fête, give the money in the account to local charities and put our feet up.'

'Sad though.' Jacqui sighed. 'How much is in the bank?'

'About two and a half thou.'

Jacqui whistled.

'It's what we need as seed corn each year – the hire of the marquees, the liability insurance, publicity, the PA system… It all costs and most of the suppliers want the money up front.'

'So if we donate the money to good causes and empty the account, the chances of us running another fête—'

'Are vanishingly thin,' finished Heather. 'I suppose we might be able to get the council to give us some start-up money but that can't be banked on.'

The pair sat in gloomy silence.

Finally Jacqui said, 'So, we've got to make a success of this one.'

'Right, then,' said Heather. 'People we should

approach…' She pulled a battered old notebook towards her and started scribbling some names in it. Jacqui got up and moved round the table to peer over Heather's shoulder.

'What about Joan Makepiece?' she suggested, as Heather paused.

Heather added the name.

'And Mags Pullen?'

'Unlikely, but you can try her.'

'Bex?'

'Yes.'

The list grew and as it did, their morale lifted fractionally. Finally Heather put her pen down, ripped out the page and then carefully tore the piece of paper in half.

'Top or bottom?' she offered.

'Bottom. Right, let's hit the phones.'

———

On the far side of town, a second group of teenagers were gathered, but this lot had more shelter than the ones on the cricket pitch, because they were huddled, out of the wind, under one of the ramps at the skate park. The foursome – Ashley, Zac, Megan and Sophie – had been friends for a couple of years. To be more precise, Ashley and Zac had been mates in primary school but they'd drifted apart when, at eleven, Ashley had moved to the local comp, while Zac had gone to the smart independent school in Cattebury. When Zac's parents, Olivia and Nigel Laithwaite, had fallen on hard times because his father had gambled away vast sums, he'd been forced to move to the comp where he'd fallen in with Megan and Sophie too.

'How's your revision going?' Megan asked Sophie.

'Revision?' yelped Zac, sitting up straight so fast he

banged his head on a cross-beam. 'Fuck,' he muttered. 'That hurt.' He rubbed his head.

'Yeah, revision. That thing you do when you learn stuff ready for exams,' said Megan, trying not to laugh at Zac.

'But the mocks aren't till after Christmas.'

'I know but there's no harm in starting early,' said Sophie. 'What's the phrase? Prior preparation prevents poor performance?'

'Shit, if I start learning stuff now I'll have forgotten it by the time we get to the exams. I'll start on Boxing Day – that seems plenty of time to me.' Zac turned to Ashley. 'You agree with me don't you?'

Ashley shrugged. 'I've got lines to learn, so I can't concentrate on mocks till the panto is over.'

Megan and Sophie exchanged a worried glance. 'Which is when?' asked Sophie.

'The week before Christmas. I'm Jack in Jack and the Beanstalk so I've a ton of work to do. But after the panto I'm not going to audition for any other roles till after the exams proper. I mean, I know having a bunch of A levels won't make any difference if I get into drama school, but what if I don't?' He looked bleakly at his mates. 'God knows what I'll do then.' He shook his head. 'It's all right for you – get the right results and you've got a university place. I have to rely on an audition. Half a day, less in some places, to convince a bunch of strangers that I can act better than the other candidates. And what if I can't?'

'But you're bound to. Everyone says you're brilliant,' said Megan with feeling.

'Of course they do. They're friends and family and such-like. Complete strangers mightn't be such pushovers.' Ashley sounded really glum.

'Then you'll just have to keep trying till you succeed,' said Zac.

'Yeah, right, but auditions aren't free, you know. You have to cough up if you want to be seen.'

'No!' Megan was genuinely aghast. 'But that's awful.'

'It is, if you don't have the Bank of Mum and Dad to run to.' Ashley shot a pointed look at Zac.

'Steady on,' said Zac. 'You know what my dad did.'

'Huh,' said Ashley. 'I bet there's still a *lot* more cash sloshing around in your house than there is in ours.'

'Stop it,' said Sophie, holding up her hand. 'Arguing about who's poorest won't change things.'

'The fact is, I'm going to have to get a job and that on top of exams and everything else…' Ashley sighed. 'Still, who wants to have any free time and fun?'

———

In her big Victorian villa, next to the town's pub, the Talbot, Bex was sitting in her cosy kitchen, warmed by the Aga, sipping a mug of tea while watching her youngest, Emily, play with her wooden railway and her favourite doll, Betsy. Upstairs, she could hear her two boys, Lewis and Alfie, playing some noisy game that involved a lot of shouting and banging. Her oldest child – seventeen-year-old Megan – was out and about somewhere with her friends.

'Watch, Betsy, the train's going through the tunnel,' lisped Emily.

'Toot-toot,' said Bex.

'Toot-toot,' repeated Emily. She pushed the train vigorously along the track and it derailed. 'Oh dear. Naughty train.'

'Gently,' admonished Bex. The doorbell rang.

Bex got up, put her tea in the middle of the table so Emily couldn't possibly reach it and went into the hall to answer it. It was her old employer and owner of the Talbot.

'Belinda! Come in. Tea? Emily and I are playing trains in the kitchen.'

'I'd love a cup.' Belinda pushed the door shut behind her and followed Bex down the corridor. 'Hello, Em,' said Belinda. 'How's my favourite little girl?'

'Hello, Beninda,' said Emily and thrust the doll at her.

'And hello, Betsy,' said Belinda accepting the gift.

'You're looking well. But then you always do,' said Bex, with truth. Belinda's blonde bob was rarely anything other than immaculate and she always had a ready smile for everyone. *It's the job. No one likes a grumpy landlady,* she'd said, when Bex had first arrived in the town a few years earlier and had got a lunchtime job as a barmaid.

'You're very kind,' said Belinda, accepting the compliment. She waggled the doll at Emily who trotted over and grabbed it back. 'Anyway, I haven't come here to fish for compliments; I came to talk to you and Miles.' Miles, Bex's husband, was the chef at the pub.

'Oh.' Bex made the tea and passed the mug to her visitor. 'So, not a social call.'

'Not exactly.'

Bex went to the hall and hollered up the stairs. 'Miles, Belinda wants a word.'

'Coming,' her husband's faint voice answered over the boys' rumpus upstairs. A few seconds later, Miles, dressed in chef's whites, clattered down the wide staircase and into the kitchen. 'Morning, Belinda. Whatever it is, I didn't do it!' he said, with a huge grin.

'It's all right, it's nothing sinister,' sad Belinda. 'But I've been having a think.'

'Steady,' said Miles as he leaned against the work surface by the sink.

Belinda raised an eyebrow. 'I'm not getting younger and I'm running out of energy.' She saw the look on Bex's face. 'Yes, I am. And I'm thinking about retirement.'

'Oh,' said Miles. 'Giving up the Talbot?' He frowned. 'So… selling the pub, or putting a manager in full-time?'

'Sell,' said Belinda. 'Frankly, I'll need the equity to fund a new home.'

'I can see that,' said Miles.

'I'm offering you and Bex first refusal.'

'Oh.'

Bex who had been standing by the Aga pulled out a chair and sat down. 'Us?'

'Why not?' said Belinda. 'Miles already has a half-share.'

Which was true.

Miles and Bex exchanged a look. 'We're going to have to think about this,' said Miles. 'I mean, I couldn't possibly afford to buy the other half outright and I'm not quite sure that with a wife and four kids, I really want to get into debt. I'm a bit long in the tooth to want a mortgage.' Bex put her hand on Miles's arm, but Miles shook his head. 'In fact, whether or not I want to keep my share might depend on who buys your half.'

'Oh?' said Belinda. The surprise in her voice indicated she hadn't thought of that possibility. She sipped her tea then said brightly, 'Still, I'm only thinking about it and I probably won't put it on the market till the spring, so you've got masses of time to weigh up the pros and cons.' She gave them an encouraging smile.

Miles looked at the kitchen clock. 'I must get going, or I'll have my boss on my back for being late.' He winked at

Belinda. 'Did you lock up?' he asked as he cast about the kitchen for his own keys.

Belinda pulled a bunch out of her pocket. 'Have mine.'

Miles took them from her, and gave Emily a noisy kiss, which made her chortle. 'Back about three,' he said. 'Bye all.'

The stained glass in the front door rattled as Miles shut it.

'He wouldn't have to get a mortgage,' said Bex. 'I could give him the money. What with the money from the London house when Richard was killed, plus the insurance payout…'

'Truly, I didn't ask you to buy me out because you're the rich widow.'

'Well… not a widow since I married Miles.'

'But still rich.' Bex didn't deny it. 'Even so,' continued Belinda, 'it's a good business; you've already got a stake in it…'

'I know. It makes sense, but running the place is a lot more work than just being the chef there—'

'Tell me about it!'

'I honestly don't know whether we've got the energy for that, as well as the kids.'

'I completely understand,' said Belinda. 'You could always get a manager in – my flat will be empty, after all.'

Bex nodded. 'We'll think about it. We really will.'

'Good,' said Belinda. 'Now, tell me all your news. I haven't seen you for a gossip in ages.'

TWO

Heather ended the call she was making, put the phone on the kitchen table and crossed another name off her list. Yesterday, it had seemed relatively easy – she and Jacqui would phone lots of people they knew to persuade them to join the fête committee. Well, she'd phoned lots of people, but her powers of persuasion were failing miserably. She wondered if Jacqui was faring any better. Probably not. She shook her head and a feeling of despair seeped through her. When had volunteering – doing something for nothing, helping others – become so unpopular? She sighed and stretched. She'd had enough of phoning people and being rebuffed; she needed to go for a walk, clear her head, maybe scrounge a cup of coffee or tea off someone. Miranda might be a good bet – and even if she wasn't in, it was a pleasant walk up the Cattebury Road and she could come back via the nature reserve.

She stuck her head round her husband's study door. 'I'm going out for a bit, Brian.' As always, when working, he'd run his fingers through his hair and his fringe now stuck up like Tintin's.

He took his glasses off and polished them, before he said, 'That's nice, dear. Will you be back for lunch?'

She nodded. 'Yes, but if I'm a bit late there's some cold chicken in the fridge – enough for some sandwiches.'

'Very well, dear. Have a nice time.'

Heather grabbed her threadbare coat off the peg in the porch and slipped her arms down the sleeves. As she shrugged it onto her shoulders a button dropped off.

'Damn it,' she grumbled, as she picked it up and shoved it in her pocket. She'd sew it back on when she got home. Luckily it was the top button, so probably not too noticeable if she left the next one down undone too and pushed the revers back. She really did need a new coat.

She left the vicarage and walked up the road, past the cricket pitch and the graveyard towards the high street. The big rookery in the oak trees that edged both locations was silent, but a robin was sitting on the churchyard wall, chiding her for encroaching on its territory. It was all gloriously peaceful, although Heather could have done with the temperature being a bit higher – it was distinctly nippy. She hurried on, knowing that the uphill gradient of the Cattebury Road was going to warm her up. By the time she rang the bell of Miranda Osborne's big barn conversion, she was puffing slightly. She crossed her fingers in her coat pocket – *please let Miranda be in.* A sit-down and a cup of coffee would be most welcome. Actually, a biscuit wouldn't go amiss, either.

A shadow darkened the frosted glass panel at the side of the front door a second before Miranda opened it.

'Heather! What a surprise. What can I do for you? You've got time for a cuppa haven't you?'

'I won't lie and say I was passing,' said Heather. 'I haven't seen you for a while and I thought I'd drop by for a chat – see how things are.'

'Come in, come in,' exhorted Miranda, opening the door fully and stepping back.

Heather stepped over the threshold, into the bright, cavernous space and, as she always did, gave thanks she didn't have to keep this place immaculate – so much white, so many polished surfaces. And she knew exactly how much work it took, because she and Miranda shared a cleaner – Amy Pullen – who frequently let off steam to Heather about how much elbow grease it took to bring things up to Miranda's exacting standards. The vicarage, with its shabby-chic, was much easier to maintain, mostly because whatever you did, it always looked faintly untidy and mildly down-at-heel. A bit like herself and Brian, she supposed.

'Tea or coffee?' offered Miranda, as Heather took off her coat and dumped it on a nearby chair. Given its age and general tattiness, it didn't merit being hung up.

'Coffee please,' said Heather, relishing the idea of real ground coffee. No instant here, although with Miranda being vegan, the milk could sometimes be a bit of a challenge.

'Black, or with soy milk?'

Heather didn't mind almond milk, but wasn't a fan of soy. 'Black, please.'

Miranda led the way across a vast expanse of bleached birch planks to her huge minimalist kitchen and the shiny chrome coffee machine, which dominated a corner of the white marble counter. She twiddled and fiddled and a minute later, handed Heather a mug of delicious fresh coffee. Thirty seconds later she had one for herself.

She led the way back to the sitting area and the four white faux-leather sofas arranged in a square. As she lowered herself very gracefully into one of them, she said, 'So your visit has nothing to do with Jacqui's phone call, asking me to join the fête committee?'

'Err… not really. Although it would be great if you'd join us. You're such an asset – all that energy.'

Miranda gave Heather a steady stare. '*Not really?*'

'No, honestly. But, you know, if the conversation got round to the fête… Did you give Jacqui an answer?'

'I said I'd think about it.'

'And have you?' She was aware she might sound a touch needy. 'But I expect you haven't had time yet. Jacqui and I only met about it yesterday.'

Miranda stood up and made her way to the kitchen, returning with a notebook and pen. 'So, where have you and Jacqui got to?'

'Asking for volunteers – that's about it at the moment. If we can't get enough we really can't run it.'

'Yes, Jacqui said something along those lines. How many do you need?'

'A dozen – maybe fewer. More than just Jacqui and me at any rate… and you?'

'And me,' confirmed Miranda.

Heather felt her body relax slightly. If Miranda was on the team she was sure they could pull things off. Miranda wasn't the sort of woman you easily said no to.

———

Ashley was up in his room, the panto script in his hand, reciting his lines while trying not to look at the text. He was horribly aware that he was still only halfway through the first act and the cast was supposed to be off-book in only a few weeks. And then there was the niggling worry that maybe he should be revising for his mocks as well.

He threw his book onto his bed and slumped into his chair.

Maybe he shouldn't have auditioned for the part. But it was more experience before he tried to get into a good drama school, and acting was what he wanted to spend his life doing. But if he didn't succeed…? Oh, why was life so diffi- cult and complicated? Why didn't he want to do something like being a solicitor, or a teacher, or something… normal? He rubbed his face with his hands. He just had to succeed; that was all there was to it. He leaned over and picked up his script again and stared at the lines. Hopeless. He was reading them, but they simply weren't going in. Ashley put the book down and went downstairs. He heard movement in the kitchen – it had to be his mum's boyfriend, Ryan, because his mum would be out cleaning, seeing as it was Thursday.

'Hi, Ry,' he said, as he wandered into the kitchen. On the work surface, the kettle was coming to the boil.

'Morning, Ash. What have you been up to?'

'Learning lines – or trying to.'

Ryan picked up the kettle and pointed at it. 'Brew?'

Ashley nodded. 'Please.' He leaned against the counter. 'Did you always want to be a fireman, Ry?'

'Pretty much. I was brought up on a diet of *Fireman Sam* and *Postman Pat* – it was that or being a postman, I guess.'

Ashley grinned. 'Maybe I shouldn't have watched *Fame* one wet Sunday afternoon.'

'Quite probably! But then you've watched *Top Gun* and *Harry Potter* and *The Hobbit* and you haven't wound up wanting to be a fighter pilot or a wizard or a dragon slayer.'

'Good point.' He watched Ryan fish out the teabags and pour in the milk. 'Did you ever wonder what you'd have done if you hadn't got into the fire service?'

'All the time. Even when I was putting on the kit for the

first time, I was expecting someone to leap out and tell me they'd made a mistake.' He handed Ashley a mug. 'You have to believe in yourself, mate, and your abilities. You're going to make it, I'm sure of it.'

Ashley took his tea. 'I wish I was so certain.'

Ryan ruffled his hair. 'Don't be so hard on yourself.'

'It's tricky. I've got the panto, mocks, schoolwork and I think I'm going to need to get a job.'

'Job?'

'I've been looking at drama schools – most auditions seem to cost about fifty quid. Where am I going to get that sort of money? Mum can't let me have it. And then there's the travel… I'm going to need hundreds.'

'Blimey, mate, I didn't know. Maybe I could—'

Ashley held his hand up. 'No, I wasn't hinting – honestly. And anyway, I've got to be able to afford rent and food and crap like that once I'm there.'

'Aren't there grants?'

'I can get a student loan but that's not going to cover everything. Maybe I should go for something more sensible.'

'Give up on your dreams? You shouldn't do that.'

Ashley shrugged. 'Yeah, well… I suppose I could wait and see how the panto and the mocks go. If they're all right maybe I'll keep on going.'

'That's the spirit. Now then, I'm going to make a start on lunch in a minute – how about a bacon butty?'

Instantly Ashley felt a little boost. A bacon butty wasn't going to solve his problems but the prospect of something so delicious was going to take his mind off them for a few minutes.

———

Heather walked back home from Miranda's, not through the nature reserve as she'd intended, but retracing her steps down the Cattebury Road. At the bottom of the hill, after the road had crossed the river Catte, it did a sharp dog-leg to the left before it headed westwards to the town centre. On the south side of the corner was an ornate, gated entrance to a large private property – the Reeve House. It was, Heather believed, a house of some considerable historic importance but she only knew this from hearsay. No one she knew had ever visited it, not even her friend Olivia Laithwaite who had once, before her circumstances changed dramatically, been the sort of person who got invited everywhere in the county.

And now, to judge by the sign nailed to the gatepost, it was up for sale. Heather expected it was the sort of house that would feature in the pages of *Country Life* with the advisory note of *price on application*; code for *if you have to ask, you can't afford it.* But even so, she was curious as to how much it might be going for and what it looked like. *Might it be on Zoopla, or Rightmove?* she wondered, before she dismissed the idea. As if it would make any difference to her life, knowing those things. But even so…

She quickened her pace as she turned the corner into Parsonage Road and the biting wind caught her head on. She clutched the lapels of her coat and resolved she'd have to find the money out of the housekeeping budget to get a new one, before the weather got seriously worse. She reached the vicarage with relief and slammed the front door against the weather.

'I'm back,' she called, as she headed into the warmth of the kitchen.

Brian came out of his study to greet her. 'I was just about to make the sandwiches.'

'Yes, dear.' Heather very much doubted it, because he

wasn't great on keeping track of the time and worse at anything domestic. 'And no need to worry about that, now I'm here.'

'Good,' said Brian happily, confirming Heather's suspicions.

'I've just seen the Reeve House is up for sale.'

'Really? That'll be worth a pretty penny.'

'That's what I thought.' Heather got the bread out of the bin and began slicing it. 'Not that we care. And I very much doubt if anyone with that sort of money will become friends of ours.'

'God and Mammon? Despite what the Bible says I'm not entirely sure they are mutually exclusive.'

Heather began to butter the bread vigorously. 'Hmm,' was her response.

After Heather had finished the post-lunch washing-up and tidied the kitchen, she got out her laptop, ostensibly to carry on with collating the parish newsletter. The cursor hovered temptingly over the Google icon. Almost despite herself, she tapped the touchpad and then started to type 'The Reeve House' into the text box. She'd only got halfway through when autofill completed the search request.

'Like it was meant to be,' she murmured, as she double-tapped. And there, on the screen, was the house's very own Wikipedia entry, complete with a series of pictures. It was, Heather had to admit, very beautiful, with all the features one might expect from such an ancient property, which had, according to the article, been added to by successive owners over the centuries. That much was apparent from the Tudor, half-timbered wing, and barley twist chimney pots, the Queen Anne architecture of the other wing and the very modern pool house in the garden. It should, thought Heather, look a mess, with all those different architectural styles, but it didn't. It looked loved and lived in and, despite its size, cosy. *Although it's probably a nightmare to heat,* Heather told herself. *And as for the upkeep…!*

She tapped the keyboard and went back to the search engine and there was a Rightmove listing for the house. Feeling a bit naughty about being so nosy, Heather clicked on that too and felt her jaw physically drop.

'Four million,' she whispered. 'Dear heavens above.'

THREE

At the north end of the town, not far from Miranda's house, Maxine Larkham was pottering about in her studio. The studio was really a large summerhouse, with an overhanging roof, and a veranda, situated at the bottom of the garden of the Edwardian villa she'd shared with her husband, Gordon, for over forty years. It overlooked the town's nature reserve bordering their property and it was where Maxine spent most of her spare time, painting. As a retired art teacher, no one had given much thought to Maxine's hobby – apart from acknowledging she was quite good and that it gave her pleasure. All that had changed, when she'd started up an art club in the town, which had ended up being the subject of a TV arts programme.

Suddenly her hobby had turned into something far more lucrative than they had ever dreamed and a Maxine Larkham original could command several thousand pounds, while signed limited edition prints went for around five hundred. And more recently, Woodford Priors, the local hotel, country club and spa had instigated a programme of cultural breaks, where guests could indulge in the finer points of various creative activities – writing, sewing and water-colour painting being the most popular. Maxine had been the artist chosen to teach watercolour painting.

'Are you sure this is something you'd really like to do?' her friend, Olivia Laithwaite, one of the hotel's assistant managers, had asked.

'Of course. I love to teach.'

'But you're retired.'

'What's that got to do with it?'

'Don't you and Gordon want to spend more time together?'

Maxine had smiled. 'Olivia, we've been married for over forty years. We've spent *a lot* of time together. Frankly, I'm quite glad when he pushes off to play golf and I'm sure he'll be equally happy to get shot of me for a few hours.'

'But the courses are for five days straight. That's a lot.'

'Only once every couple of months. That's hardly full-time. And it'll be fun and I'll meet new people… Seriously, I think it'll be wonderful.'

As a result, her first course was scheduled to start the following Monday; ten students of whom she knew nothing, apart from their names and self-assessed skill level. The majority had classed themselves as beginners, except for one student who had inserted the words *absolute, total and clueless*. Heather smiled at the honesty and looked at the name at the top… Laurence McLachlan. She wondered if he was as Scottish as his name but, either way, she thought he might be a fun addition to the group.

She carried on with what she was doing: collecting some art books on basic watercolour techniques, sorting out images of flowers and landscapes for her class to use as inspiration for their own pictures and gathering up pencils, erasers and a thick wodge of high-quality paper. Normally she wouldn't go for anything this expensive for beginners, but given the prices this group was paying for their week's tuition and accommodation, this was *not* a bunch who would appreciate cost-cutting. Besides, it wasn't as if she was picking up the tab for the materials, so she didn't actually care how much each sheet cost. The hotel itself was providing easels, boxes of paints and a wide selection of brushes – things that could be reused several times. Woodford Priors was making quite an investment in the programme; Maxine hoped it was going to succeed. It would provide a nice little earner for all the other tutors too. People rarely got paid much at all for their craft skills. She knew she was lucky to have made the break-through that she had.

Maxine stood back and looked at her pile of equipment and wondered if she had every base covered. She could always nip home and pick up anything she'd forgotten – the hotel was only five minutes up the road. Her mobile in a back pocket jangled. She checked the caller ID: Heather.

'Heather, how lovely to hear from you. What can I do for you?'

'I'm ringing to ask a favour.'

'OK,' said Maxine slowly.

'It's the fête.'

'Oh yes?'

'We need a poster to advertise for volunteers. If I organise a competition for the primary school kids, would you judge it?'

'Will there be a prize?'

'There will, when I've sorted something out. Of course, the main prize will be for little Timmy or Lottie to have their painting up all over the town, but I appreciate they might want something more tangible, too – like money or sweets.'

'Yes, kudos is all very well, but a nice voucher to spend is even better. When do I have to do it?'

'As soon as I get my act together.'

'Can you wait for a week or so?'

'Of course.'

'Only I'm running a course at Woodford Priors next week and I really don't feel I can take anything else on till it's finished.'

'That's fine, honestly. The fête isn't till August and things don't really gear up and get going till well after Christmas. We just need some more people committing in the next few weeks, so we know if it'll be possible to run it.'

Maxine had a quick think. The town had been so supportive of her and of her art club. Without that, she wouldn't be where she was now. It was payback time.

'I'll come on the committee, if you'll have me.'

'Have you?! That'll be wonderful. Really. Thank you!'

'I can't do anything very useful – I'm hopeless with accounts and I expect my minute-taking would be worse than useless, but I can help design any signs or flyers, or stuff like that.'

'Perfect. To be honest there are very few formal jobs. It's more a case of pairs of hands, people to make phone calls, pick up donations, keep a list of volunteer stallholders, that sort of thing.'

'I think I could manage most of those things.'

'Good, great. I'll send over the details for the poster and put you on the mailing list for committee meetings. Cheers.'

Heather rang off, leaving Maxine wondering if her impulsive volunteering had been entirely wise.

———

Miles and his assistant chef, Jamie, were busy cleaning down the pub kitchen after the lunch service had finished. There wasn't that much to do, because the pub's lunch menu mostly consisted of quick, cheap bites to appeal to the office workers and shoppers of the town. Toasted sandwiches and soup were highly favoured, along with chicken or fish and chips. Very few lunch customers wanted the slow-roasted pork belly, or the lamb shanks, but those were popular with the evening clientele.

Belinda pushed open one of the swing doors. 'Got a moment, Miles?'

'Of course. You're OK to finish on your own, Jamie, aren't you?'

'Sure thing, boss. See you later.'

Miles followed Belinda back out of the kitchen, into the now empty pub.

'A drink?' she offered.

'No thanks. Just necked a pint of water.'

'So… have you had any thoughts?'

'About the pub?'

Belinda nodded.

'As you can imagine, we talked of little else last night.'

'And…?'

Miles sighed. 'Bex said she could buy your share outright, so no mortgage, no debt…' He paused. 'And you're right, we could get a manager in.'

'There's a massive *but* coming here, isn't there.'

'But I'm used to working with you. You and I completely understand each other; we're a team. I'm not sure I want to begin all over again with someone new.'

'But it might work beautifully.'

'It might not.'

Belinda nodded. 'But if you don't buy me out… it puts

me in a difficult situation – only being able to sell a fifty per cent share.'

'Are you saying you want me to sell my half, too?'

Belinda stayed silent.

'Is that a *yes*?'

'It's a *maybe*.'

'I see,' said Miles. 'That puts a slightly different complexion on things.' He fell silent.

'Are you angry?' asked Belinda.

'No,' said Miles. 'No, honestly, I'm not. You want to retire and your half of the pub is your asset – your pension plan, or part of it. I get that. I just haven't considered, till now, the ramifications of one of us wanting *out* of the partnership.'

'It was always going to happen at some stage.'

Miles shrugged. 'You're right. I've been an ostrich… happily cooking away, not really thinking about anything other than my job and now my family. I can't blame you for thinking about the future, even if I haven't.'

'The future doesn't have to be just yet. I'd kind of hoped to get it on the market in the spring, as I said, but I could make it later in the year. I *really* don't want to make things difficult for you, but I have to think about myself, too. I want to kick back and have a good time while I can still enjoy myself. I want to be able to have weekends and evenings off, not to dread sunny bank holidays because I'll be rushed off my feet…' She stared at Miles.

'Yeah, I get it, I really do. I feel the same – even with Jamie helping, I sometimes wonder what it must be like to be able to go to the pub after work, have a pint to unwind and go home for supper. Don't get me wrong, I *love* being a chef, I love being in the hospitality business, but whether I'll be able to hack it still when I'm sixty…' He shrugged. 'I think I might want to retire then, too.'

'You understand.'

Miles nodded. 'Of course I do. But I've still got to work out where it leaves me.'

'We don't have to make any decisions yet. I'm sure there's a solution out there – we just have to find it.

———

Miranda Osborne was a firm believer in the old saying: 'If you want something done, ask a busy person'. Bearing that in mind, she gathered up a notebook and pencil a few days later and walked down the hill, into the town and headed for the town hall. In her experience, people who were already volunteers were more likely to offer their services, than people who weren't.

'The poster campaign might bear fruit, but it's very easy to chuck that sort of flyer in the bin. A personal approach is much harder to ignore. How many, ideally, do you need to run this fête?' she'd said to Heather and Jacqui.

'How long's a piece of string?' said Jacqui. 'We need someone to run the admin side of things – the insurance, the Health and Safety—'

'Someone to co-ordinate the stalls, to make sure we don't have duplicates and that they're adequately manned,' chipped in Heather.

'A treasurer.'

'Yes, that's essential. In fact,' Heather added, 'we need that more than almost anything else. As soon as we start paying for those leaflets and handing out a small prize we're going to have to account for the funds spent.'

'In which case, I'll focus my energy in that direction,' said Miranda. 'I'll take all the contact details for anyone advertised on the town hall noticeboard as running groups and clubs, and give them a ring. I'll report back next week.'

'Do you think that'll work?' asked Jacqui.

'Only one way to find out. And what's the worst that can happen – I get told to push off? I think,' said Miranda with a broad smile, 'I can weather that.'

Heather and Jacqui didn't doubt it. This was the woman who, when she'd first moved to Little Woodford, had maddened half the townsfolk with her vegan-inspired protest beside the butcher's stall at the weekly market. She'd stuck to her guns despite the vitriolic comments she'd attracted. Miranda was not insensitive but she had thicker skin than many.

'Go for it,' said Heather.

Miranda stood outside the town hall and carefully copied down the contact details of the groups she thought would be large enough to include a treasurer. There were only about half a dozen, which was disappointing. Clubs, like the book group, were non-starters as they required no funding, had no assets and no expenses either. With a feeling of disappointment, she put her notebook back into her handbag and headed for home.

FOUR

Laurence McLachlan had a couple of reasons for being in Little Woodford – one of them was pleasure and the other was business, of sorts. Business was the key reason; he was here to look at the possibilities of relocating back to his native UK from America and there was a house in the town he wanted to view. With that in mind, he'd decided to book into a local hotel for a few nights so he could explore the area as well as take a look at the property – and the only hotel in the town had been Woodford Priors. Hobson's choice, he'd thought. But, while on the hotel's website, he'd seen it was advertising residential courses, one of which coincided with his visit. Watercolour painting. He'd always fancied learning to paint. All his life he'd been creative, worked with creatives, lived and breathed an arty kind of world, but, while he was good with music and words, painting and drawing were a mystery.

'It's as if it's been written in the stars,' he told himself, clicking on the icon.

He read the spiel about the course, the tutor, what was on

offer… the price. Jeez! But then he realised he was going to be getting bed and full board for five nights, a highly qualified teacher – some woman called Maxine Larkham – all the materials to get started and the whole kit and caboodle was going to take place in glorious surroundings.

'And why not,' he murmured, as he clicked the 'Book now' icon and then added on a few extra days' stay, for the business of buying a house. The bill was eye-watering, but what the hell? If he got the house, it'd all be worth it. He then googled Maxine Larkham and found a whole slew of information about her on Wikipedia. Star of an arts programme on British national TV, apparently. Secondary schoolteacher, founder of the Little Woodford Art Club, married, one daughter… yadda yadda. And then he found a site selling signed prints. Cool. Her stuff was certainly good – paintings he'd happily give house room to. And Little Woodford looked even lovelier when depicted in her watercolours than it did on the estate agent's site. And, furthermore, she was a local and, if he did wind up in Little Woodford, it might be nice to be acquainted with someone who could show him around a bit. Win-win.

Which was why he was in Little Woodford in late October, staying at the extraordinarily comfortable Woodford Priors Hotel and awake at a ridiculous hour because the eight-hour time difference between LA and the UK was playing havoc with his body clock.

He threw back the covers on his bed and loped across the floor of his vast suite to the window. Outside it was a perfect autumn day, with the trees all different shades of russet and bronze, dew sparkling on the lawns and the cobwebs adorning the herbaceous border full of jewel-coloured Michaelmas daisies, rudbeckias and autumn crocuses. In the valley he could see a wispy mist rising and the clear sky promised a glorious day. Wasn't this little spurt of late sunshine called St Martin's summer? Well, whatever it was, it was too good to waste.

Laurence chucked off his pyjamas, put on some running gear and five minutes later, stepped out of the front door. Wow, the air packed a punch. He rubbed his hands together as he set off at a steady pace along the drive and then onto the main road at the end. He jogged down the hill towards the little town, while early commuters swept past in their cars. As he passed the town's boundary, he saw a sign to a nature reserve, so he followed the directions and found himself in an area of meadows and coppices, bisected by a river. Even at this early hour it was busy with dog walkers. As he jogged, he lapped up the lush scenery and gin-clear air; so completely different from anything in LA with its acres of freeways, high-rises, tall palm trees, beaches... and smog.

He ran back up the hill to the hotel and decided to explore the gardens a bit. He knew from the website that Woodford Priors was set in several acres of parkland, so he loped round to the back of the hotel to see more of the grounds.

Beside the terrace that led off from the bar, where he'd enjoyed a pre-dinner drink the previous evening, he saw a signpost advertising tennis courts, a woodland walk and the stable block where the course was taking place. Time spent in reconnaissance and all that, he told himself, as he followed the path.

And there it was... a slice of English architectural gorgeousness. It stood four-square, with a central arch set into a plain front wall of mellow, creamy stone and behind it, a cobbled courtyard was surrounded on the other three sides by the old stables, each with massive double doors high enough to admit a mounted rider or even a carriage.

All these doors were open, but the shadows inside the building were so deep in contrast to the bright sunshine that Laurence couldn't make anything out as he stood in the entrance. On the block opposite the arched entrance there was a clock tower and, on the other two sides, a dovecote.

The sound of a bell ringing made him glance at the clock. Eight – time to get back to his room, shower and then grab some breakfast before the nine-thirty start. He didn't want to be late on his first day. He turned to retrace his steps and walked back towards the hotel through a car park. It was pretty obvious that this one wasn't for the guests – no Mercs or Jags or other high-end marques. This one was full of beaten-up Mondeos and Corsas and the like. And a blue estate with an open tailgate and a woman standing beside it, staring at the woodlands in the distance. She was late fifties... early sixties? Kind-faced, attractive and tidily dressed, without being fashionable. She wasn't Botoxed or fake-tanned and her pepper-and-salt hair was natural too. In LA she'd be a freak.

Laurence couldn't help himself. 'A penny for them.'

The woman jumped.

'Sorry, I didn't mean to startle you.'

'I was miles away,' she said. 'Wondering if it's going to be warm enough to work outside this afternoon.'

'I would say it depends what you're doing. If you're a lumberjack – almost certainly. If you're doing something less energetic – maybe not. And, if I may say so, you don't look like a lumberjack.'

'I think that's a compliment,' she said, laughing. 'Although I'm not entirely sure what a lumberjack might look like.'

'No? Probably not much call for them around here.

Anyway, I need to get going. Things to do, places to be and I'll be no one's friend if I turn up all hot and sweaty.'

Laurence jogged off, passing two lads in hotel livery, one of whom was dragging a handcart. He ran up to his room to shower and change and then thirty minutes later was in the dining room, helping himself to an excellent buffet breakfast. He nodded at a couple of other guests who he had seen the previous night and wondered if they might be on the course with him. He was looking forward to it. It was going to be fun.

———

Megan and Sophie stood that the top of the drive that led to the school car park, waiting for Ashley and Zac to appear. Every now and again a big double-decker rumbled past, bringing in kids from the outlying villages. The two girls were almost exact opposites. Sophie was an archetypal blonde, with a peaches and cream complexion and blue eyes, while Megan, whose birth mother had been Spanish, was blessed with Mediterranean colouring. Kim Kardashian to Sophie's Kylie Minogue.

'Typical, isn't it,' said Sophie, as she examined her long hair for split ends.

'What is?'

'The weather over half-term wasn't great, but look at it now.' The brown, withering leaves on the horse chestnuts that edged the school playing field were gilded by the low sun and the dewdrops on the neatly cut grass sparkled like a Swarovski window display.

'I know. And I bet it'll be blazing hot when we sit our As and as soon as they're over – monsoon.'

'But just think, soon we'll be able to take our holidays

when we want to. We won't have to take them after school breaks up.'

'Don't you find that a bit scary?' said Megan.

'What?'

'Leaving school, having to get a job, look after ourselves.'

'Not really. I've been cooking and doing all that house-work stuff for years. Anyhow, I'll probably have to stay around here, 'cos who will look after Mum if I push off to uni?'

'Yeah, sorry.'

'Don't be. I'm going to apply to Cattebury College, then I can commute.'

'But—'

'Look, here's the boys.' Sophie dropped her hank of hair and waved to them. 'How's the panto going, Ash?'

'OK, thanks,' he answered. 'I kinda wish I hadn't said I'd be Jack – after what you girls said about revision. I'm getting worried I've got too much on.'

Zac yawned pointedly. 'Change the record, Ash. No one made you audition.'

'Don't be mean, Zac,' said Megan. 'Not everyone is like you and doesn't care about their future.'

'I *do* care.'

'Huh – you've got no excuse not to have started work for your mocks then,' she said.

'But they're months away.'

'Ten weeks, Zac. Ten weeks. And there's Christmas slap-bang in the middle, and we've still got course work to do, assignments to hand in, your personal statement to write for your UCAS application…'

'OK, OK,' said Zac. 'I *do* know.' He glared at her. 'I'll get it done – all of it. I got my GCSEs, didn't I?'

Which was true. They might have been considerably

better results if he hadn't fallen in with the local drug scene, but he'd managed to clean up his act and knuckle down enough to pass most of his exams with relatively decent grades – all things considered.

'Stop it,' said Sophie. 'God, if we're all stressy and edgy now, what will we be like by the summer? Live and let live.'

Megan sighed but dropped the subject. Sophie was right – she usually was – it wasn't her place to interfere in someone else's life. Besides, she had her own worries. The night before, she'd heard her parents discussing Belinda's plans to sell the pub. She hadn't been able to hear everything, because the sitting room door was shut but Miles, her stepdad, had sounded quite worried. Megan didn't understand the ins and outs, but all she could think about was that if Belinda sold up, he might lose his job. Then what? Bex couldn't go out to work, not with little Emily to look after. What would happen to them all?

It wasn't as if life had been plain sailing this far, either. It was one of the reasons she and Sophie got on so well – they'd both had tricky childhoods. Sophie's mother had MS and Megan's birth mother had abandoned her father and her when she was just two – fleeing back to Spain. Her father had employed a nanny – Bex. Both of them adored her and Megan had been thrilled when they'd married and produced two little brothers for her. But then, when she was fourteen, her father had been killed. A lorry had run a red light and knocked him off his bike. They'd made a fresh start in the country, away from the memories, and here Bex had met the wonderful Miles and fallen in love with him. But despite this happy ending, Megan was only too aware that life could still be unpredictable and nothing could be taken for granted.

Zac, however, obviously seemed to take everything for granted.

FIVE

Laurence and the other members of the art course straggled along the path that led to the stable block in plenty of time for the nine-thirty start. Having seen it once already that morning, he was prepared for the impact and was amused by the 'oohs' and 'aahs' of his fellow students. But even he was impressed when they got inside and saw the incredibly sympathetic make-over that had been wrought to turn the building into an art studio. He walked around it, absorbing all the original features: the exposed beams in the roof space, the stone water trough, the cast-iron mangers, some highly polished tack artfully arranged on trestles… It was glorious.

Dotted around the floor were a dozen easels and chairs and, beside each work station, was a table with a top-of-the-range box of watercolours, pencils, a selection of brushes in a pot, a large jug of water and an acrylic watercolour palette. At the front was the tutor's desk and, in one corner, small armchairs were grouped around low tables and there was another, larger cloth-covered one, with a small electric boiler, mugs, jugs of milk and water and a selection of every sort of tea or coffee anyone could wish for. Beside it was a small chiller filled with complimentary cold drinks. But the highlight of the room was the long exterior wall with its huge bifold doors running its length, bringing light and a magical view over a wooded valley into the room. Laurence didn't think he'd ever seen a better classroom.

Having finished his tour of the room, Laurence made his way back to the workstations to bag a vacant one for himself and saw someone else push open the main door, someone carrying a laptop and some books and heading for the front table – the lumberjack lady.

He strode confidently forward. 'Hi,' he said holding out his hand. 'Of course, I knew all along you weren't a lumberjack. Can I assume that you're our tutor?'

Laughing, the woman put down her stuff and shook his hand.

'Good morning,' said the tutor, addressing the room. 'As you have probably guessed, I am Maxine Larkham and I will be teaching you about watercolour painting over the next few days. Now, it doesn't matter if you are a complete beginner—'

'Which is a relief for some of us,' Laurence interrupted. The other students laughed.

'—or if you've already done a fair bit,' continued Max. 'This isn't a competition and my aim is to enthuse you with this medium so you feel confident about continuing on your own. If you carry on painting, whether for profit or pleasure, I will be thrilled. So, before we start, I think we ought to get to know each other and I suggest we help ourselves to a drink – there's tea, coffee or cold drinks at the back – then sit around that table and have a little chat. How does that sound?'

'Sounds good to me,' said Laurence.

Once everyone had their drink of choice and had settled into the armchairs, Maxine began.

'I think some of you might have already met up in the hotel, especially if you stayed last night, but let's go round the room so each of you can tell us your name and a little bit about yourself for the benefit of everyone else.' She pointed to a mousy woman on her immediate left. 'We'll start with you, if you don't mind.' She smiled encouragingly.

'Oh… right… well… er… I'm Brenda. My husband died last year and I've always wanted to try painting but I never seemed to have the time what with one thing and another and besides, John – that was my husband – wasn't keen on me joining things. He said clubs and suchlike were only in it for the subscriptions and didn't care about the members and were a waste of money. Well, it's my money now…' She petered out after her flash of rebelliousness and gave the group an embarrassed smile.

It seemed to Laurence that Brenda was well rid of John.

The introductions continued, but after Brenda's revelation most of the other reasons for attendance were pretty prosaic. Annie was here because she'd been good at art at school, but her career, three children and a busy life meant she hadn't had much of an opportunity to try painting, 'Apart from walls and ceilings,' till she'd retired last year. Charles's reason was an impulse buy, when he'd seen the course advertised. One student was a fan of Maxine's. Another, Peter, had recently gone through a very messy divorce and hoped he might meet someone with similar interests… and then it was Laurence's turn.

'My name is Laurence McLachlan and, as you can probably guess from my accent, I'm a Scot. I've never picked up a paintbrush in my life, but I work with a lot of creative types and I felt I ought to make an effort to understand what some of these guys do in their spare time. Besides, why not? A fabulous setting, a top-quality hotel and a world-class artist as a teacher.' He saw Maxine blush. 'Well, it's true,' he said, 'I've seen your stuff on the internet.'

After half an hour the introductions had been made, the teas and coffees drunk, and it was time to start the course proper.

'We're going to start off with the basics... drawing,' said Maxine.

She led the way to the other end of the room and the students stood in front of their easels while she began to explain about perspective.

At the end of the morning Laurence was pretty sure he'd never make an artist. Perspective, despite Maxine's best efforts, was a mystery. 'You stick to what you know, buddy,' he told himself as he reached for his rubber yet again.

———

Quite apart from being the vicar's wife, Heather was a part-time teaching assistant at the comp. She used to do more hours, but the last few years had seen her reduce her commitment to a couple of days a week. And this morning, as she sat in the staff room during the morning break and sipped a cup of tea, she wondered if she and Brian could afford for her to cut back to just one day. For a couple of years now they'd let out their best spare bedroom on Airbnb but the income from that was sporadic; none of their guests had the least problem with the setting, the tranquillity, the area or the glorious breakfasts Heather cooked but, being an outdated vicarage, their spare bedroom had no en suite. For some, that was a deal breaker. When they had guests, Heather and Brian used the downstairs loo and, both being early risers, would shower before seven, leaving the bathroom pristine. But even the promise that their guests would have exclusive use of the bathroom for ninety-five per cent of the time, wasn't enough to persuade many. And it was unlikely the Church would look favourably on them fitting another bathroom in the vicarage – even if they could afford the expense.

She was, Heather admitted as she took a bite of a chocolate hobnob, not getting any younger and when she'd arrived at the school gates this morning, after the half-term break, she'd felt devoid of energy. She'd smiled and greeted the kids she passed, she'd chatted to the teachers in the staff room as she waited for the first bell to go, but the thought of spending a whole day helping, cajoling and encouraging her assigned students, or even restraining the more challenging or difficult pupils, had made her want to close her eyes and sleep till the school day was over. But she couldn't and so she hoped that a large mug of tea and a sugar rush from the biscuit might see her through till lunch. She let her mind drift…

'What's this I hear about yet another new estate in Little Woodford?' She recognised the voice as belonging to David Johnson, head of maths and stalwart of the town's am-dram society.

Heather's ears pricked up. Another new estate? Where? And surely the town didn't need more residents? The school was full to bursting as it stood.

'Tell me more,' said Irene Blake, one of the humanities teachers.

'I don't know for sure but I've heard a rumour that the big field off the ring road, behind the churchyard, has been offered up in the council's call for sites.'

Heather gripped her mug tighter. She knew that field; it was the one they used for the fête.

'They won't give it planning will they?' asked Irene.

'Why not? It's within the town's envelope and the council is always banging on about the need for affordable housing—'

Irene interrupted David. 'Talking of affordable... have you seen what the Reeve House is being sold for?' Her voice was high-pitched with excitement.

'No, tell me.'

'Four million,' Irene squeaked. 'Or, to be more exact, offers in *excess* of four million.'

'Well, it's a lovely house, river frontage, lots of land...'

'But even so...' The pair drifted away, speculating on who might have the kind of money for a house like that, leaving Heather digesting the news that the field, used for decades for the fête, might be subsumed by a housing estate.

First it was the lack of volunteers for the committee and now this. What else would happen to try and stop their fête? Heather felt even wearier.

———

Miles and Bex were in their kitchen. Emily was in her high chair playing with Play-Doh, cutting out shapes with some old cookie cutters. The other children were back at school and their parents were revelling in the peace and quiet, after the hurly-burly of half-term.

'You don't have to get a mortgage,' said Bex.

Miles shook his head. 'I know and your offer is very generous but I am *not* going to take your money.'

'*Our* money,' said Bex.

Miles pushed back his chair and stood up. He went and looked out of the kitchen window. 'Yours, ours, mine... it's still a no. I don't want to buy Belinda out. Cooking is my life but I'm not a businessman; I know that. And I spend enough time there – evenings, weekends, bank holidays – as it is. I want to see this little one grow up. I want to take Megan to her university and help her unpack. I want to play with the boys. I want to help with their homework, watch their sports matches… If I try and manage the pub as well as cook there, do the accounts, do the ordering—' Miles shook his head and ran his hands through his hair. 'No.'

'Then sell your half share,' said Bex reasonably. She picked up a star shape and pressed it into Emily's dough.

'Pretty,' gurgled her daughter.

'But if I do that, I'll have no say in what the new owners do.'

'You can't have it both ways.'

'I know.'

'You could sell your share and find another job.'

Miles frowned. 'There's not much around here – let's face it. The Talbot is the only pub in town.'

'There's Woodford Priors.'

Miles considered this, before he shook his head. 'It'd probably mean a pay cut. They've got a head chef and, even if they've got a vacancy or two, I'd have to take a sous chef post or maybe a chef de partie role… It wouldn't be the same as being my own boss.'

'I see that, but if you stayed there…' Bex gave a little shrug. 'Promotion…?'

'Maybe. I don't think there's much of a churn at the hotel amongst the senior staff. I think it's only the kitchen juniors who move on.'

'We could ask Olivia to keep her ear to the ground for us. If the right role did come up, and you were ready, it would save them a fortune on recruiting.'

Miles sighed. 'I don't know. I really don't.'

'Suppose you tell Belinda that when she comes to sell,

your half will be up for grabs too, and we cross the bridge of *who you then work for*, when the pub is sold? You may love the new owner, you may find you fit seamlessly into the new regime, with the added bonus of having a blooming great cushion of money stashed in your bank account for a rainy day.'

'I'll think about it,' said Miles. He glanced at the kitchen clock. 'Time I went to work.' He kissed his daughter's forehead and then the top of Bex's head. 'See you about three.'

'See you. Love you,' said Bex, as Miles headed out of the kitchen.

After he'd gone Bex got out her mobile and texted Olivia.

A favour? Is there much turnover with the chefs in the hotel kitchen? Asking for a friend. ☺

SIX

On her way home from the school, Heather went into the town hall. Cynthia, the town hall receptionist, fount of all knowledge and dispenser of information to visitors and tourists, manned the desk. In front of her were glossy leaflets about the local area and a stack of maps of the town.

'Oh, hello, Mrs Simmonds,' said Cynthia, looking up as the door opened. 'What can I do for you?' Heather was a regular visitor to the town hall, usually needing notices about church services or appeals for volunteers to be placed in the town's newsletter.

'Hi, Cynthia. Is there someone I can speak to about planning?'

'Planning? For the vicarage?'

'Goodness me, no. I've heard a rumour…'

'A rumour about?'

'Parsley Field – where we hold the fête.'

'I think you'll need to speak to the clerk.' Cynthia picked up a phone on her desk and pressed a couple of buttons. 'Yes… The vicar's wife, Mrs Simmonds is here… About

Parsley Field...' She put the phone down. 'He's coming through.'

Cynthia had barely replaced the receiver, when a man unknown to Heather came through the door.

Heather, you haven't met our new clerk, have you?' said Cynthia. 'Heather, meet Tony Glenham, Tony, this is Mrs Simmonds.'

'Tony, please,' he said smoothly. A bit too smoothly for Heather's taste, as he extended a hand.

She shook it, but didn't reciprocate with her Christian name. She didn't feel they were going to be friends.

'Come through to my office.'

Heather followed him into the back rooms of the town hall. The main meeting room, with which Heather was very familiar, was on the first floor but she couldn't recall ever venturing into the space below it, behind the front desk. The inner sanctum, she thought.

The reality was less *inner sanctum* and more *workaday offices*, with drab paint and dreary furniture, manned by the few permanent town hall officers. Heather glanced through the open doors, as she followed Tony.

'Here we are,' said Tony, holding open the door to his rather bigger, plusher office with a better grade of fixtures and fittings. 'Tea, coffee?'

'No, nothing, thanks,' said Heather, plonking herself, unbidden, on a violet-coloured upholstered chair. She clutched her handbag on her knees.

'Now then... Parsley Field.' Tony sat at the swanky black leather executive chair behind his desk and swivelled gently to and fro.

'Yes. I heard it might be turned into a housing estate.'

Tony nodded.

'But it's where we hold the fête. It can't be.'

Tony sighed and stopped swivelling. 'I'm afraid it's not up to us to dictate what the landowner can and can't do with his own property.'

'But the fête is an important part of the town's calendar. Can't we object to what's being proposed?'

'Of course, that's why we have planning regulations. But the county as a whole has been told by the government it has to build over a hundred thousand new dwellings. Each parish has been allocated a quota and Little Woodford's has to go somewhere.'

'But… but…'

'This site is ideal.'

'There must be other sites.'

Tony got up and went over to a big map of the town, pinned to his wall. 'Where do you suggest? You have to remember that we need to consider what's already there, not to mention access, drainage, flood risks… For example—' he pointed at bits of the map '—here, here and here are out of the question, either because the land itself floods already, or because it'll push the water downstream and flood existing dwellings.'

'I see,' said Heather. She sighed heavily. 'So my objection is unlikely to succeed.'

Tony sat down again and steepled his fingers. 'I'm sure there is another space big enough to hold the fête. A big garden, maybe. The vicarage one?'

Heather shook her head. 'Our garden can and does host the church fête, which is a very modest affair, compared to the town's one.' Tiny in comparison – an Aunt Sally, a tea tent, a few craft stalls, a tombola… While the town fête had bouncy castles, a beer tent, the flower and produce competition, food concessions, a band playing, and all sorts of other attractions, before one even considered the book, cake and toy stalls… dozens of money-spinners and booths. The biggest garden she knew was the one at the Grange, where Miranda lived, and even that wasn't going to cut the mustard. The main marquee for flowers and produce would have to be pitched in the adjoining field in order to fit in.

'So you're responsible for two fêtes?' asked Tony. 'Isn't that a fate worse than death?' he chuckled at his own joke.

'I was given responsibility for the town fête as well, because I wasn't quick enough to say no,' said Heather.

'I'm sure you run both of them admirably.'

Why did Tony's approbation make her feel faintly queasy?

'So, back to a new venue,' said Tony, realising his compliment had fallen flat. 'What about the cricket club?'

Heather resisted the temptation to roll her eyes and explained the patently obvious in simple terms. 'Because, in the summer they have matches on it every weekend and if it isn't the first or the second elevens playing on a Saturday, it's the youth teams on a Sunday.'

'The school?'

'I wanted to use their field for a Christian folk festival some years back and was told their insurance didn't allow it.'

'I see. Might there be another field, another farmer you could approach?'

'Possibly but, almost certainly, any other field would be the wrong side of the ring road for young families to access safely. Frankly, I can't think of anywhere.' She was wasting her time here. 'Not that it's your problem, Mr Glenham. The fête isn't the council's responsibility, it's the fête committee's.' She got up to leave. 'But thank you for confirming the rumour. At least I know where we stand.'

'You could always approach the landowner – ask if he's taken into consideration the impact on the fête.'

'Mr McGregor?' Heather raised her eyebrows. *Care about the fête?* she added internally. She knew he'd tolerated it because the £200 rent for the field had been easy money, but selling it with planning permission was *way* more lucrative and even *easier* money.

'You know him?'

'We're acquainted. We have to be, because of renting Parsley Field from him for the day but we're not...' she paused for a second '...friends.'

'No?'

If Tony Glenham was expressing surprise it was, presumably, because he'd not met Mr McGregor – a difficult man; reclusive and bad-tempered and, rumour had it, handy with a shotgun. He'd caused a stir some years previously when he'd applied to have sixty houses built on his land on the far side of the ring road. In the end, the development had been pared down to twenty-five houses, which had been approved because it was classed as a brown field site due to some derelict agricultural buildings on it.

The townsfolk had all muttered that it was the thin end of the wedge because the estate broke out of the town's envelope. It had set a precedent and now the town would *sprawl*. The sprawling hadn't happened and the little estate hadn't led to anything worse, but it was apparent to Heather that Mr McGregor had discovered he could make far more from selling off parcels of land to developers than he could ever earn from the back-breaking work of being a farmer. She couldn't blame him, even if she deeply resented his current plan, but she didn't feel inclined to confront him about it.

———

Having got back from school only a short while previously, Ashley went into the sitting room, carrying the stack of spiral-bound paper that was his copy of the script and found his mum, Amy, curled up on the sofa, playing something on her phone.

'Can you give me a hand, Mum?'

'Wait a sec… bugger. I've lost.' She chucked her phone onto the table beside her, next to a half-drunk cup of tea. 'What is it, Ash? What do you want? Only I'm busy.'

Ash was perplexed. Busy? Playing Candy Crush? Oh well. 'I need testing on my lines. I need someone to read through with me.'

'Is it going to take long?'

'It's only the bits I'm in.' Ashley didn't add that it was most of it, because he was playing the title role. 'And only the first act.'

Amy sighed. 'OK, hand it over.'

'I've highlighted all my lines. I just need you to read the line before each of my speeches.'

Amy nodded and flicked through the pages. 'Blimey, you got loads to say. How do you remember all this stuff?'

'Dunno. Just by learning bits at a time and then hoping I can stick all the little bits together in the right order.'

Amy turned back to the first page. 'Off you go, then.'

Ashley began his first speech, but was interrupted by Amy after a couple of lines.

'Does it all rhyme, then?'

He nodded. 'Yeah, it's the way pantos work.' He carried on, then paused, waiting for his next cue.

'Mum?'

'What?'

'I need my cue.'

'Gawd, sorry.' She ran her finger down the page. 'Oh right… So, who am I here? Jack's mother?'

'Yes,' said Ashley, feeling his patience fraying.

His mum held the script up and stiltedly declaimed, 'Look, my boy, my purse is empty. And I for one have never dreamt, We'd be so poor we'd have to eat, Grass like Daisy. We can't have meat.' She grinned at Ash. 'How was that? Do I get the part?'

'Yeah, terrific.'

Amy carried on with another speech, ignoring the fact she was supposed to be helping Ashley.

He sighed. This was hopeless. Maybe he'd get Ryan or one of his mates to help him.

'I could get the hang of this,' said his mum. 'Except for all that learning. Could I do it with the script?'

'No, Mum. The whole point of acting is doing it without the script.'

'Spoilsports,' grumbled Amy. 'Right, where were we?'

'No, you're all right,' said Ashley. He took the script back.

Amy pouted. 'I was just starting to enjoy myself there. But have it your way.'

'When's supper?' he asked, to change the subject.

'Six. Fish fingers and chips – or don't actors—' Amy gave the word *actors* a ridiculous emphasis '—eat grub like that?'

Ashley ignored the jibe. 'Fish fingers'll be ace. Cheers, Mum. Back in a bit,' he said, grabbing his skateboard with a free hand and legging it out of the door. He'd see who was hanging out at the skate park – maybe he'd be able to persuade them to read through with him. He dropped his board to the ground when he reached the pavement and scooted his way through the council estate, past the allotments and into the park. There were some little kids on the swings, while their mums gossiped, and some girls huddled on the roundabout, heads together while they played on their phones and giggled. The skate park was empty.

Ashley dumped the script on top of a half pipe, then clambered up with his board, before he swooped down and up, performed a couple of desultory tricks and wound up back on the ledge. He parked his board, sat on the edge with his back to the half-pipe, legs dangling over the vertical drop, and opened his script. He read each cue with one hand covering his next line and then whispered his words to the trees on the far side of the park. As a way of going over his lines it worked, but it was so easy to catch a glimpse of his next speech while he was reading the cue.

'Learning lines?' A hand, belonging to Sophie, tugged the toe of his shoe.

Ashley looked down. 'Yeah, trying to.'

'Hang on.' She walked round to the lowest point of the half-pipe and then ran and scrambled up the slope, grabbing Ashley's proffered hand. She was panting from exertion as she settled herself next to him.

'Give it here,' she demanded. 'From the top and just the cues, right?'

Ashley smiled. Sophie's help was going to be perfect. Her mum, Lizzie, had been an actress, before she'd contracted multiple sclerosis and all of her ambitions had come to a juddering halt. She now helped out backstage with the theatre group and Sophie had picked up enough from her mum to know what he needed by way of support. He wished his mum would treat his acting seriously, not ripping the piss out of it. That was the trouble with acting; the more seamless, the easier, the *less* like acting it looked to an audience, the harder it was. But he couldn't explain that to his mum – she simply wouldn't get it.

'You've almost nailed the first act,' said Sophie, as she closed the script and gave it back to Ashley.

'Nearly. And thanks for your help.'

'Anytime.'

'It's great having someone who gets what I'm doing.'

'I don't, not really, not like Mum would, but I understand a bit of what it must be like.'

'My mum's no good and the school is as bad – all they care about is UCAS forms and personal statements. I asked if there was someone who might help with audition pieces but that was a waste of time.'

'Can't the theatre group help with that?'

'They do… sort of. And – I don't want to sound mean – but they're all amateurs, aren't they? What do they know about theatre schools?'

'Mum knows. You could ask her.'

Ashley stared at his feet.

'Why not?' insisted Sophie.

'I'd feel mean. It wouldn't be fair. I'd feel like I was rubbing her nose in it – *look what I'm hoping to do when your career is all behind you.*'

'Oh, no it isn't,' said Sophie.

'Oh, yes…' Ashley stopped and grinned.

'She wouldn't mind, honest. I think she'd be delighted to help. Come round after school one night – talk to her about it. It might have been a couple of decades since she was at drama school, but I shouldn't think acting has changed much since Shakespeare was starting out. How about you come round early on Wednesday, before both of you go to the theatre group? I'm sure she'd love to have a chat about it.'

SEVEN

Maxine clapped her hands, although the room was hardly noisy. Her students, working on their paintings, peered round their easels.

'In case you haven't noticed, it's four-thirty and I thought you might like to have a bit of a wash-up session before we finish, so you can tell me if there's anything you want me to do differently, ideas about the catering, the layout of the room… anything. But let's lay down our brushes, go to the back of the room, grab a drink and a biscuit and have a chat.

'Please, miss,' said Laurence, 'can I just finish a tricky bit?' Whenever he spoke, Maxine thought he sounded like Sean Connery. He really did have the most delicious accent.

'And me,' said Brenda.

Maxine grinned. 'Of course. Let's gather shortly, when you're all ready. Five minutes?'

Maxine made her way to the back and started opening mini packets of biscuits and tipping the contents onto a plate. A couple of the students had followed and were helping themselves to mugs of tea.

'This is so great,' enthused Peter. He hadn't been much of a contributor so far and she had wondered if he was enjoying himself. It was nice to have her doubts allayed.

'Who knew there was so much you could make paint do?' said Annie. 'I had one of those tin paintboxes as a kid, with hard little circles of colour in it. After a bit, the paints got all grubby and mixed up and the end of the brush just splayed out… Not the best way to encourage anyone to paint. But these—' She sighed happily. 'All those colours we've got to play with. And who knew about the ways to mix them up?'

Maxine smiled happily. *Job done,* she thought. *Well, almost.* She still had to teach most of them how to use all those lovely colours to make something recognisable. She'd already assessed that it was going to be a harder job with some than others. It was ever thus.

'So…' She smiled at the group. 'A good day?'

There were lots of enthusiastic nods and smiles and a few affirmative comments. 'Good. You'll be back tomorrow, then.' More nods and smiles. 'Any comments? Anything at all.'

'Could we have some music while we paint?' asked Peter.

'Sure, of course you can bring your own playlist and headphones. I've no objection to that at all. I often have music on in the background when I paint.'

'What do you listen to?' asked Laurence.

'Almost anything: classical, jazz, heavy metal… I have eclectic tastes.'

'And does it inspire you?' asked Brenda.

'I suppose… subconsciously. Or maybe I pick the music to go with what I'm working on. Heavy metal if I'm doing something bold and brash, some Bach for a small finicky watercolour—'

'And jazz?' asked Laurence.

'Ah… jazz. That's like a nice wine – it's a good accompaniment to almost anything.'

'A woman after my own heart.'

Not for the first time that day she thought there was something faintly familiar about him – and not just the Sean Connery voice. From the start she'd had a vague feeling that their paths had crossed previously. But that seemed supremely unlikely and, besides, he gave no indication of recognising her. And to ask 'have we met before?' was just too cheesy. Maybe, it was because his silver hair, startlingly blue eyes and a wonderful tan made him look like a film star or model. Was she mixing him up with the guy in the Marlboro cigarette ads of her youth, on whom she'd had a bit of a teenage crush and which had prompted her to have a brief flirtation with nicotine? It was possible.

He gave her a devastating smile. Was he flirting with her? No, he was a charmer… It was his default setting. Maxine cleared her throat. 'But back to the course… anything you want altered, changed, different…? Was lunch OK? Enough veggie options?' No one looked inclined to speak or to comment. 'And I'm not going too fast?' Again a lot of blank looks. 'Nothing?' She looked at her students. 'In which case I'll take it that we're on the right track. So, if you'd like to rinse out your brushes and put them in the pots provided, and leave your paintings on your easels to dry overnight, you're free to go. Don't worry about your palettes, I'll get them cleaned. Right, I'll see you all tomorrow. Have a lovely evening.'

A little burst of applause rippled round, making Maxine feel really chuffed. The first day had gone without a hitch. The students were lovely. All she had to do was keep going along the same lines and the hotel would probably be happy too. High five!

She went to the front of the room and began to pack up her own kit – it was just her sketchbook, her handbag and her laptop she wanted to take home with her. The rest of it she'd leave in the room overnight. But first she wanted to make sure she had the right slides for the lesson the next morning. She was plugging a memory stick into the side of her laptop when Laurence hove up.

'A jazz fan, eh?' said Laurence.

'I was a bit of a jazz geek when I was at art college. Less so now.'

'Did you like all jazz styles?'

'Quite a few of them.'

'Free jazz?'

'No, I tried, but never really got into it – no key, no harmony, no beat... I want to be able to hum along, tap my feet, dance.' She shrugged. 'I did try, but kept coming back to the likes of the Duke, Fats, Dave Brubeck and John Coltrane.' She stared at him. 'You're going to tell me I'm not adventurous enough to be a proper jazz fan, if I don't like free jazz.'

'Absolutely not.'

'So are you into jazz?'

'A bit. I like all music. Changing tack... is there a nice pub round here? The hotel's just fine but it's a bit...' he searched for the right word '...*corporate*.'

'I know what you mean. Well, there's the Talbot in town. If you follow the road down the hill and around the bend, it's on the right. You can't really miss it – it's the only pub on the high street. They do food too, if you're interested. Pub grub but extremely *nice* pub grub.'

'Sounds ideal. I may play hooky one night and give it a go.'

'The landlady's called Belinda. She'll look after you.'

'Belinda? I dated a Belinda years ago. Had a soft spot for that name ever since.' Laurence returned to his easel and began to pack up. He hummed a tune as he dealt with his brushes and tidied up his table, before heading for the door, with a cheery 'See you'.

Maxine half recognised the tune, but couldn't quite place it. It niggled for a second or two but, the more she wondered why it was faintly familiar, the more ethereal the memory became until, like a wisp of bonfire smoke on a breeze, it vanished altogether.

The other students, now a proper group of friends and acquaintances, had gone with Laurence in pairs and three-somes, chatting as they left, making arrangements to meet up for pre-dinner drinks and talking about their achievements... The silence that followed was lovely. She quickly checked her memory stick for the pictures she wanted, before switching her laptop off. She then rang the reception desk and asked for a porter to come over and collect the dirty cups, plates and palettes and for the room to be cleaned and tidied, ready for the next morning, before she picked up her computer and bag, shut the door and headed for the staff car park.

She saw Olivia unlocking her bike. She waved at her friend.

'From the feedback I've had so far,' said Olivia, 'you're doing a brilliant job.'

'They seem happy enough, which is all I ask for. And now I am going home, in the hope that Gordon might cook supper. I'm bushed.'

'And if he doesn't? The pub?'

'Maybe. Or Deliveroo.'

Olivia prepared to mount her bike. 'Good idea. See you tomorrow, bright and early.'

'Not so early tomorrow – I don't have to worry about the

set-up or the arrangements any more. I'll get here about nine.'

'Then I'll give the room a check when I get in – just to make sure it's all in order.'

Olivia rode off and Maxine wearily got into her car. No way was she going to cook tonight. Pub, take-away – she didn't care.

'How did it go?' said Gordon from the kitchen as she dumped her stuff in the hall and pushed the front door shut with her foot.

'You look knackered,' he added.

'I feel knackered.'

'Hard work, eh?'

Maxine rubbed her face with her hands. 'Yes, but rewarding. They're a nice group, all very engaged, but I am hugely aware they've paid *a lot* of money to be there, which puts the pressure on to make it perfect. Quite apart from the fact that they probably want to end up painting pictures they're proud of.'

'Will they?'

'Early days, but a couple have got a bit of a spark. Some of the others… they may be late developers.'

Gordon went over to the freezer and got out an ice tray. 'Is that *teacher-speak* for no?'

Maxine raised a tired smile. 'Maybe. I'll probably try and get them interested in abstracts.'

'That way no one can see how hopeless they are,' he said as he cut two slices off a lemon.

Maxine grinned. 'Nice big jolly blocks of colour… What's not to like? And I had a chat with them, just before we finished for the day and they were all pretty happy. No complaints, no gripes… all good.'

Gordon plopped a few ice cubes into a pair of tall glasses,

sloshed in a generous shot of gin, dropped in the lemon and filled them to the brim with fizzing tonic.

'Sounds like you did really well. Now, have this, while I run you a nice hot bath, then while you have a soak with a second gin, I'll ring the pub and book a table. How does that sound?'

'Like heaven on earth.' Maxine sank back into her chair as Gordon clumped up the stairs. As she sipped her drink she thought what a good man Gordon was. They'd had their ups and downs in their forty-odd years of marriage, but they'd come through them all and it was little thoughtful gestures like this that had kept them strong.

The worst 'down' had happened only a few months previously, when Gordon had a brief dalliance with one of Belinda's bar staff. Maxine had been up to her eyes, dealing with the fact that half their family had taken up residence in their house and she'd had to become a carer to her mother-in-law. It had been incredibly stressful. Tensions in the house had resulted in Gordon spending more time than was necessary at the pub. And *that* had resulted in him falling under the spell of Ella, who looked a little like Catherine Zeta Jones. Younger, attractive, voluptuous and hanging on Gordon's every word... No, it was no surprise that he'd fallen a bit in love with her – right up until the penny dropped that she was really after his assets – a big house and decent pension. They'd weathered that and their marriage had come out of it in one piece – perhaps stronger, now they both realised how much failure would cost them emotionally.

She closed her eyes and let her mind drift over the day and for a fleeting second she felt she knew the music Laurence had hummed. But... then it was gone...

———

Miranda was in her kitchen preparing delicious roasted vegetable filo pastry tartlets as a starter for supper that evening. Like Maxine, she was sipping a gin. It was, she thought, handy that most spirits were vegan, being partial, as she was, to a G and T while she cooked. She was surprised by a ring on her doorbell. Roddy was up in his study, doing whatever he did up there – Miranda suspected dozing, quite often – so there was no point in expecting him to answer it. She covered her tartlets with a damp tea towel – filo could, and often did, dry out so quickly – and crossed the floor to the front door.

'Heather? What brings you here at this time?'

'Miranda, sorry to bother you but I've just heard some really disturbing news.'

'Then you'd better come in.' She led the way to her kitchen area. 'I hope you don't mind if I carry on. Filo pastry can go wrong so easily.' She whisked the tea towel off the little cases and began coating another tissue-thin sheet with olive oil. She deftly sliced it into six squares, layered them into the muffin tin to make a sixth tartlet, then took a mixing bowl of brightly coloured roasted veg and dolloped a tablespoon into each case. Heather watched, riveted by the process.

Miranda opened the eye-level oven, wincing slightly as the blast of hot air hit her square in the face, and then slid in the tray and slammed the door.

'Sorry about that,' she said, as she set a timer. 'Now… gin?'

'Oh…' Heather didn't often drink gin. Sherry was all they ran to at the vicarage. 'Well, maybe a teensy one.'

Miranda ignored the *teensy*, as she mixed Heather's drink, and then led her over to the vast white sofas that dominated the minimalist sitting room. She folded herself down elegantly and crossed her ankles. Heather plonked down opposite her.

'So what's the disturbing news?'

'Parsley Field is being sold for housing.'

'Parsley Field?'

Heather quickly apprised Miranda of the location, its importance to the fête and their chances of finding something else both large and central enough to replace it.

'To coin a phrase, that's a bit of a spanner in the works.'

'More like the whole tool box,' said Heather glumly. She took a glug of her drink and almost gasped. She wondered if finishing it was wise.

'Then we need to find somewhere else.'

'But where?' Heather stared at Miranda over the rim of her glass. 'I've lived here for years and I can't think of anywhere that might be suitable.'

Miranda snorted. 'There must be.' She put her drink on the table and went to fetch her laptop. 'Google earth,' she said, as she switched it on and waited for it to warm up. 'I love the way it lets you have a good snoop around.' She entered her password and hummed a little tune to herself as she swirled her finger over the touch pad and then tapped it with her beautifully polished fingernail. 'Here we go,' she murmured as her fingers flew over the keyboard, typing in *Little Woodford*. She patted the sofa next to her. 'Let's have a look together.'

Heather moved across. 'So this is Parsley Field,' she said, pointing out an expanse of green behind the church.

'Big space,' observed Miranda.

'We don't use all of it – about half – but it's the access from the town centre, which is almost as important as the size.' Heather waved a finger around the aerial picture of the town. 'There are loads of fields round and about – any one of which we might be able to borrow – but to get to them, people would have to cross the ring road.'

'What about the rec?'

'The play park and the skate park get right in the way of everything. The cricket pitch is in use at the weekends… And we obviously can't use the nature reserve.' Miranda paused and peered at the screen. 'What's this place?'

'That's the Reeve House. It's up for sale – four mill is the asking price, apparently.'

Even Miranda was impressed. 'Goodness. Has it got a buyer yet?'

'No idea.' Heather took another sip of her drink. Now she knew what to expect, she rather enjoyed the hit of alcohol. 'I don't move in those sorts of circles.'

'No, well, but if they're churchgoers…'

'We can't bank on that or even that the place will be sold in time for us to make overtures to the new owners. Besides, people with that sort of money may not want the hoi-polloi tramping all over their country retreat.'

Miranda looked slightly sceptical. 'It's good enough for the owners of Chatsworth and Longleat.'

'It's still a long shot,' said Heather. She had another sip. This gin was really awfully good.

'There's a couple of houses up near Maxine's that have big gardens. I could ask them.'

Heather peered at the screen. 'I don't think we'd get the marquee in,' she said.

'Could we do it without the marquee?'

'The flower and produce competition is one of the main attractions.'

Miranda sighed and flipped closed her laptop. 'There has to be a solution. Leave it with me – I'll work on it. There must be somewhere.' A timer pinged in the kitchen. 'Tartlets,' she said.

Heather drained her glass. Time for her to get going too, to make Brian's supper. She followed Miranda to the kitchen area, carrying her glass. She felt strangely light-headed – definitely squiffy, she decided. She hoped she'd get home without mishap and Brian wouldn't notice.

EIGHT

It was seven-thirty when Maxine and Gordon pushed open the door to the pub. It was pleasantly busy, but not over-crowded and Belinda, from behind the bar, pointed at a table by the window, set for four, with a reserved sign on it. As it was Monday night, Belinda wasn't expecting a rush and could afford to let a couple, dining alone, have a bigger, nicer table.

'Another gin?' asked Gordon, as Maxine made her way towards it.

She shook her head. 'Better not. I don't want to pitch up tomorrow with a banging hangover. Why don't we just split a bottle of wine with our meal?'

'OK,' said Gordon. 'I'll get that and bring the menus over.' He was back in a couple of minutes carrying two glasses, the menus and a bottle of Rioja. 'And Belinda said to tell you that Miles's fish pie is glorious.'

'OK.' Although Maxine wasn't entirely sure fish pie was what she fancied. When she went out to dinner she usually liked to pick something she was unlikely to cook at home –

and fish pie definitely didn't come into that category. She perused what was on offer... ooh, confit of duck with a sour cherry sauce. Yum. Decision made, she took a sip of her wine.

'Thank you, for this,' she said. 'A perfect end to a really good day.'

Gordon smiled at her. 'Make the most of it. Tomorrow it'll all be back to normal – no gin in the bath, and supper may be only mince and mash.' Gordon wasn't a natural cook and rarely ventured into the kitchen, so his repertoire was limited.

'I don't care. And tomorrow will be a whole heap easier. In fact, tomorrow I probably won't be as shattered. If I give you a list of things to shop for, I may take over the cooking.'

The relief on Gordon's face would have been visible from space. 'If you're sure?'

'Yes, I know everything works, the students aren't tricky—'

'Did you expect them to be?'

'To be honest, when I looked at the fee for the course—'

'Which is?'

'They're paying two and a half grand a pop for five days' tuition.'

'What?!' Gordon spluttered.

'Mind you, it includes five nights, all-found, at a five-star hotel, plus my fee, plus all the materials, so possibly not *completely* ridiculous.'

Gordon nodded. 'Five nights fully catered at Woodford Priors isn't going to come cheap.'

'No. And people who can afford that may be used to getting the best.'

'Which is why the management asked you to teach their first course.'

'Daft bugger. They asked me because I'm local and they wouldn't have to give me a room for the duration. That must be quite a cost saving.'

'Now, who's being daft?' He smiled at her fondly.

'You two lovebirds ready to order?' asked Belinda, coming over with a notebook and pen.

'The duck for me,' said Maxine.

'And I'll have the entrecote – medium rare,' said Gordon.

'There'll be a wait of about twenty minutes,' said Belinda. 'Fancy something to nibble on first… olives, some bruschetta?'

'No, I think we're fine,' said Maxine.

Belinda returned to the bar and passed the order through to the kitchen while Maxine and Gordon lapsed into comfortable silence, till Maxine said, 'You should see the course room.' She described it to her husband.

'So, did they convert it specially?'

'It looks like it. Of course it'll be perfect for other things they've got lined up.'

'Even so, quite an investment.'

'Exactly, which was why I was so worried about mucking up. A shitty review or two on Tripadvisor and I could scupper things for years to come.'

Gordon nodded. 'I can see that. Still, that won't happen – the students haven't rioted yet or asked for their money back, so it's unlikely they will. You said it was all happy vibes at the wash-up. The hotel would be mad not to have you do this on a regular basis.'

'And I won't have to do so much prep for the next one – just wheel out what I did this time.'

'Unless you get return students.'

Maxine gazed at him. 'Well, that would be a bit of a compliment. Unless they felt I hadn't managed to teach them

properly the first time round – which might be a possibility.'
She grinned.

While they ate, the pub began to fill with the after-supper drinkers – the townsfolk who popped out for a catch-up with friends, after their evening meal, rather than those who dropped in for a drink after work. Maxine was chewing her last succulent mouthful of duck, when she saw the door to the pub open and a familiar figure stride in. Without thinking, she stood up immediately and waved, making Gordon swivel in his seat to see who his wife had spotted.

'Who's that?' he asked.

'One of my students.' Maxine waved more vigorously. 'A chap called Laurence. Oh good, he's seen us. Nice guy,' she added, sitting down again. She watched Laurence make his way towards them. 'You don't mind, do you?'

'Apparently not,' said Gordon, looking as if he rather did.

'Maxine, hi!' said Laurence, radiating bonhomie and charm. He bent down and shook her hand. 'And this is…?'

'Gordon, my husband.'

Laurence transferred his grip to Gordon's hand and shook it energetically. 'You've got such a talented wife. She's a gem. The patience of a saint. I'm Laurence, by the way – the class dunce.'

Gordon looked pleased but slightly bemused. 'Oh… er… thank you.'

'And he isn't,' said Maxine, 'the class dunce. Won't you join us?'

'No,' said Laurence. 'You're eating. I've no wish to disturb you. But you're right – this is a lovely pub.'

'We like it. Anyway, we've finished, haven't we, Gordon?'

'Have we?' He caught the look in his wife's eye. 'Oh, yes.'

Laurence picked up their wine bottle on the table. 'And

this is almost dead. How about I get a refill?' And before they could answer he was heading for the bar.

'Have we met him before?' asked Gordon. 'I almost feel I recognise him.'

'That's weird,' said Maxine. 'That's what I thought, when he pitched up this morning, but I don't recognise the name. Laurence McLachlan – mean anything to you?'

Gordon shook his head. 'Nope. He must just have one of those faces.'

Laurence came back with a glass and no bottle. 'The nice lady will bring the wine over when she comes to clear the plates.'

Maxine shared the last of the wine in their bottle between the three of them. 'Can't have you dying of thirst, while you wait.'

Laurence laughed. 'Hardly.'

Belinda arrived with the Rioja and a couple of menus. 'Pudding?'

'Don't let me stop you,' insisted Laurence. 'I ate very well up at the hotel.' He patted his stomach.

'And the *nice lady* is called Belinda,' said Maxine.

'Oh – so *you're* Belinda,' said Laurence, fixing his blue eyes on her and noticing her properly. 'Love that name. I'm Laurence.'

Belinda returned his gaze. If it had been a cartoon, thought Maxine, there would have been drawings of lightning bolts or a picture of a gigantic magnet. The attraction couldn't have been more instantly obvious. Maxine's eyes flicked between the two of them, spotting the dilation of their pupils, the momentary flare of nostrils and Belinda's blush. For a second Maxine felt a thump of jealousy. Laurence was *her* friend. She didn't want him looking at

Belinda like that, or Belinda reciprocating the look, for that matter.

Get a grip, woman, she told herself. *Stop being so childish.*

Then Belinda cleared her throat. 'Pudding?' she repeated.

'Just a coffee for me,' said Maxine.

'Gordon?' asked Belinda.

He glanced at the specials board before he shook his head. 'No, just coffee too.'

'I'll bring it over in a minute,' said Belinda as she took away the dirty plates.

'Did Maxine tell you, I accused her of being a lumber-jack, this morning?' said Laurence, refocusing on his companions.

'A what?'

And Laurence recounted the tale, although Maxine rather wished he hadn't. 'Lumberjack' wasn't exactly flattering.

'Yes, well…' she said a bit stiffly.

'It was quite funny at the time,' insisted Laurence.

'Hmm.'

'This is a lovely town,' said Laurence, smoothly changing the subject. 'I walked up as far as the town hall. It's so pretty.'

'We like it. It's a proper little community — lots of things happening, lots of clubs and activities.'

'I can see that. It's got a nice buzz. And a cracking pub with a cracking landlady.'

'She's quite nice,' said Maxine petulantly.

'She looks it,' said Laurence studying her again.

'Oh, well,' said Maxine, forcing Laurence's attention back to her. 'Let me tell you about all the other things that go on here.'

It was a good half hour before they called for the bill and

Maxine felt irritated to note that she and Gordon only got part of Belinda's attention as she swiped their credit card.

'That Laurence chappie seemed a nice bloke,' said Gordon, as they made their way across the nature reserve. 'Very charming.'

'Belinda certainly thought so,' said Maxine crisply, before she relented. It wasn't Belinda's fault she'd been charmed by him. 'The other students really like him too – funny, charming... He's got this way of being able to talk to everyone and anyone. No artist though, and I don't think, even with my best efforts, he's going to become one.'

'One for the abstract route?' asked Gordon.

Maxine nodded.

'What's his day job?'

'I've got no idea – although he said he works with creatives.'

'That hardly narrows it down.'

Maxine laughed. 'I can't give them all the third degree.' She put on a cod-German accent. 'Ve haf vays of making you talk.'

'It's just,' said Gordon, 'I *still* feel I almost recognise him.'

'I know – it is weird, isn't it. Maybe he *looks* like someone recognisable. A doppelgänger. Because, I know for a fact, I've never come across Laurence McLachlan before in my life.'

———

Maxine was incredibly touched and thrilled when, as the students prepared to pack up and go at the end of the Friday afternoon, Laurence disappeared out of the course room and reappeared with a huge bouquet of flowers.

'We all chipped in,' he said. 'We felt you need a special thank you for being so endlessly patient, for teaching us so much, for being so encouraging...' He smiled at her. 'To be honest, I had business here in Little Woodford and I booked the course because it was there on the hotel's website and I thought... what the heck? I never expected to enjoy it half as much as I did, nor to get so much out of it.' He proffered the flowers. 'So thank you.'

Maxine could feel her face burning with pleasure and embarrassment as she stepped forward. 'Honestly, you shouldn't have. It's been a delight to teach you all. I've had a blast so I feel a complete fraud accepting this. But thank you. Thank you for being lovely students and I truly hope you feel inspired and confident enough to keep on painting. If you do, it'll bring me even more pleasure than these flowers – and that's saying something.'

The little group of students started to gather up their possessions – the sketchbooks which were theirs to keep, their finished paintings, a cushion to be returned to their hotel room, an overall or two... One or two swapped mobile numbers, one or two were in a hurry, with trains to catch – but most drifted around, as if they were reluctant for the week to end. Maxine stacked her art books on her table at the front, before unplugging her laptop and projector and adding them to the heap.

'How are you going to get that to your car,' said Laurence, eyeing the pile.

'Same way I got it here. I'll ring for the porters and they'll bring their trolley round. It saves on multiple journeys.'

'If there's a problem I can give you a hand.'

'Very kind, but I'll be fine. I expect you want to head off.'

'Nope. The business I came here for isn't scheduled till tomorrow. The art course was a bit of holiday before the main event. I'm in no hurry to be anywhere.'

'OK.' An impulse overtook Maxine. 'If you're at a loose end this evening, do you fancy coming to ours for supper?'

'No...' But he sounded as if he was wavering. Then, more forcefully, 'I couldn't impose. Thanks, but no thanks.'

'It wouldn't be an imposition. Honest. I thought I'd cook a curry.'

'Curry?' Laurence's eyes widened. 'I haven't had a good curry in an age.'

'I cook a mean rogan josh. And poppadoms and garlic naans, maybe some dhal and some saag aloo. There's going to be masses. Heaps.'

Laurence threw his hands up. 'OK, I give in. You're sure now?'

'I wouldn't have asked, if I wasn't. Seven o'clock.' Maxine grabbed a scrap of paper and scribbled her address on it. 'And my phone number just in case you get hopelessly lost, but we're easy to find. As you come down the hill towards the town, there's a right turn signed to the primary school. Turn into that road and we're number five.'

'I think even I can manage that. Thanks Maxine, I'm really looking forward to it.'

Laurence loped out of the workroom and Maxine phoned for the porters. As she waited for them to arrive with their trolley, she hoped Gordon wouldn't mind. And when was the last time they'd done a bit of impromptu entertaining? It was going to be fun.

NINE

Laurence McLachlan wasn't the only person in Little Woodford to get an invitation to supper; Ashley Pullen was about
to head over to Sophie and Lizzie's.

'My food not good enough for you?' asked Amy.

'Mum, it's not like that. I need to talk to Lizzie about
drama school.'

'Jeez, not that again. I thought you were going to learn
how to do something useful, like being an electrician or a
plumber, like Ryan said.'

'I know… only…'

'Only what?'

'Only it's not acting. I want to do that more than
anything. I know getting an apprenticeship and a trade is a
good idea. I know what I *said*, but I want to do *this, now.*'

Amy sighed and shook her head. 'You won't get no hand-
outs from me, if you do this.'

'I wouldn't expect to. I'm going to get a job and save up.'

'What?' Amy screeched. 'And when are you going to find
the time to do that? You've got your A levels, you're doing

this stupid panto and now you want a job too? Shit, Ash, what planet are you living on? There ain't enough hours in the day for all of this.'

'I'm living on the same planet as you, Mum. How many jobs do you do? You manage.'

Amy sighed and shook her head. 'And I wouldn't have to do all them jobs if I'd stayed on at school and got my exams.' Her voice softened. 'I want better for you, Ash. I want you to do well, I want you to earn decent money, I want you to have a nice house not a poxy council one like this.'

'This house is OK.'

'Don't you want better than *OK*?'

Ashley shrugged and caught sight of the kitchen clock. 'Look, Mum, I know you want what's best for me and so do I. I happen to think that's being an actor. But I need to get going, else I'll be late, and that'd be rude.'

'At least I've managed to teach you manners,' said Amy.

'Mum, you've taught me heaps. I'll be all right. Trust me.' Ashley shot out of the door before his mother could delay him further and headed across town to his friend Sophie's.

The smell of garlic and onions greeted him when Lizzie opened the door and he could hear the sound of someone busy in the kitchen of the little house.

'Soph's made a lasagne,' said Lizzie, after they'd settled in the sitting room. 'I hope you like it.'

'Sounds lush,' said Ashley. 'I think I ought to learn how to cook.'

'It's not tricky.'

'No, I get that.'

'You implying that if my Soph can do it, anyone can?' But Lizzie was grinning as she said it.

'Hey,' said Sophie, coming into the room. 'I heard that.'

Ashley went brick red. 'That wasn't what I meant at all.'

'And I was joking, as well you know!' said Lizzie.

'Good.' Sophie flicked her with an oven glove she was carrying.

Ashley watched the banter between the two and felt a twinge of envy. He couldn't have treated his mother like Sophie did hers, or he'd have been given a thick ear. But he supposed their relationship was defined by Lizzie's dependency on her daughter and maybe that was a high price to pay. Too high a price.

Sophie sat on the chair next to her mother's wheelchair. 'But being able to cook is a useful life skill. I mean, how are the likes of someone like Zac going to cope at uni? I bet he can't even make toast.'

'I can do a bit,' said Ashley. 'With Mum holding down so many jobs, I had to learn to fend for myself when I got home from school.' He paused. 'Not that I could cook a lasagne. I don't think my mum can either – she buys hers ready-made.'

'Well, mine is made from scratch and it'll be ready in about twenty minutes. So while we're waiting, what do you want to ask Mum about auditions?'

Ashley shrugged. 'I'm not sure I know where to start.'

'OK,' said Lizzie. 'So how about I tell you about my experiences. Things may have changed since I went to drama school but probably not completely.'

Ashley nodded. As far as he was concerned, any information was good – when you knew almost nothing, the only way was forward.

———

The doorbell rang at ten past seven, as Maxine was busy cooking.

'I'll get it,' called Gordon from the sitting room.

Maxine stirred the dhal and checked the seasoning of her curry, as her iPhone, docked into a speaker, filled the kitchen with soft music from one of her playlists. On the table, set for three, her glorious bouquet was prettily arranged in a vase and the recessed lights glinted off the cutlery and glasses. The aroma of spices filled the air and she felt she could do no more, beyond cooking the rice at the last minute.

'Maxine, this is wonderful,' said Laurence, as he followed Gordon into the kitchen. He handed over a heavy bag before he kissed Maxine on the cheek. 'A contribution.'

Maxine peered into the bag. It contained a bottle of wine, a bottle of port and a box of chocs.

'I wasn't sure which you'd prefer,' said Laurence, 'so I bought all three.'

'That's ridiculously generous. But thank you,' said Maxine. She returned to stirring the dhal while Gordon poured drinks – glasses of wine all round – and then the men settled themselves at the table.

She was vaguely listening to the conversation – mostly a discussion about microbreweries and nice pubs they'd visited over the years – and trying to work out when she needed to put the rice on to boil, when she clocked a complete change in Laurence's tone of voice.

'Is this some kind of a wind-up?' He slammed his glass down so hard that some of his wine slopped onto the scrubbed wooden table and he glared angrily at his hosts.

Maxine and Gordon stared at each other, utterly bemused. Maxine switched her gaze to Laurence.

'I'm sorry…?' she stuttered.

'That.' He pointed an accusing finger at her iPhone.

Still Maxine was at a loss. And then she tuned in to the music. It was the theme tune to the 1970s enigmatic cult science fiction movie, *Ninety-nine*. The theme had won an

Oscar for best original score and been likened to Dave Brubeck crossed with Jean-Michel Jarre.

And then her brain began to make connections. She remembered a film about the cracking of the Enigma code and how the giant early computer, the Bombe, had wheels and tumblers that whirred and turned and then stopped in sequence as they hit the right solution. This was exactly what seemed to be happening inside Maxine's head.

The music Laurence had hummed. *Whirr, whirr, click, clunk.*

The faint feeling she recognised him. *Whirr, whirr, click, clunk.*

He worked with creatives. *Whirr, whirr, click, clunk.*

Laurence McLachlan... Lozza Lachlan, the film music composer and jazz musician. *Whirr, whirr, click, CLUNK.*

'Good God,' she whispered as she stared at him. 'Lozza Lachlan.'

'You're telling me you didn't know,' said Laurence. 'Seriously?'

Maxine nodded. 'Truly.'

'In which case I'm sorry about my reaction. It's just... well. I like anonymity these days and I was kind of hoping for an evening of complete normality.'

'Honestly, you've achieved that. I didn't have a clue. Although I thought you looked kind of familiar. Gordon did too.' Gordon nodded. 'But the last time – well, the only time we saw you in the flesh – was at the Albert Hall. Gordon won some tickets in a Student Union raffle, when we were both studying in London. Nineteen seventy-six? Seven?'

'Seventy-seven,' confirmed Laurence. 'You were there?'

They both nodded vigorously. 'Fabulous concert,' said Maxine. 'Although our seats were up in the gods, about as far away from the stage as it was possible to get.'

'So the music you were playing just now wasn't a hint that you'd rumbled me.'

'Shit, no! Truly, I had no idea.' Maxine remembered her dhal and swore again as she stirred it and found it had started to stick to the pan. She whipped it off the heat and put it on a trivet. 'The dhal may be off... We'll see.' She sat on a chair next to Laurence. 'So, where have you been? You were huge here in the Seventies, touring all over the country and then...' She clicked her fingers. 'Poof, you disappeared.'

Laurence sighed. 'The States, Germany – they love me in Germany – but mostly I was in LA, writing stuff for films, TV... anything. My kids were growing up there, in school there. I couldn't afford to come back here because of the taxes and then the UK went off the jazz scene. You guys seemed to fall out of love with it, so I didn't tour here again.'

'That's sad,' said Maxine.

'It's fine,' said Laurence. 'I'm not exactly on the breadline.'

'This business you're here for,' asked Maxine. 'Would that be arranging another tour?'

Laurence laughed. 'Hell, no. Getting too old for that. A different hotel room every night, endless travel, late nights, sex and drugs and rock 'n' roll... Well, not the last three obviously – not at my age.'

'Pfft,' said Maxine.

'No, I'm here to buy a house. My earnings aren't what they were, so I don't have to give *everything* to the taxman, my kids have long since flown the nest and have their own lives and my marriage isn't looking too flash – hasn't done for years—'

'I'm sorry,' said Maxine and Gordon simultaneously.

'Don't be. It's been on life support for about the last fifteen years. Besides, I miss England. I miss *weather* as opposed to *climate*, I miss warm beer and cold winters, I miss pubs… And I've got a couple of old retainers – although they'd kill me for calling them old – who are loyal to me and I kinda feel I owe them… Anyway, they want to retire back to their roots in Scotland and they can't house-hunt from the States, so it suits all of us if I come back here.'

'So, where are you thinking of buying?' asked Maxine.

'Here, in Little Woodford. The Reeve House.'

'The Reeve House?' said Maxine and Gordon in unison, once again.

'I'm viewing it tomorrow. Do you know it?'

'We know of it,' said Gordon. 'I don't know of anyone who has actually seen it. It's in massive grounds, and the people who own it are either total recluses, or are never there – no one knows which, for sure. I don't think I've ever seen the gates open. Have you, Max?'

Max compressed her lips. 'Not that I can recall. Strictly off limits that place. Not that there's anything wrong with the owners wanting their privacy. I don't think I'd like all and sundry tramping up our drive to have a gawp at this place. But I believe the house is very beautiful, so it seems a shame that it's hidden away.'

'Maybe, when I live there, *if* I wind up buying it, I might change all that. What's the point of falling in love with a place because you just love the sense of community, and then cutting yourself off from it?'

'Good point,' said Gordon.

'And I'm sorry I got a bit riled a minute or two back. I suddenly had a feeling your very kind invitation to dinner had a subtext. That's what living in LA does for you – makes you kinda paranoid about friendships. Are those people being nice because they want something? *What's in it for them?* I should've known you wouldn't be like that.' He smiled at

Maxine. 'But, I'd like to be just some newcomer in this town, until I really get a feel for the place, get accepted for just being me. You understand.'

'Perfectly,' said Maxine. She would be more than happy to be his gatekeeper, if that's what he wanted.

TEN

In November Heather realised with a jolt, that if she didn't get her act together, nothing would be ready in time for the fête next year, regardless of whether they'd found a venue or not. The plan to co-opt a treasurer from another community group had come to nothing and nor had she managed to find anyone else to help with the organisation. She needed to be more proactive. A fortnight later, she'd got hold of the primary school and organised the poster competition, got the results back, and called a committee meeting to pick a winner. Olivia promised to see if she could wangle a few hours off to join them.

'But I may be late,' she'd warned.

In the end, they gathered, without Olivia, in Heather's kitchen.

'Right, the poster competitions,' she said pulling a stack of A4 sheets off the counter and plonking them in the middle of the table. 'I suggest we look at each one in turn, you all give it a thumbs up or a thumbs down and anything unanimously accepted goes through, in its appropriate age group, and everything else is an also-ran. Once we've whittled them down, I suggest Maxine picks the final three for each group.'

It took a lot less time than any of them had expected. Some of the posters hadn't included the vital information, a couple seemed to show skills vastly superior to what could *possibly* be expected of a child of around five or six, some were dreary and some were a complete mess. That left a handful of real contenders. While Maxine went through the finalists, Heather made them all tea and got out her best biscuits.

'Excellent choices,' said Jacqui, after they'd decided on the winner and runners-up.

'Now then,' said Heather, 'our next headache is the loss of our venue. Parsley Field is being sold to developers and we need to find somewhere else PDQ.' She looked around at the group. 'Thoughts?'

'The primary school field,' suggested Maxine.

'The PTA isn't keen, Partly because of insurance issues, and partly because they're afraid it might spoil attendance at their own fête later on.'

Everyone conceded this was a valid point.

'What about asking if we could have temporary pedestrian lights on the ring road and using a field on the other side.'

'Anything to do with highways is always expensive,' said Miranda, 'and we certainly won't get lights for nothing.'

Silence fell again.

'It's a long shot, but...' said Maxine. She paused.

'Yes?' said Heather encouragingly.

'There was a guy on my painting course... He's hoping to buy the Reeve House.'

'Good grief,' said Heather. 'But it's on the market for millions.'

'I know. So there's a lot of "ifs" involved. But *if* he buys it and *if* he moves in before the summer, there might just be an outside possibility he'd consider letting us use the grounds.'

'*If* he did, it would be utterly perfect,' said Heather. 'But as you say, there are quite a few *ifs*. Can I ask who it is?'

Maxine screwed up her face. 'I'd better not say. I mean, he said he'd like to be a part of the community if he does wind up living here, but what he *says* and what he *does* might be two different things. And I think he'd rather be anonymous, till he gets to know people – so he can judge if they like him for himself, or if they want to be friends because of his money and his name.'

'I can see his point,' said Heather. 'Not that I've ever had that problem.' The others laughed. 'However, if the Reeve House falls through, have we got a Plan B?'

The laughter died as they considered the bleak fact that they didn't.

———

'Ashley Pullen!'

Ashley jolted awake and saw Miss Watkins, his English literature teacher, staring at him.

'Late night, was it?'

'No, miss.'

Her eyes narrowed sceptically, although she didn't pursue the matter. But when the bell went at the end of the class, she stopped him from leaving.

'A word,' she said, putting her hand on his arm. 'It's not like you,' she said, when the classroom was empty, 'to doze in my class. What's going on?'

'I've got a lot on, miss.'

'To the detriment of your schoolwork. Maybe you should look at your priorities.'

'Can't, miss.'

'I beg your pardon?'

'Miss, my priorities might be different to yours.'

'*Not* performing to the best of your abilities in your A levels is hardly in line with either *our* expectations or *your* interests. You've got a good head on your shoulders, Ashley; you're bound to get at least a B grade in English literature – if not higher. You want that, don't you?'

Ashley shook his head. 'I don't think drama school cares about grades.'

Miss Watkins stared at her pupil. 'You know, Ashley, I sometime regret casting you in the school panto. You're university material. If you get a good degree, the world's your oyster.'

'So?'

'So – job security, a career, good pay—'

'Massive debts, three years studying something, just for the sake of it… It may be what the school wants but it's not for me. I want to act – which is why I'm in the Players' panto. That's why I'm knackered. I'm sorry but there it is. I can't give up now. I've got a cracking part and it wouldn't be fair on the drama group, not at this stage. Anyway, I need the experience before I start auditioning properly.'

Miss Watkins rolled her eyes. 'But you could join a uni drama group. There's plenty of actors who have made it big that way.'

Ashley sighed angrily. 'This school wants me to go to uni, so it'll look good on your website – bump up the figures. It's not about me, it's about the school.'

'That's what you want to think, Ashley, but you're wrong.'

Ashley trailed off to the sixth form common room. He

liked Miss Watkins, he really did. She was a great teacher and she'd got him interested in drama in the first place, but if he didn't put himself and his ambitions first, who would? As he went into the common room, he saw the tatty old sofa in the corner was empty. He'd planned to use his free lesson to start an essay for his history teacher, but now decided he'd grab some zeds instead. The essay would have to wait, even though he had another rehearsal that night, the essay had to be in by the end of the week, and time was running out.

————

The printing company produced the posters on glossy A4 paper in under forty-eight hours. Most shops along the high street were more than happy to stick one up in their windows. The town hall put one on the noticeboard. The library, the schools, the surgery and of course the church also obliged. By the time Heather got back home to make supper, she felt pretty sure people would have to be blind not to spot them.

She had only just got her key out her handbag, when she heard the house phone ringing. Thankfully, Brian had a dedicated line in his study, so Heather didn't have to be the gatekeeper for her husband's calls. She slipped off her coat as she raced down the hall to answer it before the caller rang off.

'Hello,' she panted.

'Hello,' said a voice with a slight northern burr. 'I'm ringing about t' town fête.'

'Really?' Heather was astounded. The ink on the posters was barely dry.

'I have got t' right number, haven't I?'

'Yes,' said Heather quickly. 'But I've only just got back from putting the posters up and I wasn't expecting a response this fast.'

'So, you still need people?'

'Need people?! Yes.'

'I used to be an accountant… Is that any good?'

Silently, Heather thanked God, before she said, 'Are you offering to be our treasurer? We'd love you to take over the books. It's not difficult. Would you like to come round to the vicarage so you can see what's involved?'

'Yes, yes, that'd be a very good idea.'

'When would be convenient…? I'm sorry, I don't even know your name. I'm Heather, Heather Simmonds.'

'And I'm Diane Maskell. I've not long lived in Little Woodford and I'd like to get to know people. Helping out with summat seems a grand way of doing it.'

'That sounds brilliant. Are you free tomorrow? Come and have a coffee here and I'll show you what's what. I may even be able to round up another committee member or two so you can meet them too.'

'Grand. See you at eleven.'

'And you know how to find us?'

'You're opposite the cricket pitch, aren't you?'

'Sadly, we're not in the Old Parsonage. If you go past it, we're the next house… the new one.'

'I'll find you.'

They exchanged farewells, before they rang off.

In the next couple of minutes, Heather phoned Miranda and Jacqui.

'She seems really nice. And an accountant,' said Heather to Miranda. 'The answer to our prayers. Well, mine anyway. I know you're an atheist.'

'I am thrilled,' said Miranda. 'And I'm glad you think your prayers had something to do with it. Personally, I'll put it down to carpet-bombing the town with posters.'

November segued into Advent and the town got caught up with the excitement of Christmas. Ashley's panto rehearsals reached fever pitch, Sophie and Megan were buried in their books revising for their post-Christmas mocks and Miranda, hoping the season of goodwill would move local companies to sponsor the following year's fête or pay for advertising space in the programme, was relentless in her pursuit of their CEOs. When Heather wasn't up to her eyes helping organise the Christingle service, decorating the church, and sorting out her own family's celebrations, cards and presents, she was frantically busy at the school helping out with the children's Christmas activities. But at the back of her mind was the knowledge that the clock was ticking relentlessly, that it would soon be the new year and then there would only be six months left to find a new venue for the fête, with all the health and safety issues it would entail. At least, she thought, as she dusted down the lovely ancient carved wooden crib, at least Diane, her new treasurer knew what she was doing. She'd met Heather, Jacqui and Miranda and had impressed everyone with her knowledge of accounting.

'I'll put all this on a spreadsheet,' she'd said, having taken a look at the books. 'No one does accounting like this anymore. This is out of the Stone Age.'

Heather had felt a bit nettled by the comment, but she did appreciate that the world had probably moved on from double-entry book-keeping.

'And you seem to have some people, authorised to sign for stuff, who aren't on the committee. That's wrong. We need to get them taken off, new mandates put in place for signatories who *are* on the committee and get it all above board.'

'If you say so,' said Heather.

'You leave it to me, chuck, I'll get all the paperwork done. And what's this?' She held up an invoice.

Heather peered at it. 'Oh, this is from the printer who did the recruitment campaign posters. I'd clean forgotten. That needs paying pronto, please.'

'OK.' Diane took it back and turned her attention to the bank statements. 'And we can probably get a better bank than this one. I mean, I know interest rates are low but you've got money on deposit that isn't earning a penny. We need to get that sorted, too.'

After she'd gone, the other three members of the committee had stared at each other.

'She's right, of course,' said Miranda. 'Fresh eyes… always good for shaking things up.'

'A real asset,' said Heather, smiling. 'If we can just find a new venue, we'll be all set for another great fête.'

ELEVEN

The panto, which played to packed houses in the run-up to Christmas, was a triumph. Even Miss Watkins acknowledged the Little Woodford Players had pulled off a brilliant production.

Suck on that, Miss Watkins, Ashley thought rudely, as the school broke up on the Friday lunchtime and pupils spilled out of their respective classrooms. But, despite his defiance, he knew he was going to have a pretty grim Christmas, if he was going to make up for his lack of revision. No slobbing around in front of the TV, watching seasonal films and Christmas specials. He cheered himself up with the thought that it was only mocks and he had another five months before the real exams. He told the Players that he wasn't going to take on any other roles until he'd sat his A levels. This was partly so he could concentrate on his schoolwork, but it was also to leave every Saturday free for a part-time job. If he could save up some money, even if it were only a few hundred quid, it might make all the difference when he went

– *if he went* – to drama school. He kicked at a stone on the pavement as he headed for home.

'Coming to the skate park, Ash?' called Sophie. She was walking along the drive, a few yards ahead of him, arm in arm with Megan, the pair of them wearing Santa hats.

Ashley hadn't planned to but, what the heck? 'Yeah, why not?'

He caught up with the girls and together they headed past the turning to his house, past the allotments, to the Rec.

'Miss Watkins was a bit tough with that snidey comment about your mocks,' said Sophie.

Ashley shrugged as they reached the half-pipe and crawled into the space beneath, to hunker down away from the nippy breeze. 'She's got a point. I've done bugger all for the mocks but I'll knuckle down over the hols. Besides, if I can learn a whole play, I can learn a few facts.'

Megan and Sophie exchanged a glance. 'But it's not a *few*, is it?'

'I'll be fine.' Ashley's tone meant the topic was closed. 'I'm going job-hunting over the holidays.'

'But you're supposed to be revising,' said Megan.

'I can do both. And I can't revise twelve hours a day. No one can.'

Megan nodded. He had a point. 'What do you want to do?'

'Anything… probably just part-time. So, shops probably. Got to be local, 'cos I can't drive and I don't want to waste money on bus and train fares. I need to save for when I leave home. Like I said, I've got no Bank of Mum and Dad.'

Sophie snorted. 'Join the club. Anyhow, good luck, because I wouldn't think there's much going in a place like this – not *after* Christmas.'

'Who says anything about *after* Christmas. The sooner I

start the sooner I can save. I'm not proud; I'll do anything. Someone, somewhere must have a vacancy.'

'If we hear of anything, we'll tell you, won't we, Soph?'

'Thanks,' said Ashley. He shivered. 'Sorry, I'm going home – too cold for me. Besides, I want some lunch and after that, I'd better get revising. I'll make a start today and then tomorrow I'll go job-hunting.' He saw the look the girls gave him, as he crawled out of the space. 'It'll be fine – I can juggle it. And happy Christmas, you two. See you next year.'

The girls watched him lope off, back across the tatty grass of the town's play park.

'I hope he's right about being able to juggle. He deserves to succeed, doesn't he?' said Megan.

'But we both know life isn't fair.' Sophie gave Megan a steady stare. 'What you deserve and what you get aren't necessarily the same thing.'

'No, no they're not.' They both had reason to know that.

———

When Megan got home, the house was filled with the smell of her stepmother's baking – mince pies – she decided. From the sitting room came the sound of her half-brothers, Lewis and Alfie, playing something that involved a great deal of noise and upstairs she could hear the sound of Amy hoovering.

Megan slung off her coat and schoolbag in the hall and headed into the kitchen, where Bex was busy cutting out pastry shapes. Emily was in her high chair, eating some grapes.

'Hiya, Bex,' said Megan.

Bex looked up. 'How was your last day?'

'Mostly quite fun. The assembly was good, I've got a

whole heap of cards and my tutor group loved your spiced biscuits—'

'I'm glad.'

'But Christmas won't be Christmas with mocks hanging over us.'

'It won't be that bad. You can take a few days off. You've been revising so hard already.' Bex walked around the big table and gave her stepdaughter a hug. 'You're going to be fine – you'll sail through them.'

'Maybe,' said Megan, sounding less than confident. 'And I'm worried about Ashley; he's been so caught up in the panto, he hasn't even started revising yet and now he's talking about getting a job…' Megan's forehead wrinkled. 'He keeps saying he won't need A levels if he gets into drama school, but supposing he doesn't?'

Bex smoothed Megan's hair. 'Given how totally terrific he was in the panto I'd think any drama school would bite his hand off to have him. Anyway, he's not your responsibility.'

'No, but…'

'No *buts*,' said Bex firmly. 'Besides, he's practically a grown-up—'

'Actually, he *is* a grown-up. He's had his eighteenth.'

'Then I'm sure he can juggle a part-time job and school-work. He can't revise every hour in the day.'

'That's what he said.'

'Well, then… And anyway, with Amy here, I don't think we ought to be discussing her son.'

Megan knew her stepmother had a point, but her kind heart wasn't going to stop worrying just because it had been told to.

———

Miles came home a couple of hours later – the lunch service having finished at the pub. He slumped onto the sofa, put his head back on a cushion and shut his eyes.

Bex, who had heard the front door bang, followed him into the sitting room.

'Where are the kids?' asked Miles, sitting up and trying to look alert.

'Emily is having a nap, the boys are playing on my iPad in the kitchen and Megan is in her room. She may be revising or she may be on TikTok – who knows. Tea?'

'I could murder a cup.'

Miles shut his eyes again till Bex reappeared with his drink.

'You look shattered,' she said.

'Well it's the last Friday before Christmas so it was wall-to-wall office parties, Christmas shoppers… The pub was mad. Honestly, Belinda is going to have to get someone to help us out in the kitchen – Jamie and I can't cope. We were running out of plates, pans, prepped veg…' He sighed. 'People popping into the pub for lunch don't want to wait half an hour for a toasted sandwich.'

'No, I can see that.' Bex paused, while she thought. 'Would it have to be someone skilled?'

'We need a kitchen porter, not another chef.'

'Could anyone do that?'

'Why?'

'Just asking.'

'It's hard work – lots of washing-up, cleaning down surfaces, loading and unloading the dishwashers… But, no, not skilled.' He stared at her. 'Why?' he repeated.

'Because Megan's friend, Ashley, was talking about job-hunting, apparently. Something part-time.'

'But he's got exams.'

'He still wants a job and, if you don't employ him, someone else will.'

'What does his mother say?'

'How should I know? At any rate, you'll only need him for the busy times. Let's face it, you and Jamie have coped so far.'

'I suppose. And if he's like his mother, he won't be afraid of hard work. How many jobs does Amy hold down?'

'Exactly. Shall I tell Megan to talk to him?'

'Why not?' Miles picked up his tea and took a slurp.

———

Amy put her three bags of shopping down and eased her shoulders. Her little council house was silent. Did that mean she was alone, or that Ryan was having a kip and Ashley was working?

'Anyone home?' she called. She heard a chair scrape back upstairs.

'Hi, Mum.' Footsteps thumped on the stairs.

'Put the kettle on, there's a love,' said Amy as her son appeared at the foot of them.

Ashley tramped off into the kitchen and she heard the kettle being filled.

'Got some good news, Mum.'

Amy hung her coat on the newel post and picked up her shopping. 'What's that?' She hefted the bags onto the counter with a grunt.

'Got a job.'

Amy sagged back against the work surface. 'You've what?'

'Got a job.'

'Are you barking mad?' she yelled.

Ashley shook his head. 'I thought you'd be pleased.'

'You thought wrong. What about your exams?'

'I'm revising; I'm working hard on them.'

'Huh.'

'I can do both.'

'Really?'

Ashley stared at his mum defiantly. 'Yes I can. And it's only part-time.'

'What are you doing?'

'Working at the pub – in the kitchens.'

Amy shook her head. 'But you can't cook.'

'I can wash up.'

'Washing-up? That's no job for a man.'

'It's work, Mum – paid work. And I'll give you money towards my keep out of it. It's win-win, Mum. You'll have more; I can save for when I leave home, and when I *do* leave home, I'll have something to put on my CV.'

Amy didn't look convinced. She sighed. 'I can see you've made your mind up and got it all worked out.'

Ashley nodded.

'But promise me something,' said Amy.

'What?'

'If you muck up your mocks, you'll give it up. Promise?'

The kettle boiled. Ashley concentrated on making the tea. 'So what would you call mucking up?'

'Failing them.'

'I won't.'

'You better not. When do you start?'

'Monday – Miles said he'd be too busy to train me over the weekend.'

'Then you'd better get back to your books, hadn't you? You ain't got time to lay around and enjoy yourself.'

'No, Mum.'

TWELVE

'Is that the Larkham household?' said the voice on the phone.

'It might be,' said Maxine, warily. She'd already had one cold call that morning asking about her household security arrangements. 'As if I'd tell a complete stranger about our burglar alarm,' she'd muttered to herself, putting the phone down while the caller was mid-sentence.

'Excellent. It's Laurence here.'

'Laurence! How lovely. I'm sorry I was rather cool but... you know... spammers.' She felt stupidly flustered and pleased by the call.

'No, I fully understand.'

'But, how did you get my number?'

'You gave it to me, remember; the night I came for that truly excellent curry.'

Maxine had forgotten. But now she'd remembered she'd scrawled it on a horribly scrappy piece of paper. He'd kept it? Goodness.

'Anyway, I'm ringing because I want to return the favour.'

'Honestly, you don't—'

'I've moved into the Reeve House. Would you and Gordon come to dinner with me – help me make the house seem lived in?'

'Oh... We'd love to. That'd be delightful. When?'

How about the first Friday in January? You'll be busy over Christmas and I'm sure you've already got plans for Hogmanay.'

'Hog...? Oh, New Year's Eve. Er, no actually.'

'Really? Then why not come here? What could be nicer than celebrating with friends?'

Maxine felt flattered that he thought of her as a friend. Lozza Lachlan, a celeb, calling *her* a friend.

'That sounds wonderful. I mean, I'll have to check with Gordon – just in case he's made secret plans for a surprise party.'

'Well, of course.'

Did Maxine detect a note of amusement in his voice? 'I'll get back to you.'

'I'd better give you my number. Got a pen?'

Maxine scrabbled around in the drawer under the phone and found a pencil and a bit of scrap.

'Shoot.' She scribbled down the digits.

'And I'd better also ask if there's anything you don't eat?'

'Tripe,' said Maxine promptly.

'Oh, no! That's what I planned for the main course.'

Maxine laughed. 'Seriously, we're really easy to please. Anything. No allergies, no intolerances, nothing.'

'Just the kind of people my housekeeper likes.'

Maxine had to bite back an exclamation. *My housekeeper?!*

'So, assuming Gordon hasn't made plans you don't know about, I'll see you on the thirty-first – say, around eight? And don't dress up, please. Just wear what you're comfortable in.'

'Coo,' said Gordon, when Maxine found him in the potting shed, sharpening his lawnmower blades. 'Fancy us – mixing with the rich and famous.'

'I know. It's all a bit surreal. We ought to take a house-warming gift.'

Gordon stared at his wife. 'Really? What do the likes of us give a man who's just bought a four-million-pound house?'

'I could give him a painting – only… that might be a bit boastful. I mean, with money like that, he could have a house full of proper artists.'

Gordon shook his head. 'There you go again.'

'You know what I mean – pictures worth hundreds of thousands rather than hundreds.'

'For what it's worth, I think he'd love a picture of yours. Perhaps one of the town. A view of the church, or the town hall…'

'If you think so.'

'I do.'

———

Christmas came to Little Woodford, with the usual range of expectations, from the quiet and lonely older inhabitants, who simply wanted to get it over and done with, to the raucous young families, who were on tenterhooks with excitement. Christmas at Bex's house of course fell into the latter bracket, with even Emily, now nearly three, realising something was afoot. Lewis and Alfie were completely hyper in every waking moment while Megan vacillated between enjoyment of the celebrations and despair about revising for her exams. Miles was just looking forward to Christmas Day itself, when the pub would only be open for a couple of hours with no food served and Boxing Day, when it would be completely shut. Two whole days off.

'How's Ashley doing?' asked Megan, as she helped Miles prepare the veg for the following day's Christmas feast.

'He's a hard worker, I'll give him that,' said Miles, cutting a cross in a trimmed sprout and chucking it in a pan. 'He needs to sort out some of his time management, but he'll get there.'

'In what way?' Megan cut the potato she'd peeled into four and put it in another pan.

'If we're running out of saucepans, it's no good him wanting to load the dishwasher with crockery instead. And when a delivery arrives, he needs to deal with that and stop peeling potatoes. He needs to work it out for himself and not be told by me or Jamie.'

'But you're going to keep him on?'

'Hell, yes. To be honest, I don't know how we managed before and he's only been with us a few days.'

'That's good. I still don't know how he's getting any schoolwork done. I'm finding it tough enough and I don't have any excuses.' Megan finished the last of her spuds and swept the peelings into a compost caddy. 'Anyway I can't hang around in the kitchen enjoying myself. Got to get back to my revision notes.'

'Thanks for the help, Megan,' Miles called after her.

Megan climbed the two flights of stairs to her attic eyrie and sat at her desk, which looked out across the front garden to the high street. The weather outside was wintry rather than Christmassy and rain pattered against the window and dripped off the eaves. She saw Belinda open the front gate and walk up the drive. She wondered idly what she wanted.

———

'All set for Christmas?' asked Miles, as Bex ushered her visitor into the kitchen.

'If you mean *have I sent all my cards and got the tree up?* then the answer is *yes*. If you mean *am I ready in any other way?* then the answer is an emphatic *no*. On the other hand, when you're a single woman with no close relations, you don't have to worry about anything much, except what's on the box.'

'Actually,' said Bex, as she pushed the kettle onto the Aga hotplate, 'that sounds quite attractive.' She got out a teapot and spooned in some tea.

'It has its pros and cons.'

As Belinda spoke, Alfie and Lewis erupted into the kitchen, both crying, both blaming each other for a broken toy, each shouting the other down.

Miles got up and took them away, suggesting it might be possible to fix the damaged plaything. He shut the door as he went and the decibel level in the kitchen dropped exponentially.

'I can imagine, but right now, the idea of a quiet Christmas has a certain appeal.'

'They're fine now and again. It gets a bit dreary when it's the norm.'

Bex's shoulders sagged a little in sympathy. 'Yes, I'm sorry. I was being flippant. I can see you're right.' She smiled an apology at Belinda. 'But don't you normally go round to Bert and Joan's for a slap-up lunch?'

'Yes, sometimes,' said Belinda, sounding falsely bright. 'But this year they're off to a niece's.'

'So, you're going to be alone? All day?'

Belinda shrugged. 'As you say, it has its advantages. It's very peaceful. No squabbles to adjudicate over, no fights over the TV remote—'

'And no company,' said Bex. 'Look, I know this is probably your idea of hell, but if you fancy finding out what the seventh circle is *really* like, you'd be more than welcome to join us for lunch.'

'I couldn't.'

'Why not? It isn't as if there won't be enough food to go round. You know what it's like with Miles catering! Truly, we'd love you to come.'

'But it's a family occasion.'

'And you're practically family.'

Miles, having restored order with the boys, re-entered the kitchen.

'Tell her, Miles,' said Bex.

'Tell her what?' The kettle on the Aga was jetting out steam, so Miles poured boiling water into the pot.

'That she should come here tomorrow for lunch.'

Miles looked at Belinda. 'Of course you must come.' He paused. 'I mean, if you want to. You might think slow disembowelment preferable to the bedlam that goes on here but... well, the offer is very much on the table.'

Belinda's face was transformed by a broad smile. 'If you're sure? What can I bring?'

'Yourself. Truly, that's all. Come round as soon as you get rid of the Christmas drinkers. We're planning on eating around two. Does that suit?'

'It sounds perfect,' said Belinda.

After she'd gone, Miles said, 'Do you think that's why she came round – to wangle an invite?'

'Maybe. But maybe we should have checked she was OK for Christmas.' Bex smiled. 'In a way I take it as a huge compliment that she wants to spend Christmas Day with us. Three hyped-up kids and a stressed-out teenager isn't everyone's cup of tea.'

Miles nodded. 'You're right. Well, next year, we'll get our invite in first. That's if she's still in the area.'

'You don't think she'd move away, do you? All her friends are here.'

'And it's a lovely place to live but... well, maybe she wants a fresh start, or the seaside... There's lots of reasons why she might want to go.'

'And there's even more to stay. Oh well, it's not our problem, nor is it our business. What *is* our business is that she should have a brilliant day with us.'

'And that's well within our skill set,' said Miles.

THIRTEEN

Belinda arrived at her hosts' house in time for lunch, bearing two bottles of good champagne and another of port. She could hear the shrieks of overexcited kids as she was shutting the gate at the end of the drive. She took a deep breath before she walked up the path, slightly apprehensive – ridiculously so, she told herself – about spending so much time with small children. Grown-ups in every form she could handle, but kids… She didn't have a clue. Still, it wasn't as if she was going to be flying solo – Bex and Miles would be there. All she had to do was to be nice to them.

When Bex opened the door, the smell of the roasting turkey was almost as overwhelming as the volume of noise.

'Happy Christmas! Sure you don't want to change your mind?' she said, as behind her, Alfie waved an inflatable dinosaur that was almost as big as he was, and chased Lewis, yelling in mock-terror, across the hall.

'No, no it's fine. Lovely,' she said, while wondering if children came equipped with a 'mute' button. Even with Alfie and Lewis in the sitting room the racket in the hall was ear-splitting.

'Come into the kitchen and say *hi* to Miles.'

Belinda followed Bex and put her carrier bag of bottles on the counter.

'Happy Christmas to you both,' she said.

'I'll put something on the TV for the kids,' said Bex. 'It'll keep them occupied so we can talk in relative peace and quiet.'

Ah, thought Belinda, *TV is the mute button. Jolly good.*

'And happy Christmas to you,' said Miles. He clocked the gift. 'Naughty, we said just bring yourself, but it's very welcome nonetheless.'

'The fizz is chilled.'

Bex had obviously found something to entertain the boys, because silence suddenly descended. A few seconds later she reappeared and saw Miles extract a bottle of Bollinger from the bag.

'Gosh.' She looked at Miles. 'All we normally run to is Prosecco, so this is a real treat. It would be rude not to try it,' she said. 'I'll get the glasses.'

Belinda sat on one of the kitchen chairs. 'I think this is the point at which I offer to help with the cooking and you say there's nothing to do.'

'You're right, and there isn't,' said Miles. 'Except that you can pop the cork, if you like. That's something I know you've got more skill and practice with than I have.'

Belinda took the bottle and peeled off the foil, then removed the wire cage. She waited until Bex returned with the champagne flutes, before she gripped the cork and slowly twisted the bottle. The cork popped out almost silently, apart from a faint hiss and a little puff of vapour.

'Yes, I know a huge pop and an explosion of bubbles is more exciting,' said Belinda, 'but all that does is waste the fizz.' She deftly half-filled the three flutes before topping them up to the brim, as the first burst of the bubbles subsided. 'Cheers.'

'Cheers,' Miles and Bex replied.

'And,' said Belinda, 'I know this might not be the right moment, but it isn't often I get to see you both together. Any more thoughts about the sale of the pub? Only, come the spring, I'd like to get it on the market.'

Miles and Bex exchanged a look.

'Well…' started Bex.

'The thing is…' said Miles.

'You want to keep your half,' said Belinda.

'No, that's the thing,' said Miles. 'The town has got the pub and then there's the hotel and they cater for different ends of the market. Pub grub – *nice* enough but nothing spectacular – or fine dining. What the town doesn't have is anything in between – a bistro, that sort of thing.'

'Go on,' said Belinda.

'If I sold up my half, I wouldn't mind opening up my own place. Nothing big – maybe fifty covers – catering for people who want somewhere a bit quieter than the pub, but still affordable.'

'You sure?'

Miles and Bex nodded.

'In which case,' said Belinda, 'we'll wait for the winter blues to pass and then we'll approach a commercial property agent.' She smiled at them both. 'Thank you. That's my best Christmas present ever.'

Miles put his glass down and got on with the cooking, while Bex and Belinda, both redundant, watched. Belinda was mesmerised by her chef's efficiency.

'I rarely get to see him in action,' she said. 'Poetry in motion.'

Miles was getting the huge golden bird out of the Aga, as she said this. 'It'll be poultry in motion, if I drop this,' he grunted. He slid the roasting tin onto the counter and covered it with foil and a couple of tea towels. With the turkey resting, Miles then finished off the veg, the gravy, the bread sauce and all the other trimmings.

Periodically Bex went to check the children were all behaving – the boys were now glued to a Disney cartoon in the sitting room while Megan helped Emily dress her new doll in a seemingly endless variety of outfits.

Finally, all was ready, Belinda and Bex ferried most of the food into the dining room and, when the children were all seated round the big table, Miles brought in the vast turkey.

Alfie's eyes almost popped out of his head.

'Wow!' he said.

'It's bigger than you,' said Belinda. 'I think Mummy and Daddy are fattening you up for next Christmas.'

For a second Alfie looked as if he believed her, before he said. 'Don't be silly, Mummy and Daddy wouldn't eat me.'

'Not unless I was really hungry,' said Miles, brandishing a carving knife. 'Just as well there's plenty to eat today, isn't it?'

It took a while to serve everyone, to pass round the side dishes, the gravy, the pigs in blankets, the cranberry and bread sauces, for glasses of juice or wine to be filled and for everyone to declare at last they had everything they wanted.

Belinda raised her glass. 'To the chef.'

A hour later they were all stuffed to the brim, Emily had gone up for her afternoon nap, Megan had retired to her room to revise, the boys were slumped in front of another cartoon and Bex and Belinda were ferrying the pudding plates into the kitchen, having told Miles they would clear up.

'I may have a quick snooze on the sofa,' he said.

Belinda surveyed the disaster area that was the kitchen. For a second she wondered where to start. 'Do your glasses go in the dishwasher?' she asked Bex.

'Not these ones.'

Belinda went to the sink and began to fill it with piping-hot water. As the washing-up bowl filled, she began to stack the dishwasher. She had the plates and cutlery in it, before she needed to switch off the taps and with an area of the counter clear, she laid out a couple of clean tea towels and began on the glassware; rinsing it in the sink before putting it to drip on the cloths.

'You are a powerhouse,' said Bex admiringly, as she watched order being restored.

'One of the few benefits of spending one's life in hospitality,' said Belinda.

The pair worked in tandem, until everything was sorted. The remains of the turkey were in the larder, piles of clean saucepans were on the table, the dishwasher was full and running, and the glasses were dry and sparkling. And the house was silent. The massive meal was being slept off by everyone else.

'Coffee?' said Bex.

'I'd love one.'

A couple of minutes later, Bex put two steaming mugs and a plate of home-made chocolate truffles on the table.

Belinda eyed them. 'You have to be joking,' she said. Then she added. 'That was lovely. A perfect Christmas.'

'Noisier than Bert and Joan's.'

'It certainly was. But more fun. Christmas really is for kids, isn't it?'

Bex nodded. Emboldened by fizz and a glass (or two) of

port she asked, 'Was not having a family a conscious decision? Don't answer, if you don't want to, but I'm curious.'

'Yes and no… At first I liked being a career woman, running my own business, being good at what I did and it was more than enough.' Belinda took a sip of her coffee. 'But then, as the years passed, I got set in my ways. It gets very difficult to accept someone else in your life when their set ways don't match yours. Which is why Miles and I never worked out.' She stared at Bex. 'But I am *so* glad you and he did. Really, you two are perfect together. Anyway, it was around the time he and I split that I realised that it was never going to happen for me.' She stared at the steam rising from her mug. 'I don't mind – most of the time. Oh, not about Miles, hell no… *or* not having kids. No, I mind that I don't think there's ever going to be anyone significant in my life. No one to wake up next to every morning, no one to snuggle up against on a chilly winter's night.' She smiled sadly at Bex. 'I think that ship has sailed. Actually it's sailed, docked in New York and is on the return leg. I have to accept I'm going to wind up a lonely old spinster.'

Bex shook her head. 'I don't think so. I think there'll be someone out there for you.'

'I did meet someone, very briefly a few weeks back. There was an instant attraction. He was *very* gorgeous and the way he looked at me… well, I haven't been looked at like that for quite a while.' She wasn't going to admit to Bex that she still fantasised about it, about what it might have led to, if things had a bit different. If they'd met under other circumstances.

'Oooh,' said Bex.

'But he was passing through.' She shrugged. 'Still,' she added as lightly as she could, 'it's nice to know that some basic human reactions still function. Even with my advanced years.'

'Bollocks. And besides, when you're not so busy you'll have more time to look. Gosh, if I look half as good as you, when I'm contemplating retirement, I shall be more than delighted. And everyone says how lovely you are as a person – which is true.'

'Shut up,' said Belinda, blushing.

'You can't deny it. And, in the words of the immortal Jane Austen: "It is a truth universally acknowledged that a single man in possession of a fortune must be in want of a wife." Only in this case we can dispense with the *possession of a fortune* bit.'

'Oh, I don't know,' said Belinda. 'I wouldn't mind swapping comfortable living for the lap of luxury.'

Bex laughed. 'I don't think anyone would disagree with that.'

———

A week later Maxine and Gordon walked through the now-open, ornate, wrought-iron gates at the top of the drive to the Reeve House.

'Fancy living behind gates like these,' said Gordon, gazing at the intricate wrought iron.

'Frankly, I'm thankful I don't. Think of painting them.'

'We'd get a man in to do it.'

'I suppose. I can't imagine having that sort of money.'

Gordon put his arm round her waist and gave her a squeeze. 'With your paintings doing as well as they are, it's not such a pipe dream anymore.'

'Daft bugger,' said Maxine.

They crunched up yards and yards of gravel drive, lined

with ancient copper beeches, and old-fashioned street lamps that made Maxine think Mr Tumnus ought to be standing under one of them. And then, through the bare branches, they saw the house.

'Wow,' breathed Maxine.

Ahead of them the drive divided and formed a grassy turning circle. In the centre of this grass was a large ornamental pond, with a bronze statue of a boy holding a turtle, from which spouted an elegant jet of water that splashed onto the rocks at his feet. Behind this was the house.

'"Last night I dreamt I went to Manderley again",' murmured Maxine.

'It is a bit, isn't it?' agreed Gordon.

They paused and took in the building, floodlit in the dark night. In front of them was a weathered stone two-storey tower with crenellations and a massive oak double door, overlooked by a beautiful mullioned window. It was breathtaking.

Gordon assumed a passable Loyd Grossman accent. 'And who do you think lives in a house like this?'

'A very lucky, very rich man,' said Maxine. 'Come on,' she said.

The bell pull, predictably, was a big brass handle connected to a rod. Maxine gave it a yank. After a few seconds, during which they wondered if the bell had actually rung, they heard the scraping of the lock, one of the doors was flung open and there was Laurence, dressed in slacks and an open-necked checked shirt.

'Welcome, and come in out of the cold.'

Behind the door was an enormous hall with a hammerbeam roof, a gallery running around it, a large and beautifully decorated Christmas tree and a flagged floor, covered with a selection of glorious Persian rugs in vibrant reds and blue and greens. On the walls hung some massive portraits, and in the middle of the wall opposite the stairs was a monster fireplace with a roaring fire burning merrily. It was, thought Maxine, the sort of fire that should have had a whole ox rotating on a spit over it. Soft jazz played in the background. It was a perfect English Christmas scene as imagined by Hollywood – almost too good to be real. Except here it was.

A woman appeared from a small door on one side of the massive oak staircase leading up to the gallery.

'This is Mrs Huggins, Elspeth. She's my housekeeper – or, at least she is for the time being.'

'Now then, Laurence, you know perfectly well that John and I won't be going anywhere till you're sorted with replacements.'

Maxine remembered what Laurence had said about old retainers wanting to move back to Scotland.

Laurence smiled fondly at her. 'Yes, I know. Now then, give your coats to Elspeth and I'll get you a drink. Name your poison.'

Maxine asked for a gin and tonic, Gordon fancied a beer, and Laurence went to a small bar tucked into the corner and began to get out glasses and bottles. A few minutes later they were settled on the vast antique chesterfields flanking the fire.

'Gosh, this is cosy,' said Maxine, as she sipped her drink. 'And such a beautiful house. Oh, before I forget…' She produced a long cardboard tube from a bag. 'I hope you don't think me presumptuous, but I brought this, as a bit of a house-warming present.' She handed it to her host.

It took Laurence a few seconds to extricate the picture and to unroll it.

'Oh Lordy,' he said. 'For me? Really?' He looked at the watercolour of the Little Woodford high street in the summer, with real pleasure. 'This is wonderful.'

Maxine felt ridiculously made-up by his reaction. 'I'm glad you like it.'

'Like it?! I love it.' He swooped over to her and planted a big smacker on her cheek. 'I hope you don't mind, Gordon.'

'Carry on, old man.'

'It just shows what can be achieved when the artist has real talent,' he said admiring the picture again. 'Something I totally know I don't have.'

'I could try and help you some more with technique,' offered Maxine.

Laurence gave her a steady stare. 'Maxine, I think we both know what a waste of your time that would be, lovely though the offer is.'

It was almost two a.m. when Maxine and Gordon finally tottered back down the road, full of excellent food and rather too much champagne. It had been an epic evening complete with fireworks let off at midnight.

'And that must have cost a bob or two,' observed Gordon.

At Maxine's insistence, they'd also enjoyed a rendition of Laurence's famous theme tune *"Ninety-nine"* at the grand piano in his study, a room as big as Maxine and Gordon's sitting room.

'That was some house,' said Gordon as they toiled up the hill.

'It's a big old place to rattle around in on your own,' agreed Maxine.

'He's got Mrs Huggins.'

'I don't think that's anything other than professional. It must be all very well having staff but it's not the same as family is it? Judging by what he told us a while back, he doesn't seem that close to his kids and his marriage is on the rocks. That's not a great place to be, is it?'

'Just shows that money isn't everything – it can't buy you happiness.'

'But you can be miserable in a degree of comfort.'

'I think,' Gordon said, stopping and turning to his wife, 'I'd rather be happy with you, than have what Laurence has got.' He dropped a kiss on the end of her nose, before they began walking up the hill again.

'I hope he didn't mind me saying he should offer his garden for the fête.'

'If he did,' said Gordon, 'it really didn't show. And he did say he wanted to be a part of the community.'

'Although I know we still mustn't let on who he really is – or not for a few more months.'

'You can't blame him. He wants to make friends with people and know they like him for himself, not because of anything else.'

'Someone will work it out. They're bound to be interested in whoever has bought that house.'

'Maybe,' said Gordon. 'Only I don't remember anyone really caring who owned that place before.'

They turned into their road. 'True, except the previous owner bought it before we had the internet. It was a lot harder to pry, back then.' Maxine got her key out, as they turned into their drive. 'Anyway, although his house is glorious, I think I'd rather live here. Just think about getting the cobwebs down in that great hall.'

FOURTEEN

Heather was up a stepladder, getting down her decorations, when Brian showed Maxine into her sitting room.

She put a little clutch of baubles on the top step and made her way gingerly back down to the floor.

'Maxine, what a lovely surprise.'

'I hope it's not a bad time.'

'No, I was about to have a break and make Brian and me a coffee. You'll join us, won't you?'

'Lovely.'

'I'm the bearer of good news,' said Maxine as Heather got out mugs and filled the kettle.

'Better and better.'

'You remember I told you I'd met someone interested in the Reeve House?'

'Yes.'

'Well, they've bought it and agreed to open the grounds for the fête.'

Heather's face lit up. 'No!'

'Yes. Isn't that great?'

Heather clapped her hands. 'What a brilliant start to the new year. I can't wait to tell the committee; they'll be thrilled.'

'How's the recruitment drive going?'

'Really well. We've got a new treasurer – who under-stands accounting, so that's a relief – and a couple of people who are happy to be gofers, so we're pretty much quorate. And now we've got a venue, we can start planning in earnest. I am *so* pleased. Thank you.' Heather plugged the kettle in. 'So... who's the new owner?'

Maxine pursed her lips. 'I know this sounds a bit loony, but I'm not at liberty to say.'

'You're joking.'

'No. The person in question is a really nice, genuine soul, but would like to be anonymous for a while longer.'

Heather shook her head. 'Well, it all sounds a bit odd to me, but I trust you and it's only a garden we're borrowing, so I suppose it's none of my business. But obviously he or she is rich and famous.'

Maxine grinned at her friend. 'Stop digging. My lips are sealed.'

'Worth a try. But I'll need a contact phone number or email, or something. We'll have to do a recce of the garden and ask about where we can hook up for power and water. I mean, you could be the go-between, I suppose, but it'll mean an awful lot of work for you.'

Maxine nodded. 'The owner has a housekeeper, Mrs Huggins. She'll sort you out and I'll let you have her number.'

'Housekeeper, eh?'

'Yes, all very Mrs Danvers and Manderley but the owner is no Maxim de Winter – or Rebecca, for that matter – although the house could certainly be used as a location, if they wanted to do yet another remake of the film.'

'You've seen it?' Heather couldn't hide her envy.

'Had dinner there. And it's very, *very* beautiful. That's when I got the owner onside.'

Heather tugged her forelock. 'I can see I'm going to have to be super-nice to you, now you're mates with the rich and famous.'

Maxine grinned. 'I didn't say anything about anyone being rich and famous.'

'Well, they've got to be rich to buy that house and if you're being so coy about naming whoever, they've got to be famous. QED,' said Heather smugly, as she made the tea.

The pub, that lunchtime, was quiet. It was always the way after Christmas and the New Year. The guys from the allotments – Harry, Bert and a couple of others – were there having their usual lunchtime pint and busy putting the world to rights. There were a couple of men in suits, poring over a laptop at another table but, other than that, the pub was empty. Belinda was busy stocking one of the shelves with mixers, when the door opened and a man strolled in. It took a second for Belinda to process who it was. Maxine's pal. Laurence, she remembered. How could she forget the man who'd given her *that look*? The man whose stare had made her knees tremble. The man she thought she'd never see again.

Oh dear God.

'Hello,' she said, straightening up. She hoped her voice sounded normal. 'What can I get you?'

'Hello,' he responded, settling himself on one of the stools at the bar and contemplating the beers on offer.

That accent. She'd forgotten how meltingly delicious it was. And those eyes!

'What would you recommend? I'll admit to not being familiar with any of these beers. And it's Belinda, right?'

Oh… he'd remembered. She wanted to bounce up and down with happiness, possibly waving a cheerleader's pom-pom. Instead she confined herself to saying, 'Yes. Well remembered.' She swallowed to keep her voice steady. 'The beers are mostly from local breweries. I can recommend this one.' Belinda put her hand on the pump. 'You can have a taste if you like… er… Laurence, if my memory serves me well.'

'I'm impressed.' His oh-so-blue eyes twinkled at her. 'Yes please.'

Belinda sploshed a quarter of an inch of amber liquid into a glass and handed it over.

Her customer tasted it. 'Nectar,' he pronounced. 'A pint of that, please. And the lunch menu?'

'Sure.' Belinda concentrated on pouring the pint. 'So… what brings you back to Little Woodford?' she asked as she rang up the sale.

'I've just moved here.'

He'd *moved* here?! 'Then I hope you'll be very happy. And I hope to see more of you.' She handed him his change. A *lot* more of you, she thought. All of you.

'I'm sure you will.' Laurence took his pint and the menu and went to a window table, quite unaware that Belinda was staring after him.

'Phwoar,' she whispered to herself. 'If only…'

───────

With the festivities well and truly over, life for pretty much everyone fell back into the old routines. The Christmas lights round the town were switched off and the decorations came down, people went back to work, schools returned and Zac, Ashley, Sophie and Megan were almost relieved their mock exams had actually started. Over at the vicarage, Heather was staring at a piece of paper with a number written on it and wondering if she had the brass nerve to ring it.

'Brace up,' she said to herself, as she picked up the phone and began to dial the local number. The phone was answered after half a dozen rings.

'Hello,' said a soft female voice with a Scots accent.

'Erm… is that Mrs Huggins?'

'It most certainly is. And who is calling?'

'I'm Heather Simmonds, the vicar's wife. I'm ringing about the fête.'

'Oh, yes. Mrs Larkham told me to expect a call. What can I do for you?'

'Well, I have no idea what the grounds of the Reeve House are like and I need to do a site visit, for a risk assessment and to discuss matters like power and water and other stuff like emergency access.'

'I see. When would you like to do this?'

'Ideally, as soon as possible.'

'This afternoon?'

'Goodness.' Heather paused. She hadn't expected anything quite so soon. But she had nothing planned. 'Yes, that'd be perfect.'

'Come around two, if that's convenient. Looking forward to meeting you.'

'Thank you, me too. Goodbye.'

Heather put the phone down and realised she was quite

excited about going to the Reeve House. It wasn't often being a vicar's wife meant you scored a perk – what a bonus.

Several hours later she walked through the wrought-iron gates and up the long drive. At the far end she could glimpse pale grey stone and her curiosity made her quicken her pace slightly.

Feeling diffident, she tugged the bell pull and waited, trying not to feel as if she was a trespasser. The door opened and she saw a stoutish woman with grey hair piled into a cottage-loaf bun, and a floral pinny.

'Mrs Simmonds?'

'Please call me Heather. You must be Mrs Huggins.'

'Elspeth. Come in and we'll go and talk in the kitchen.'

Heather stepped into the great hall and tried not to goggle too obviously, but it was very difficult. To someone who had spent most of her adult life in rather inadequate vicarages, a private house on this scale was quite surreal.

'Lovely, isn't it?' said Elspeth.

'Stunning.'

Elspeth opened a door under the stairs and led her down a long panelled corridor to the kitchen. With its worn flags, dressers stacked with china, a massive refectory table in the middle and polished copper pans above the Aga, she half expected someone like Mrs Patmore or Carson to make an appearance. She noticed that one end of the kitchen was rather more modern with a wall of fitted cupboards and a granite counter. She hoped, for Elspeth's sake, that there were also some integrated appliances, like a dishwasher and a washing machine.

'Take a seat,' said Elspeth. 'Tea?'

Heather nodded and smiled, too stunned to speak.

The tea was, of course, made in a pot, with milk in a jug and served with home-made biscuits. As they ate and drank,

Heather told Elspeth about the town and the fête and Elspeth reciprocated with a bit of the house's history. Heather was dying to ask who her employer was, but didn't dare. And she was longing, with almost equal intensity, for Elspeth to offer to show her around the rest of the house but, when they'd finished their tea, Elspeth led her out into the grounds, through the kitchen door and Heather knew she'd have to be content with the little bit she'd seen.

Naturally, the grounds were as glorious as the house, with a terrace leading down to a formal parterre, a wonderful walled vegetable garden and an enormous, manicured lawn that swept down to the river Catte. Even in the bleak, cold January light, the garden was looking well-tended and Heather could imagine summer picnics on the lawn, or drinks parties on the terrace – and, of course, a proper garden fête, with bunting, music and fun and games.

'We thought you could hold the fête here, on the lawn. It'd be big enough, wouldn't it?' said Elspeth. She had her back to the river and was looking towards the house. Heather followed suit and contemplated the space. It was perfect, as far as the size was concerned, but she worried about the river. 'Would your boss object to us fencing it off – only I'm not sure running water and overexcited small children are a great mix?'

'I'm sure he'd be OK with that.'

'We'd pay for it, of course.'

Elspeth turned and faced Heather. 'I think he'd prefer for the fête to maximise its profit.'

'You mean…?'

'I'll have to check, but I'm pretty sure that's what he'd want.'

Heather was almost speechless with gratitude.

'Now,' said Elspeth, 'let me show you where the outside

taps are and where there are some external electric sockets. I don't know if you need many.' She began walking back towards the house and Heather fell into step beside her.

'Really, we only need one socket for the PA system and another for the hot water boiler in the catering tent. We've made do with a bowser and a small generator in the past, but mains utilities would be a luxury. And is your boss happy about marquees going up and people walking all over this lovely lawn?'

'He's fine. It's only grass – it'll grow back.'

'Your boss seems to be quite a remarkable person.'

'He is, he's lovely.'

Which left Heather wishing again that she knew who he was – if only so she could pray for his health and happiness, which she felt was the least she could do.

FIFTEEN

The next meeting of the fête committee had to be held in the community centre because Heather's kitchen was now too small to squeeze everyone in. The atmosphere had changed too and everyone was buzzing with the news that the fête would be held at the Reeve House. Heather was finding it difficult to keep them focused on the agenda.

'Right,' she said, tapping her water glass with a pen. 'Sponsorship. Miranda?'

'On the basis that the new venue is bound to increase footfall, I've had some success,' she said. 'The sponsors think, once word gets out, half the town will pitch up, even if only to rubberneck. And because of that, I've managed to get some new ones on board.'

'That's brilliant news,' said Heather. 'Can I ask who?'

Miranda listed a farm machinery supplier, a printing company and the local brewery. 'Which takes our total sponsorship to date to nearly four grand.'

'Well done,' said Heather. 'That's going to help a lot. Which brings us neatly to the treasurer's report. Diane?'

'Indeed. Now,' said Diane, as she put a document case on the table. 'Remember me saying that the accounting system needed a bit of an overhaul?' The old committee members nodded. 'Well, we need new bank mandates to allow me to sign stuff off and to remove a couple of signatories who are no longer on the committee. I've got the necessary paperwork here.' She pulled a wodge of papers from the case. 'So, after the meeting, if Jacqui, Miranda and Heather could stay behind and sign all this lot, I can get on and move our funds into a more advantageous account.'

Heather smiled at Diane. 'Thank you. It's a good job we've got someone on board who knows what they're doing.'

'And the bank balances are two thousand six hundred and fifty-four pounds and eight pence in the deposit account and three thousand seven hundred and fifty in the current account. I've taken the liberty of looking at the previous accounts and I've gone out to tender to a number of marquee companies, requesting the same spec as previous years. If that's OK?'

Heather sat back in her chair. 'That's brilliant.'

'I can do the same with the other contracts, if you'd like?'

'If you don't mind. That's one big job I can tick off my list.' Heather sighed happily. Maybe everything was going to be all right after all. In fact, more than all right.

———

An hour later, while the meeting in the community centre was packing up, Belinda was unlocking the front door of the Talbot before she returned to the bar to start slicing lemons and limes ready for the day. She heard the door open – someone was keen – and looked up. Laurence. Her heart raced.

'Hello,' she said, pretending nonchalance. 'A pint of Rabbit Punch?'

'Is that what I had last time?'

'It was.'

'That's some memory you've got, Belinda.'

Her heart thumped harder.

'First, you remembered my very first visit, and my name and now you remembered what beer I drank on my second visit. Is this your party trick for every new customer?'

Just the ones I fancy. 'But you remembered my name too,' she countered.

'One of my first girlfriends was called Belinda. Always had a soft spot for that name.'

Belinda felt herself blushing and turned away to ring up the sale. 'Three-sixty,' she said, once she felt under control. 'Anything else?'

'One of your excellent tuna baps, please.'

'Good choice.' She rang in that sale too and gave him the new total. 'Another couple of visits and I'll start thinking of you as a regular.'

'That's an ambition to aspire to.'

Belinda laughed. 'So, do you work locally?'

'I'm kind of freelance.'

'Doing?'

'This and that.'

Belinda knew when she was being given the brush-off and felt wary of annoying him and spoiling things. 'If you want to take a seat, I'll bring your bap over when it's ready.' She gave him her best smile, to show she didn't mind. Even if she did, rather.

The pub was deathly quiet, which she found unusually unnerving; she kept wanting to exchange a comment or an observation with Laurence, but didn't feel he wanted the company so, to distract herself and to fill the silence, she decided to put on some music. Mostly Belinda avoided background music; when the pub was busy, as it so often was, there was no need for any other noise. She flicked through the playlist. Sixties greatest hits… That'd do. She turned the volume down as 'Waterloo Sunset' drifted through the pub.

Laurence looked up. 'One of my favourites,' he said.

'Mine too. Always wish I'd gone to see the Kinks live.'

'Why didn't you?'

'I don't know – too busy, too broke, too lazy…'

'All poor excuses.'

'I know. I suppose I always thought there'd be another time, another gig.' Belinda shrugged. The kitchen door opened. It was Jamie with the tuna bap. Belinda ferried it over to the table.

'Can I get you anything else? Any sauces?'

'No, this looks perfect. So, what other music do you like?'

As the pub was still empty, Belinda decided to sit down. 'The Beach Boys—'

Laurence nodded.

'The Stones.'

'That's a given.'

'The Moody Blues, The Who, Dire Straits…'

'What about classical?'

Belinda shook her head. 'Nope, I'm a philistine in that department.'

'Folk?'

'Nope.'

'Jazz?'

Another shake of her head.

'Fancy being educated?'

Belinda laughed, as the door swung open and some more customers came in. She returned to her position behind the bar and, as she took new orders, wondered just what Laurence had in mind.

———

'Stop writing and put down your pens,' said Mr Johnson, head of maths at the comp.

Ashley, who'd been checking his answers for the last ten minutes of the exam leaned back in his chair with a sigh of relief. The last of his mocks was over. He now had a clear week, a week where he could start getting his act together for auditions. His weekend shifts at the pub had paid fifty pounds a time and he now had almost enough put by to start submitting applications. Travel was still a problem. There was an outside possibility that Ryan might help out with lifts, but he couldn't rely on that. And if an audition was scheduled for the weekend, he wouldn't be able to work to earn more money.

Mr Johnson swept up his paper along with the rest, leaving Ashley free to go. His fellow students were busy discussing the questions, their answers and trying to work out how well – or badly – they'd done. Ashley couldn't see the point of picking over something that couldn't be changed and headed for home. He reached the end of the school drive and hesitated. He had a free week. He had to learn his audition pieces, but maybe he could squeeze in a shift or two at the pub – if they wanted him. Maybe he should nip down to the Talbot and see if there might be some extra hours going. And after he'd been there, maybe he could have a word with Lizzie about his auditions... what to expect, what they might ask of him, what he should wear? His mates off to uni had it so much easier compared to him; they were being spoon-fed every step of the way, but none of the teachers seemed to have a clue about how to help a budding actor. Thank God for Sophie's mum.

When Ashley pitched up at Sophie and Lizzie's front door, some thirty minutes later, having scored an extra shift at the pub on Friday evening, he had a whole raft of questions buzzing around his brain. Sophie let him in.

'You've finished?' she said. She looked tense and stressed. 'You jammy bugger – I've still got two to go. And, as I'm up to my neck in revision notes, if you and Mum want tea or coffee, you can make it yourselves.' She disappeared back upstairs and Ashley heard her door click shut. He made his own way into the little sitting room where Lizzie sat in her wheelchair, flicking through a magazine.

'Poor old Soph,' said Ashley. 'I'm lucky, my mocks are all done.'

'It's a stressful time,' agreed Lizzie. 'But auditions are going to be worse – you are going to be judged, *to your face* in front of other people. At least your exam answers are a private matter between you and the guy marking your papers. Being told you're not good enough or not right for the part... being rejected, *in public*, is hideous. Because you will be. It doesn't matter how talented you are as an actor, when you audition, the casting director already knows what he wants – the age, the voice, maybe even the way he thinks the character should walk – and if you don't fit that bill... *Next!* Are you sure you're strong enough?'

'I've got to be,' said Ashley.

Lizzie rubbed her hands together. 'Right then, let's hear your pieces.'

———

Three weeks later Ashley stood in a large room, facing a panel of five, trying to gauge how sympathetic or otherwise they might be. The girl who went before him had looked wrung out as she'd walked back into the waiting room. The others flicked smiles in her direction, but she just stared morosely at the floor. No one spoke, but they vibrated with nerves, while desperately trying to look cool and nonchalant. As actors, they were all producing brilliant performances, until you looked at the shaking hands and the nervous fidgeting.

As Ashley stood before the panel, his knees trembling, he wished he knew what they were really looking for. During the workshop in the morning, he'd made friends with a couple of the others and they'd exchanged worries, doubts and ambitions, along with mobile numbers and a promise to share results. And now, as he waited to do his monologues, Ashley was pretty sure what the outcome of his audition was going to be. He wanted it to be otherwise but deep down he was convinced this wasn't going to be his moment. His self-doubt demons were out in force.

The waiting room was a little way along a corridor, which meant no one had really been able to hear the other auditions properly, hard though they'd tried. Ashley knew they'd all be trying equally hard to listen to him. Nerves, and this sudden plummeting of his self-belief and self-esteem, almost made him turn and run. And yet... he pulled his shoulders back. Shit, he'd paid forty-five pounds for the privilege of being here, to say nothing of a train fare. He might as well do this, even if it was a waste of time and money because, at least, it would be experience to tuck away, experience that might help him in the future.

'When you're ready, Ashley,' said one of the panellists.

Ashley took a deep breath. 'I'm doing a piece from *The*

Graduate – a speech made by Benjamin Braddock, the one where Benjamin is asking Elaine's forgiveness for an affair with her mother.' He could hear the nervous tremor in his voice but he hoped it wouldn't be discernible to anyone else. But, as he spoke, he realised that his nerves perfectly mirrored Benjamin's nerves. He stopped trying to suppress the tremor and let it dominate his voice. He finished to the sound of pens scribbling on paper and waited till someone said, 'And the Shakespeare...'

'Thank you,' said one of them when he finished. Ashley was escorted back to the waiting room.

On a table under the window was a hot water boiler, jugs of cold milk and water and some sachets of teas and coffee. Ashley poured himself some water.

He turned and looked out of the window at the view of the car park and beyond, to a row of bare trees.

He had followed Lizzie's advice not to do his first audition at his top choice of drama school.

'Wait,' she'd said, 'till you've got a couple under your belt, till you see how the land lies, how others approach them, before you aim for your preferred choices.'

He'd protested about the cost, but Lizzie had shrugged and said it was up to him, if he wanted to end up with a compromise, rather than at the place where he really wanted to study. Now, in this waiting room, he conceded she might have had a point. This place would *do* if nowhere else came up trumps but he wasn't particularly drawn to it. He thought about what else she'd said: about how the process would be brutal – he'd thought she was exaggerating, but now realised she'd told him nothing but the truth.

The atmosphere in the room was oppressive, with his fellow auditionees either staring at the floor or their phones. The seconds ticked by, then the minutes. Ashley finished his water and dropped his paper cup into a wastebin. The sound of the stiff card hitting the metal made a couple of the wannabes look up, before they returned to their phones. But when the doorknob rattled, everyone sat up, tried to look engaged, positive… hopeful.

One of the panellists strode into the room. Ashley's heart rate went off the scale.

'Firstly I'd like to thank you all for coming today,' he said. 'I'm afraid we won't be calling any of you back.' And with that he turned and left the room.

That was it. Dismissal. Rejection.

Everyone stared disbelievingly at the slowly closing door.

A lad said, 'I don't know why I bothered,' before he pushed his chair back, stood up and stamped off. The girls gathered up their bags and coats, the boys picked up their jackets and, one by one, dejectedly left the room.

Lizzie had warned him it would be hard, that rejection would hurt, but he hadn't expected it to be quite so visceral. No feedback, no tips on how to do it better, nothing. No glimmer of hope, no 'We all thought you did well, but you're not for us'. Just, fuck off. As Ashley headed back towards the station he wondered what the hell he was doing. At least, he thought, his mocks hadn't been an unmitigated disaster, so other avenues might just be open to him – not that he wanted them to be, but it was a slight comfort to know that, if all else failed, he would be able to get another qualification.

He wasn't sure he had a thick enough hide to take many such scouring rejections.

SIXTEEN

Belinda was crouched down behind the bar, rearranging a shelf of mixers ready for her lunchtime customers, when she heard someone clear their throat somewhere above her head. She stood up and came face to face with Laurence.

'Oh,' she said, slightly startled and suddenly flustered.

'The door was open, so I kind of assumed the pub was too.'

'Yes, yes. It is… I was just… Never mind,' said Belinda. She didn't think Laurence would be the least bit interested in her mixer shelf. 'What can I get you?'

'A pint of the usual? Isn't that what a regular asks for?'

'Oooh,' said Belinda, pulling the pint. 'I'm not sure I've promoted you to that status yet.'

Laurence leaned on the bar. 'Jeez, what does a customer have to do to reach those lofty heights? Take the landlady out to dinner?'

Belinda concentrated on bringing the beer up to the pint line on the glass, as she composed herself. It took two deep breaths. 'I'm being offered a bribe,' she said with exaggerated horror, when she felt calmer. 'I might have to report this to our local special constable.'

'Please, Guv,' responded Laurence in a cod-cockney accent. 'I didn't mean no 'arm. Don't report me to the rozzers.'

Belinda laughed as she handed the pint through the pump handles. 'I'll let you off, just this once.'

'Good.' Laurence took his pint and handed over a fiver, but kept a grip of his end as he said, 'but you still haven't answered my question. Dinner?' He let the note go. 'Please,' he said, staring into her eyes.

Belinda paused for a second, not wanting to look needy, before she replied, 'Yes, that'd be lovely. I'll have to fix cover. When have you got in mind?'

Laurence shrugged. 'What about Tuesday.'

'Tuesday? That should be fine.' She whipped out her phone to consult the calendar 'Oh… it's Valentine's Day.'

Laurence feigned innocence. 'Is it? That won't be a problem, will it?'

Belinda thought on her feet. She'd be employing extra staff that night, anyway; it was always a busy one, with couples wanting a romantic dinner. If she was going to hire one extra person she might as well hire two – but they would have to be from her list of regulars, who could cope unsupervised and wouldn't get flustered. If she and Laurence went out to dinner reasonably locally, they'd be back by nine-thirty at the latest and she could help cash up and close. 'No… no, Tuesday will be fine.'

'Oi,' said Bert, one of her regulars, from the allotments.

Belinda jumped as if she'd been stung.

'If you two lovebirds have finished canoodling, I'd like a pint of best, please.'

Ashley managed to get to the Talbot about a minute before he was due to start work for the evening service. He'd been engrossed in writing an English literature essay and had forgotten the time, so had had to jog all the way from the council estate to the other end of town.

'Sorry I'm late,' he said, as he barrelled through the door.

Miles was busy mixing a big bowl of batter for the fish. He glanced at the kitchen clock and saw it read five-thirty. 'You're not, and I wouldn't dock your wages, even if you were.'

Ashley put on a white jacket over his T-shirt. 'No, but...' He didn't want to piss off Miles. He needed another favour from him – more time off.

'You get the work done and graft when you're here, so that's what matters.'

'Thanks, chef,' said Ashley.

'If I didn't work here, I'd still employ you.'

Ashley stopped buttoning up his jacket. 'I'm not with you.'

'There's a chance I might be moving on, later in the year.'

'Really?'

Miles nodded. 'Jamie knows, but it's not common knowledge yet, so keep it under your hat. Belinda wants to retire and she's selling up her half. I think I'm too long in the tooth to start working for a new boss and Jamie is well up to running this kitchen as head chef, if the new owners want to keep him, so I'm going to sell my half too. And then I'd like to open my own restaurant. If you want to move with me, I'd be happy to take you.'

Ashley was completely wrong-footed. 'Oh,' was all he could think of saying.

'I'd need a good kitchen porter and I'd still be happy to give you time off for auditions. Of course, if you make it to drama school, then that'd be that, but if you'd like a safety net... Well, the offer is there. Think about it.'

'Yeah, sure. Thanks.'

Miles clapped him on the shoulder. 'Right, time to rock and roll. You know what needs doing.'

Ashley looked around the kitchen – a bin needed emptying into the big Biffa container outside, the industrial dishwasher's light was flashing to indicate it had finished its cycle and there was a sack of spuds that probably needed peeling. That was him sorted for the next hour, he reckoned. He got busy. But while he was working, he thought about Miles's offer and the fact that Belinda mightn't be running the Talbot for much longer. He thought there'd be quite a few people in the town who wouldn't be happy about that. Still, not his problem.

At six-thirty the kitchen was relatively quiet. Miles and Jamie had prepped everything, and the first of the orders for the evening meal had yet to come in. Now was a good moment to get that favour from Miles.

'Chef,' said Ashley, as he stacked clean saucepans on the rack of shelving in the kitchen. 'You know what you said about auditions?'

'Yes?'

'I've got another one.'

'When?'

'Next week.'

'And you'll want the evening off?'

Ashley nodded. 'Probably. It's over in Surrey and I haven't checked the train times yet, but I'll have to cross

London in the rush hour to get back here and I can't see me making it for the start of service.'

'What day?' said Miles, trying not to sigh.

'Tuesday.'

Miles tried hard not to roll his eyes. 'But that's Valentine's. It's always busy.'

'I'm sorry. You managed without me last year.' Ashley crossed the kitchen to pick up more clean saucepans.

Which was true. Miles nodded. 'You're right. We did.' But he'd got used to having Ashley now and he had become much more of a help than a hindrance. He could be trusted with prepping the veg, as well as keeping things clean and tidy. 'Ashley?'

'Yes.'

'Working here, doing your auditions... you are keeping up with your schoolwork, aren't you?'

Ashley put the pans down on a counter. 'You're sounding like my mum.'

'Sorry.' He wasn't. 'But Megan is feeling the pressure and she isn't doing half what you are.'

'No.' Ashley stacked his pans. 'But she's got a social life, which I haven't. I can't remember the last time I saw my mates outside of school.' He turned and faced Miles. 'I don't mind, because if I get into drama school, it'll all be worthwhile.' He stared at Miles. 'Go on... say it.'

'What?'

'And if you don't get into drama school?'

Miles stared back. 'Firstly, I don't like to meet trouble halfway. And secondly, you are so determined, you're working so hard, that if there's *any* justice at all, you will.'

'You didn't see my last audition.'

'You said you didn't get through. I bet you weren't the only one.'

Ashley shook his head. 'None of my group did.'

'There you go. Someone once said, *"The harder I work, the luckier I get"*. I think there's a lot of truth in that and you are working very hard. You'll get there. So yes, go to your auditions, any ones you like, just let me know in good time when they are and we'll work round them. And my earlier offer still stands.'

Ashley gave Miles a smile. 'Thanks, that's really good of you.'

'No probs. Now then, back to work!'

———

The next morning Heather unlocked the community centre and began to arrange a couple of tables and the chairs ready for the next fête committee meeting. She hummed as she did it, because she was feeling happy and upbeat and the sun was shining. OK, it was only thin, watery, February sunshine, but the snowdrops and crocuses in her garden were out, the camellia in the churchyard was glorious and the birds were singing their hearts out, as they competed for mates and territory. Spring was, most definitely, in the air and it wasn't long till the equinox, when suddenly the winter would be behind them.

'Morning, Heather,' said Miranda, as she stepped into the hall, shrugging off her rather beautiful fawn coat.

Heather would have bet it was made of finest camel hair but because Miranda was vegan, she suspected it was probably something equally pricy but synthetic. Oh, to have that sort of money, she thought, glancing at her own, threadbare coat from the Oxfam shop.

'You sound very chipper,' continued Miranda.

'*Spring is sprung, the grass is riz...*' replied Heather. 'I love this time of year. So full of hope.'

'And the fête is going well.'

'It certainly is. Such a turnaround from where we were before Christmas.'

'Do you know yet who our benefactor is?'

Heather shook her head. 'No, still a big mystery. Not a clue. But it would be nice if it were someone famous—'

'As opposed to just rich.'

Heather nodded. 'Because then we could ask him to open it.'

'So, you know it's *him*?'

'Yes, but that's all I know. I mean, if it's some wealthy hedge-fund manager, no one will want to come and see him in the flesh — or I think it's pretty unlikely — but if it's someone like... oh, I don't know... Michael Caine or Rod Stewart, the punters'll be queuing round the block.'

'Which is why he wants to keep anonymous.'

'I suppose. Anyway, it'll all theoretical because his house-keeper gave absolutely zero away when I met her.'

'But Maxine is certain he wants to become a part of the community and he's already demonstrated this by lending us the Reeve House, so does it matter who he is?'

'You mean,' said Heather, 'I ought to ask him to open the fête, anyway?'

'Definitely,' agreed Miranda.

Most of the rest of the committee were now approaching the community centre across the cricket pitch.

'I'll write the housekeeper a letter,' said Heather. 'I think that would be easier. And she can ask him in her own time and if the answer is a "no", it's easier to say it in writing.'

'Good shout,' said Miranda, just as the rest of the committee trooped through the door.

It took a good ten minutes to get everyone settled round the table and for business to commence. It was all terrifically positive: the bank balances, according to Diane, were looking very healthy; sponsors were, said Miranda, being more than generous and almost everyone who had taken or run stalls in previous years were on board again for this year.

'Well,' said Heather, 'I think this is going to be an absolute bobby-dazzler of an event. I have been involved for about a dozen years now and I can't remember ever feeling so confident at this stage of the proceedings. Pats on backs all round, ladies!' She checked her notebook and saw one item still outstanding. She turned to Diane, 'One more thing, where are we with the marquees?'

'Oh, yes,' said Diane. 'I knew there was something I was supposed to mention, chuck.' She pulled a document from her briefcase. 'Sorry it's all a bit fuzzy. My printer seems to be playing up.' She passed an invoice across to Heather. 'I asked several companies for quotes and these guys, from last year, came back with the lowest. As you've used them before, I took the liberty of giving them the job and paying the deposit. Their prices have gone up marginally, but only in line with inflation.'

'No, that's fine,' said Heather. 'Well done. Then, I think that's everything. We'll get the minutes to everyone in a few days and see you all in a few weeks, at the next meeting.'

Miranda waited until only she and Heather remained in the hall.

'All we need now is good weather.' She smiled at Heather. 'I shall leave it to you, Brian and your boss to sort that one out.'

SEVENTEEN

Ashley wasn't sure if he was more nervous about this audition than the previous one. At least this time he knew pretty much what to expect, he was confident his audition pieces were good and he knew his choice of clothes was about right – comfy, loose trousers and top in neutral shades (not black. Someone at his previous audition had said, black was a no-no) stuff he could move about in, which wasn't distracting to those assessing him. But, on the other hand, he knew how crushing the disappointment of being rejected was, he knew how many people he was competing against, how slim his chances were and he knew how hard it was to tell his friends and family that he'd failed. He tried to tell himself that this time he wouldn't get rejected but self-doubt was sitting on his shoulder, whispering into his ear that of course he would; working-class kids from council estates didn't belong at drama school, he was out of his depth and, even if he got accepted, he'd never amount to anything.

'Never mind, Ash,' his mum had said, after the last audition. 'Take a gap year and apply to go to uni after. You've got a job with Miles whatever happens. And not just in the short term, if he's to be believed.'

'Mum, you haven't said nothing about what Miles told me about the pub, have you? That Belinda might be selling it.'

'As if,' said Amy, affronted. She'd only told her mum, so that didn't count. 'Never mind about that, we're talking about you. I've always thought you should ditch this drama school notion. How much did traipsing off to this audition cost you? I tell you something, I'm glad it's you footing the bill, not me. Still, your money, your lookout. Didn't I always say you'd be better off getting a proper qualification…?'

Ashley had switched off at that point. He knew she meant well, but a bit of sympathy wouldn't have come amiss.

The format was much the same as last time; about a hundred of them had been gathered into a huge rehearsal room, where they'd done some warm-up exercises for both their bodies and voices. They'd done some improv work and then they'd been divided into smaller groups for the individual auditions.

While he was doing the improv, Ashley felt he was performing really well. He and a woman in her twenties had been paired together, to act out having a row during a shopping trip. They'd both managed to sound really angry with each other and the words had flowed, despite the fact they were doing it off the cuff. But… 'Thank you,' one of the panel had said, as they were in mid-flow. Was that a good thing? Had they sufficiently impressed the jury? Or had they been stopped because they were trite?

They'd walked to the edge of the rehearsal room to approving looks from the other hopefuls. Ashley's morale rose.

'Thanks,' whispered his partner, as the next pair were being given their instructions.

'No, thank *you*,' murmured Ashley. 'You were great.'

She preened smugly. 'Yes, well…'

She'd thanked him for showing up, for being her foil. Ashley's morale sank.

———

A few hours after the lunch service had stopped, Belinda was in her flat over the pub, trying to work out what to wear out that evening. She wished she knew where they were going; if it were Woodford Priors she felt a skirt and blouse would probably be appropriate, but if it were the Wetherspoons in Cattebury, then jeans and a T-shirt would rate as overdressed. The truth was, it was almost certainly going to be one or the other. There were some seriously nice restaurants in the county, but they were all a fairly hefty hike from Little Woodford and she didn't think Laurence would want to drive miles and miles in February, on unlit country roads. She made a guess they'd be going to Woodford Priors and picked out her favourite maroon ballerina-length skirt, which she was going to team with a shell-pink blouse. She knew it complemented her blonde hair and blue eyes, without appearing to try too hard. And if they did wind up in Wetherspoons – well, what a treat for the regulars.

Happy with her choice, she ran a bath, poured in her favourite Jo Malone bath oil and had a long soak, before she painted her toes and fingernails and carefully applied her make-up. She couldn't remember the last time she'd spent quite so long getting ready for an evening out. She almost allowed herself to think *getting ready for a date* but she quashed that; they were just friends… acquaintances. They were too old for any of that mushy nonsense – even if it was Valentine's Day. Even so, she felt stupidly excited – like she had in her teens when getting ready to go to the local discos.

'Grow up,' she muttered to herself, as she lowered her lids to apply mascara. 'Who are you kidding?'

Laurence had said he'd meet her in the bar at seven o'clock and, as she grabbed her coat and had a last check in the mirror, she realised she was late. On balance, that probably wasn't a bad thing. Straight down to the bar and straight out. Hopefully she'd get away without too many comments and observations from the regulars.

She opened the door at the bottom of her stairs and peered into the bar. It was pretty full and almost every table was taken. Her staff were dealing with the press at the bar and for a second Belinda was tempted to put her coat on a peg and help out, but then she saw Laurence standing near the door.

'Bye, girls,' said Belinda and she dodged through the open flap in the counter to greet him.

'Wow!' said Laurence. He smiled his dazzling Hollywood smile, as Belinda pulled open the door and hustled them both outside, before any of the regulars could twig she was off for dinner with a man.

'Sorry I'm a bit late,' said Belinda, suddenly feeling rather breathless.

'It was worth the wait. You look sensational.'

Now she felt completely flustered. 'Do I? I wasn't sure what to wear. I didn't know if jeans and a sweater might be more appropriate.'

'You're perfect.'

Belinda shivered. It was perishing out here on the pavement.

'Here,' he said, helping her on with her coat. 'Although

you may not need this. The engine's running and the car's warm.'

'You left it running?!' Belinda was incredulous. 'I know this is a sleepy market town, but that's one hell of a risk.'

'It's OK. My driver's there too.'

'Driver?!' Her astonishment went off the scale. Just who the hell was this guy? And could she ask that question, point blank?

She could, she *must*, because she suddenly realised just how bonkers she was being. She was about to get into a car with him *and* his driver, or someone he *said* was his driver, and she had no idea who he was or what his plans for the evening were. Just because he was well-spoken, came to her pub and spent money there, didn't mean he mightn't be a mad axeman or a rapist. She knew absolutely *nothing* about him. She didn't know where he lived. Hell, she didn't even know his surname. If she heard of a teenager behaving like this, she'd despair at the stupidity and wonder why the girl hadn't been given better advice by her parents.

She stopped walking alongside him.

'This may be a bit late in the day, but, given that we're about to go out to dinner, I think I ought to know a bit more about you. I mean, I was brought up not to take sweets from strange men and yet, here I am, about to jump in your car, when I don't even know your full name'

Laurence didn't seem to be overly put out, and grinned his devastating smile. 'You're absolutely right. I could be anyone couldn't I? Mind you, whatever I tell you now could be a total fabrication. I might still be some random psycho. Except that, as you know, I'm friends with Maxine Larkham, and she doesn't seem to think I should be behind bars, as a danger to society.'

'Of course – Maxine. And if Maxine thinks you're all right, then the chances are you're OK.'

Laurence laughed. 'The *chances are*…? That's an advance on being compared with a strange man offering sweets to little girls. Supposing I tell you that my surname is McLachlan.'

'Delighted to meet you, Mr McLachlan.'

'*Enchanté.*'

'And would it be too much to ask where you live?' Belinda didn't think her knowing this would make the least difference, when her murdered body turned up in the river Catte. But all the same…

'The Reeve House.'

'The Ree…!' Belinda squeaked. She could feel her eyes goggling. Probably only her extra-thick mascara stopped them from falling out completely. She cleared her throat. 'The Reeve House. Hence the driver.'

Laurence nodded happily. 'Yup, one of the perks of being filthy rich.'

Belinda nearly choked. 'But why didn't you say?'

They began walking again. 'Because,' said Laurence, 'call me old-fashioned, but I wanted to make sure you liked me for myself, not my money.'

Belinda nodded. 'I do like you. You make me laugh,' she said.

Laurence took her arm. 'Good. Job done. Now…' He stopped walking. 'This is the car.' He opened the door of a silver Range Rover. 'And John, here, is our driver for the night. John, meet Belinda.'

'Evening, madam.'

He didn't have a cap, noted Belinda, who was rather expecting a clone of Lady Penelope's Parker, but he did have a jacket and tie on. And… madam!

'Nice to meet you, John,' responded Belinda, as she climbed into the back seat.

The car was, as Laurence had said, toasty warm, so she slipped her coat off again.

'Can I ask where we're going?'

'I thought the Flower Pot.'

Belinda was glad of the darkness of the car, because her eyes goggled again. 'Lovely,' she said, trying to sound nonchalant.

'Have you been there?' asked Laurence.

Belinda suppressed a guffaw – on her income? 'Erm... no. I've heard it's very good.' Which was possibly an under-statement. The restaurant had a couple of Michelin stars. She'd also heard what the prices were like. Lunch, she knew, started at over a hundred pounds a head and that was before anyone drank a drop of anything other than tap water. As for dinner...

'So I believe.'

'You were lucky to get a table,' said Belinda. 'Given it's Valentine's Day.'

'Oh... you know.' He sounded really casual about it.

'Oh?' *You know?* You know... what? Her curiosity was piqued. 'So, you're friends with the maître d'?'

'No'

'Then how? Come on, Mr McLachlan, just exactly who are you?'

'You don't know.' It was a statement not a question.

'What do you mean I *don't know*? Should I?'

'Not really. Your mate Maxine didn't, even though she might have done, because our paths kind of crossed years ago. Don't get me wrong,' he added hastily, 'I quite like that. It's nice being anonymous. Where I used to live, *no one* was anonymous.'

'And where was that?'

'LA.'

Jeez, thought Belinda. It was like being on the Somme – one bombshell after another. She stared out of her window to hide her face. 'You told me you were some sort of free-lancer... That's not the whole truth is it?' she said turning back.

'It kind of is. I'm a musician.'

That made sense – what with his interest in her musical taste. 'This is going to sound rude, but I've not heard of Laurence McLachlan.'

'What about Lozza Lachlan – the jazz musician?'

Belinda fished about in her memory banks. 'Er... no.'

Laurence hummed a tune.

Belinda was ridiculously excited that she did at least recognise this. 'Shit! I know that. I can't place it, but I know it.'

'*"Ninety-nine"*.'

'My God. *That* movie. *You* wrote the music?'

Laurence nodded. 'And some other stuff, well... quite a *lot* of other stuff, heaps of other stuff, but that's the one *everyone* remembers.'

'You should see his collection of gold discs,' said John.

'Oh my,' said Belinda. '*"Ninety-nine"*.' The music that had been used in countless ads and TV programmes.

'And in LA, I had some weird jazz groupies, verging on stalkers, who dogged my every move. It was flattering for a bit, but then along came social media. I couldn't sneeze without someone posting stuff on the internet.'

'So being here, being able to walk into your local pub where no one has a clue who you are—'

'Is really rather nice.'

'But people will suss it eventually.'

'Maybe. But I don't think the people of Little Woodford will be quite as intrusive as some Americans can be. We Brits respect privacy – the *Englishman's home is his castle* stuff.'

'Except you're Scottish.'

Laurence laughed. 'Maybe you can adopt me. I'm house-trained. Aren't I, John?'

'So my missus says.'

'John's missus is my housekeeper.'

This time Belinda did allow herself to laugh out loud. 'This is surreal. Chauffeur, housekeeper… the Flower Pot. I'm glad I didn't know, when I was wondering what to wear tonight. I'd have had a nervous breakdown.'

'As I said, you look perfect,' said Laurence and even in the gloom, Belinda could see his wonderful smile. 'Elegant and understated.'

Belinda glowed.

EIGHTEEN

Amy let herself into Heather's house the next morning and picked up the post.

'Coo-ee,' she called. 'It's only me,' she added, as she went into the kitchen, put the pile of letters and junk mail on the counter, unhooked her apron from the back of the door and then filled the kettle. She could do with a cuppa before she started and with luck, if she made one for Brian and Heather too, they might offer a biscuit to go with it. As she waited for the kettle to boil she got out her box of cleaning things and then leafed idly through Heather's post. Nothing very exciting – mostly things that looked like bills, a flier for a new pizza place in Cattebury... but the last letter. Top-quality stationery, handwritten...

She heard Heather coming down the stairs so she shoved it under the pile and tried to look nonchalant, but inside she was longing to know what it was. A posh invite? Mrs Laithwaite used to get a lot of that sort of thing, before Mr Laithwaite went bust. Mrs L used to put them on the mantelpiece – to impress the hoi-polloi, thought Amy. Not that she was impressed, but she wouldn't have minded being a fly on the wall at one or two of the dos – the Lord Lieutenant's garden party, for starters. She reckoned that would be well lush.

'Morning, Amy,' said Heather, as she came into the kitchen. 'Oh good, you've got the kettle on. Be a love and make a cup for me and Brian too. And get the biscuits out, won't you. You know where I keep them.'

Amy certainly did, although she still hadn't worked out where the posh ones were stashed. But a digestive was better than nothing, she supposed.

'And the usual this morning, please.'

'That's fine.' Amy stretched up to get three mugs out, oblivious that her skirt rode up and exposed a huge amount of mottled thigh and her most of her pink knickers. 'I brought the post in too.' She put down the mugs and handed the pile to Heather. She hoped Heather would open the letter while she was present, but Heather flicked through the pile, dumped the junk straight in the recycling bin and put the bills and the other letter back down.

Bugger.

'I've got to go out this morning, Amy, so you'll be able to get on in peace and quiet. Don't bother with Brian's study.' Heather went into the hall and came back with her handbag. She took out a couple of notes, which she put on the counter. 'I'll leave your money here for you, in case I'm not back before you've finished.'

'OK, Heather.'

The kettle boiled, Amy made the tea, put some biscuits on a plate and took one for herself. 'I'll get going upstairs, shall I?'

'That's fine.'

Amy took her box of cleaning things, her tea and her biscuit, balanced on top of her mug, and went to start on the vicarage bathroom. She'd just finished, when she heard the front door slam. Instantly she nipped downstairs as silently as she could and had a quick look in the recycling. There were the envelopes to the bills and the posh handwritten one. But where were the contents? She cast around the kitchen, keeping one ear open for Brian. She couldn't see anything that looked like that morning's correspondence. She tried the dining room, where Heather sometimes worked on the big table. Zilch.

What about the sitting room? She walked in, but couldn't see anything obvious. Maybe she'd taken everything into the study. If she'd done that, Amy was on a hiding to nothing because she could hardly go and have a rummage while Brian was in there. However, there was a little bureau in the corner of this room. Quietly Amy opened the flap. Woo-hoo. There it was.

The Reeve House
Little Woodford
Monday 13th February

Amy heart did a little jump – the Reeve House!
Dear Heather (if I may),

Mrs Huggins passed your request to me and I was delighted and thrilled to be asked to open your fête. Given it's in my garden, it couldn't be more convenient for me to do this. Of course, you may decide, when I reveal who I am, that I'm not particularly suitable. I gather you are after a 'celebrity' and an ageing jazz musician, which is what I am, mightn't fit the bill. In which case please feel free to look elsewhere; I promise I won't hold it against you, and I promise you can still use the garden. But, this ageing jazz musician once composed a piece of music that was quite well known in its heyday – it was called "Ninety-nine" and most people know me as Lozza Lachlan, although I prefer my real name of

*Laurence McLachlan nowadays. I hope, now you know my identity, that
I still get the gig.*

*If that's the case, could I ask you to keep quiet about who I am,
until nearer the time? I am not a recluse by any means but I'd like to try
and make friends and become a part of this delightful little town through
my own efforts and not due to the reputation of being a faded ex-some-
body. I hope that that makes sense and you understand.*

*Mrs Huggins has given me the date and it's in my diary. Let me
know in due course what you need me to do on the day – if you still
want me!*

I look forward to meeting you.

Yours sincerely,

And then an outlandish squiggle that could have been
anything.

Amy put the letter back, shut the bureau and crept
silently back upstairs, where she recommenced her cleaning
noisily, clattering around on the landing to try and make sure
that Brian thought she'd been upstairs for the duration.

"Ninety-nine"? Lozza Lachlan? Neither meant a thing to
her. Having assuaged her curiosity as to the contents of the
envelope, she was now riddled with a need to find out who
this guy was. Apart from stinking rich and someone who was
a jazz musician.

Amy picked up her cleaning materials and went into the
Simmondses' bedroom, where she sat on the bed, whipped
out her phone and began to google. She clicked on a link and
music blared out. Shit! Hastily she hit the mute button. In the
ensuing silence she listened for any signs of Brian and was
reassured by the stillness of the house. Carefully she cranked
up the volume a tiny bit and with the phone to her ear,
pressed the link again to listen to the music.

It was, she concluded, faintly familiar, but she mostly
listened to *Radio 1* and this was some jazzy, orchestral stuff, so

it was hardly surprising it wasn't really on her radar. She wondered if her mum would know it.

As luck would have it, Amy cleaned for Olivia on a Wednesday afternoon and she lived bang opposite her mum. If she could scrounge a lunchtime sarnie off her ma, she could kill two birds with one stone. It would save walking back to her own gaff for a bite. Win-win! She just needed to make sure her mum was going to be in. Still sitting on the bed, she rang to check.

'I've got something I need to ask you,' she told her mother.

'Which is?' Mags sounded wary.

'Oh, nothing serious. Just want to pick your brains.' Amy left a pause. 'And a sandwich wouldn't go amiss.'

'Cheeky cow,' said her mother, with no malice. 'Just as well I've got some nice ham in.'

'Perfect. See you about half twelve.'

A couple of hours later, Amy pocketed her money, called goodbye to Brian through his still-closed study door and slammed the front one behind her. A brisk wind whipped the last of the previous autumn's leaves into tiny tornados round her feet and chilled her fingers as she made her way up the road to the high street. At least it wasn't raining, she thought.

'Come in, come in, keep the heat in,' exhorted Mags. 'I've got some soup on, as well as sarnies. I thought you'd need something warm inside you.'

'Gosh, thanks, Mum. You're the best.' Amy followed her mother into the little kitchen, which smelt of tomato soup. On the counter was a plate of sandwiches.

'Be a love and take them through to the lounge,' said Mags. 'I'll bring the soup.'

'So what is it you want to pick my brains for?' asked Mags, between spoonfuls.

Amy swallowed and took her mobile out of her pocket. 'Does this tune mean anything to you?' She clicked on the link.

She saw her mother smile. 'It certainly does. Gosh, I must have seen that film about four or five times in about a week. I loved it.'

'Five times?!'

'You've got to remember, in the early Seventies we only had three TV channels; no satellite, no Netflix, nothing. The cinema was the place to go. Besides... there was the back row, if the film wasn't up to much.' She gave her daughter a wink and Amy wrinkled her nose in disgust.

'Jeez, Mum, talk about TMI.'

'Anyway, the film was called *Ninety-nine* and was set in space. Back then space travel was all the rage.'

'I suppose.'

'Why do you want to know?'

'Because the man who wrote the music has moved into the Reeve House.'

'*Really*?!'

'I don't think he wants people to know, though.'

'How come you do?'

'Heather left a letter from him lying around,' said Amy, with not the least twinge of her conscience. 'She's asked him to open the fête. I think they're planning on holding it in the grounds.'

'The Reeve House. What I wouldn't give to see that! I've lived here all my life and the closest I've ever got is peering through the gate.'

'Well, come the summer, the whole town'll get a chance.'

'What's this chappie's name?'

'Lozza Lachlan.'

Mags thought. 'Yeah, that's right. He was quite well known in his day – along with the likes of Burt Bacharach and Henry Mancini.'

'Who?'

'Before your time, but they produced some good stuff. *"Moon River"*, *"Raindrops Keep Falling on My Head"*…' Mags put her spoon in her bowl as she went into a little daydream. 'They don't write them like that anymore. It's all this rap and gangsta stuff now. Not proper tunes.'

'Yeah, well.' Amy scraped her bowl clean and helped herself to a sandwich. 'As I said, he don't want people knowing about him just yet, so don't you go telling no one.'

'As if!' Mags looked shocked that her daughter thought she might.

NINETEEN

Belinda hummed happily as she served her customers in the pub. Her date with Laurence had been glorious and the food wonderful. She'd never eaten at such a posh restaurant before and had been stunned by the level of service. From the amuse-bouche they'd been served in the bar with their aperitifs on their arrival, to the individual linen hand towels in the ladies' loo, which Belinda had visited shortly before the drive home, everything was perfect. She'd been amused to note that her copy of the menu didn't feature any prices. In a way she was glad she didn't have a clue how much it was going to cost – she suspected she'd have been horrified – but equally, she was curious to know. Just *how* much could a place like this charge for a plate of food? And as for the wine list… It was the size of a blockbuster novel. Laurence and the sommelier had a discussion about the best choice to go with turbot, which showed he knew his vintages. Belinda knew what her customers liked to drink and bought appropriate grape varieties, but beyond that, she was no wine buff at all. Vintages? Terroir? Nope – all Greek to her. The wines, however – a white, a red and a dessert – were total nectar. And if the wines were nectar, the food was ambrosia. Every mouthful was joyous. Even the coffee and the ravishingly pretty petit fours, served in the bar afterwards, were exceptional.

Laurence asked John to drop her at the door of the pub, when they returned. It was only ten and the pub was still open and full of customers.

'Fancy coming in for a nightcap?' Belinda asked.

'That's a lovely offer but I think I'll pass. John would like to get back to Elspeth and I suspect your regulars might subject me to the third degree, if they saw me walking in with their landlady.' He'd gazed into her eyes. 'Do you mind?'

She did, but she lied. 'That's fine. Another time, maybe.'

'Oh, there will be. Thank you,' said Laurence.

She sighed happily at the memory. What an evening. What a date. And it looked as if it wasn't going to be a one-off.

She leaned on the bar. Yes, the evening had been exceptional. Laurence had been amusing and a wonderful raconteur about life in LA and the bonkers things some of the people he knew got up to. She reckoned they'd have had almost as much fun if the date *had* been at the Wetherspoons in Cattebury.

'Penny for them,' said Bert.

Belinda snapped back to the present. 'Sorry, Bert. Miles away. Another pint?'

'Yes please. I reckon you were daydreaming about your fancy man.'

Busted. 'I was not,' she lied. 'Besides, I don't have a *fancy man*, as you put it.'

'Ha! That new guy spends a lot of time making sheep's eyes at you, and you at him.'

'So? He's a nice-looking guy. It's called window-shopping,

but that's all it is.' At this rate her nose would rival Pinocchio's.

Bert raised his eyebrows. 'If you say so, missus,' he said as he returned to his seat with his drink.

At that moment the door pinged open and in walked Laurence, with a newspaper tucked under his arm.

'Ha!' said Bert loudly from the corner.

'Morning. A pint of Rabbit Punch and a tuna bap,' said Laurence.

'It's afternoon,' said Belinda, nodding at the bar clock.

'In my world, it's morning, till I've had lunch.'

Belinda lowered her voice. 'I'm surprised you're hungry. I'm not.' She glanced over at Bert who appeared to be looking out of the window but was certainly straining to hear every word. 'And thank you for last night. I know I said so at the time, but it was wonderful.'

'Thank you for agreeing to come. Life is so much more fun with a companion.'

A group of office workers clattered in through the door and Laurence took his drink over to his usual table.

Between pulling pints, clearing tables and serving lunches, Belinda noticed that Laurence was making his lunch last an inordinately long time, mostly by seeming to do the crossword on the back page. He was barely halfway down his second pint, when Belinda called time. Bert had long since gone home to his wife for lunch and the pub emptied, as the last of the customers drank up and left. Laurence folded up his paper, picked up his glass and brought it to the bar. He downed the dregs.

'Now… about that nightcap,' he said.

Belinda moved out from behind the bar and locked the front door.

———

Heather, having finished her lunch and rung to check Maxine was in, retrieved Laurence's letter from her bureau and then walked briskly up the hill to her friend's house.

'Good news,' she said, after the two had exchanged greetings and Miranda had made them both a coffee.

'What is?'

Heather fished the letter out of her bag and handed it over. She sipped her coffee as Miranda read it.

'My, oh my,' said Miranda, handing the letter back. 'Lozza Lachlan.'

'That was rather my reaction,' said Heather. 'Anyway, it solves the problem of who's going to open the fête.'

'And what a very gracious letter. He sounds utterly charming.'

'There's a telephone number at the top... Do you think we should ring it?'

'I think *you* should,' said Miranda. She picked the handset off its stand and passed it to her friend.

Heather hesitated before she took it and then put the letter on the counter, so she had a free hand to dial with. She could feel her heart rate accelerating with every ring.

'The Reeve House,' said a female voice.

'Elspeth?'

'Speaking.'

'This is Heather Simmonds. I was wondering if I could speak to Mr McLachlan.'

'I'm afraid he's out at present. Shall I ask him to call on his return?'

'Yes, please.'

'Of course. I've got the number on the phone here. I don't know – all this modern technology...'

'Oh… no, I'm not ringing from home. The vicarage number is…' Heather reeled it off and then said goodbye. She pressed the button to disconnect. Miranda's face mirrored the disappointment she felt. 'Silly to feel let down,' she said, 'but it's not often a vicar's wife gets the chance to talk to someone rich and famous.'

'But you will. He'll ring back.'

'And silly to be so starstruck at my age.'

'You and me both. I loved his music in my youth. Of course,' she added, 'It was all a bit retro by the time I came across it at uni – the jazz club seemed a cool thing to belong to, although I didn't like a lot of the music the others all pretended to love. But Lozza Lachlan's stuff…' She sighed. 'Fancy him coming to live here.'

———

Laurence got back from the pub at around half past three and went to see Elspeth in the kitchen.

'Nice lunch?' she asked, as she creamed butter and sugar together in a big bowl. On the table were two sandwich tins greased and ready. Laurence felt a little burst of pleasure. It looked as if there'd be a Victoria sponge for tea; one of his favourites.

'Very nice,' he said.

Elspeth looked at him and raised her eyebrows. Laurence returned her gaze steadily.

'You were gone a while. Quite a while, in fact.'

'Was I?' He feigned innocence, but as the large kitchen clock was showing the time, he could hardly deny it.

'That was a long lunch, by any standards.'

'Maybe.'

'John said she's very nice.'

'She is. I like her. No side.'

'It's just…'

Laurence dipped his finger in the pale mixture and licked it. Elspeth moved the bowl away from him.

'It's just what?' said Laurence.

'Well… after what you've been through.'

Laurence sighed. '*Going* through. It's not over yet, but trust me, Belinda is quite different.' He thought he heard a muffled 'harrumph'. He decided to ignore it. He was over seventy, for God's sake. And yes, his ongoing divorce was a nasty, messy business and his ex-wife – Jessica – was being far from reasonable, but just because she was a prize-winning cow, didn't mean that Belinda was going to be the same. 'Anyway,' he continued, 'can we stretch dinner to feed an extra mouth?'

'Belinda's?'

'It might be.'

Elspeth gave him a steady stare, before she muttered, 'That'll be a *yes*, then.'

Laurence coolly returned the gaze. 'I'm not completely sure she can make it yet.'

'Why not?'

'Because I've only just thought of inviting her.'

'So, earlier… you had other things on your mind, did you?'

God, Elspeth could be infuriating.

'Why,' continued Elspeth, 'don't you ring her now, so I know what I'm doing this evening?'

'Because I don't have her phone number.'

Elspeth gave him a look of disbelief.

'Look,' said Laurence, 'until now it hasn't mattered. If I want to talk to her I wander up to the pub.'

'If you say so. Oh, and by the way, while you were

enjoying—' was that the faintest of pauses? '—your *lunch*, the vicar's wife phoned. I've got the number and I left it on the piano in your study. I said you'd call back.'

'Fine. And you haven't answered my question... about dinner.'

'Since I know how stroppy you can be if you don't get your own way, the answer is yes, only I'll need to get more meat out of the freezer.'

'Do that. Please,' he added as an afterthought. 'And I don't get stroppy.' Elspeth stared at him. 'Do I?'

'You're used to being in charge, so I guess you're entitled to call the shots. Och – it doesn't cut much ice with me.'

'Which is why I love you.'

'Get away.'

'Anyhow, she may not be able to come.'

'Indeed. The lassie might have other plans. In which case there'll be food wasted.'

'I'm sure we can find a way to eat up any leftovers.' Laurence knew Elspeth had a total aversion to waste, and throwing food away was right up there with kicking kittens.

'Righty-o,' said Elspeth. 'You're the boss.'

'I'll go back to the pub when it opens and ask her then. I'll let you know in good time.'

'That's fine.' Only Elspeth managed to make it sound as if it were anything but.

Laurence left her making her sponge cake and went off to his study to check his emails and kill time before the pub reopened. His study was a cross between a music room and a snug as well as having his computer lodged there, on a desk under the big bay window. Beside it was a comfortable armchair and opposite was a huge fireplace with a big wood burner and a sofa facing it. In a corner was his grand piano and the walls were covered in framed gold discs. It was his favourite room in the house.

He looked at his watch. He still had almost two hours to kill before opening time. The first thing he did was to open up the damper on the wood burner, so the flames leapt into life again, then he got out his phone to ring the vicar's wife.

No, I'll do it in a minute, he thought. He couldn't get Belinda out of his head. Kind, funny, attractive and completely normal. Such a change after LA, where people got neurotic if they didn't have neuroses. He stretched as he thought about being in bed with her that afternoon. It had been a long drought and the sex had been glorious, but almost more glorious had been the snuggling together afterwards, the pillow talk, the cosy companionship, until she'd told him to go because she had to get ready for opening time.

'But we can do this again,' she'd said.

'Tomorrow?'

'Sounds like a plan.'

But, on the way home he realised he didn't want to wait till tomorrow. He wanted her in his bed tonight. He wanted to wine and dine her, then have her to himself for more than just a couple of hours. But until the pub opened, there was nothing he could do.

He got up, moved to the chair in front of his computer and switched it on. He clicked on the email icon and instantly his inbox began to fill with messages. His solicitor and his ex-wife's had obviously been busy across the pond. He read through them – or, at least, skimmed them – and wondered if his legal team really were worth what he was paying them. It seemed to him that almost everyone wanted a piece of him and created problems for their own gain. And yet he'd been the one who had earned the money everyone now seemed to be fighting over. He could feel his blood pressure rising every time he looked at his depleting bank balances and investments. He was never going to be destitute, but he might have to start being more careful than usual. He was a Scot, he could do frugal, but he liked luxury – he'd got used to it – and it grated badly that he might have to tighten his belt while Jessica, their lawyers, his agent and various other hangers-on might not.

He knew the solution was to go on tour again, if his agent, Mylo Robbins, could arrange one. And it was a given that Mylo would. Mylo was a genius regarding that sort of thing quite apart from having a brain the size of a planet when it came to knowing what was what with rights, contracts and the music business in general. All those ticket sales would probably restore his finances to pre-divorce levels, but he liked being retired. He could see Mylo jumping with joy if he suggested it, but he wouldn't be the one having to wake up in a different hotel every morning, or sit on a tour bus for hours on end. Mylo wouldn't have to deal with the fans and groupies, or expend exhausting amounts of energy on stage three or four times a week. What on earth would he feel like at the end of a three-month tour, at his age?

He could feel his pulse throbbing, as his blood pressure rose. He needed to calm down and music would do that. He went over to his grand piano and opened the lid. He played a couple of chords, then a couple more. He repeated the little riff. It was good. He played it again and added a few more bars. He changed the key from major to minor… And as his fingers moved over the keys, he found he wanted to give the piece a title. Ta-*de*-dah, ta-*de*-dah… Didn't The Beatles use the words *scrambled eggs*, before they came up with the title 'Yesterday'? He needed something with three syllables and the right cadence to fit the tune. He'd think of it.

'So am I feeding an extra mouth, or not?'

Laurence jumped. 'Elspeth, you frightened the crap out of me. I was miles away.'

'So I could see. But I need to know what I'm doing tonight.'

Laurence glanced at his expensive wristwatch. A quarter to six. Bugger, he'd missed tea… and cake. And, if he was going to get to the pub for opening time, he needed to get going. He closed the piano.

'Cook for Belinda. If she doesn't come, I'll eat it for lunch tomorrow.'

'That you will,' said Elspeth, dryly. 'And that was a good tune you were playing there.'

'Thank you.'

'A new one?'

'It might be – not sure yet.'

'Och… well. It's about time you did some composing again.'

'I'll see you later, Elspeth, and I'll ring if I can persuade Belinda to come to diner.'

'See that you do,' said Elspeth to Laurence's back.

TWENTY

Bollocks, he thought, as he reached the top of his drive – he hadn't phoned the vicarage. He might as well call in; he was going to pass the end of Church Road en route, so it would only be a quick detour.

A few minutes later Laurence pressed the bell on the vicarage door. Heather opened it.

'Mrs Simmonds?' he asked.

She nodded.

'Sorry to turn up out of the blue, but you rang me earlier...'

'Did I?'

'Laurence McLachlan. I was practically passing, so I thought I'd drop by.'

She squeaked, 'Oh.' Then she flung the door wide. 'You must come in.' She beamed at him. 'So sorry I didn't recognise you.'

'No reason why you should and no, I won't stop – I need to be somewhere else very shortly.'

'But… even so… I should have—' She looked flustered.

'Most people know my music but they haven't a clue about me, apart from the die-hard fans. So, is it good news? Do you want me for your fête, or were you going to let me down gently?'

'Let you down? Glory be, no! We'd be thrilled if you'd do the honours. Truly. Usually the best we can rise to is the local mayor and occasionally the MP. But to have a properly famous person…' Heather clapped her hands in delight. 'And on top of letting us use your garden…'

'That's fine. It's my pleasure. If I could just ask you to keep it under your hat for a bit about who the new owner of the Reeve House is. I'm enjoying the anonymity and I'd like it to last a bit longer.'

'Yes, yes of course. There's only one other on the committee who knows who you are and she's a retired lawyer. I think you can rely on the pair of us to be discreet.'

'Thank you.'

Laurence left Heather and made his way back up the road towards the pub. As it was now gone six, he knew the evening regulars would already be in but he was sure he could still have a quick word with Belinda.

He pushed open the door and saw there must be about a dozen customers there already – all keen to slake their thirsts after a long day at work. There was music playing quietly – Carole King. Good choice. He went over to the bar, where Belinda was busy serving another customer. She glanced his way and her eyebrows registered surprise.

Laurence waited patiently for his turn at the far end of the bar, as far away from the other punters as he could reasonably get.

'Rabbit Punch?'

'Yes, please.' Then in a much lower voice. 'And thank you for earlier.'

There was a hint of a flush around Belinda's neck. 'Don't mention it,' she murmured.

'And your mobile number, please.' He went to get his phone from his pocket and couldn't find it. Bugger, he must have left it on his piano.

Belinda grabbed a beer mat and a pen and scribbled it down, while the beer was pouring.

'And come to dinner at mine tonight,' said Laurence.

Belinda looked up at him. 'You're kidding, aren't you? With this lot in?'

'Can't you get cover?'

She shook her head in bewilderment. 'Possibly, with a few days' warning, but not at an *hour's* notice. This is a business, Laurence, and I provide a service to the community. The locals expect their pub to be open and for me to be here pouring pints. I can't just turn them out onto the street and shut up shop on a whim.'

'So when *can* you come to dinner with me?'

'When I can get one of my girls in on shift. And that might take a while to arrange.'

He felt ridiculously disappointed. But surely Belinda would have a whole list of people she might be able to call on for emergency cover.

'But can't you give someone a ring? Surely there'll be someone who could step in?'

'No.'

He thumped the counter. 'You're not even trying,' he snapped.

The sound of his hand hitting the bar reverberated through the pub; conversations stopped mid-syllable and heads turned.

Belinda glared at him. 'No – and I won't be spoken to like that in my own pub.' She didn't bother to lower her voice.

Thwarted, embarrassed and frustrated, Laurence left his pint untouched on the bar and stalked out. As he reached the door, he could hear the conversations start up again and guessed most of them would be speculating about what had just passed between him and the landlady. It riled him further.

He needed to calm down before he returned home and Elspeth began to enquire as to why his dinner invitation had been refused. He walked down the lane to the nature reserve and sat on a bench in the meadow. A chill wind nipped at his ankles and wrists and tried to burrow its way under his collar, but his irritation and the burning embers of his pride were keeping him warm.

He knew he was in the wrong. And what's more, Elspeth was right – he could be stroppy when he didn't get his own way. He'd just demonstrated that in public, big time. He knew he ought to apologise to Belinda, but she'd been in the wrong too. Couldn't she have offered to make a call or two? Couldn't she have made an effort? Hell, it wasn't much to ask, was it?

He was doing it again. He took a bunch of deep, calming breaths. Slowly his blood pressure lowered, his pulse slowed and reason managed to assert itself. He became aware of the cold. Wearily he got off the bench and rubbed his hands together, to get the circulation going again before he went home.

'She turned you down, then,' said Elspeth when she saw the look on his face.

'Apparently so.' He took off his jacket and dumped it on the back of a kitchen chair.

Elspeth shook her head. 'She's got a business to run. She can't just drop everything when you whistle.'

'Thank you, Elspeth, I'm aware of that.' He could feel his jaw clenching and his teeth gritting. *Breathe,* he told himself.

'Still, I've heard a rumour in town that she's trying to sell up, so maybe, if she finds a buyer, she'll have more time on her hands. That is, unless she's planning on getting another pub somewhere else.'

'Who told you this?'

'I heard it in the post office queue. There's a lassie behind the counter, who is a mine of information. I'm amazed this town needs a local paper – all you have to do is post a parcel and you can find out everything you need to know. Any day now I'm expecting the population to rumble who you are.'

'I do hope not. As far as I know it's only a handful who know – five at the most, excluding you and John –and they've all promised not to say anything, until nearer the time of the fête.'

'Well, good luck with that because, from what I've seen, there are no secrets at all here. Now, I've got cooking to do and you're in my way. Besides, you need to ring your agent. He's phoned several times trying to get hold of you.' Elspeth flapped a tea towel at her employer to shoo him away.

Laurence went to his study and grabbed his phone from the piano. He wondered what Mylo wanted but he could guess that it was more than likely something to do with Jessica. So, what now?

'Jeez, Loz, where the fuck have you been?' Mylo's Bronx-accented voice bellowed at him.

'Out.'

'Yeah, I get that. Didn't you think to take your cell phone with you?'

'Not this time. What can I do for you?'

'You need to get your ass over to LA. I've booked you on the overnight from Heathrow. You'll have to slum it in business class – first was full – but by my reckoning you've just got time to catch it.'

'But…?

'Your ex and her lawyer have involved the IRS in your finances. It's a fucking mess at this end. They're crawling all over your stuff. I need you here and I need you here *now*. If you want to come out of this with anything left at all, I suggest you do as you're told.'

'But…?'

'Just do it, Loz. The flight leaves at ten forty-five. Be on it. I'll text the details to you.' And with that, Mylo hung up, leaving Laurence staring at his screen.

He sighed and made his way to the kitchen. 'Change of plan, Elspeth. I'm flying to LA tonight. I'll need John to bring the car round in fifteen minutes, which should just about give me enough time to pack for a few days.'

Elspeth rolled her eyes and switched off the stove. 'Best you get moving then. Do you need a hand?'

'I'm fine.'

Laurence took the stairs to his bedroom two at a time, grabbed a small case from the cupboard and flung it on the bed, before he headed for his wardrobes. If he needed to stay longer than a week, he could buy stuff. As he was packing Elspeth appeared.

'Can I do anything to help?' she asked. She watched him shove a couple of shirts in the case, before she removed, refolded and put them back tidily. Laurence left her to pack his clothes, as he grabbed some trousers, pants, socks and his washing and shaving kit.

'How long do you think you'll be gone?'

'I don't want it to be less than a week. I can't cope with a double dose of jet lag in seven days.' He rummaged in a drawer for a passport. One of the benefits of having a house in the States and paying US taxes was that he didn't have to worry about a visa.

'Would it be all right, then, if John and I went up to Scotland for a few days? We've got a yen to start looking for somewhere to live up there.'

Laurence nodded enthusiastically. 'Of course, take the car. I can give you plenty of warning before my return. Just make sure you leave the house secure.' He pulled a blazer out of the cupboard and slipped it on over his shirt. Elspeth nodded approvingly – he looked quite smart.

By the time he got downstairs again, John was waiting for him in the hall.

'Where to, sir?' he asked, taking Laurence's case.

'Heathrow.'

'Terminal?' asked John

'I don't know yet.' As he jumped into the front seat he felt his phone vibrate. 'Terminal Two. Check-in closes at eight forty-five.'

'I'll do my best.' John slammed his door and pulled away from the front of the house.

'Elspeth says you might use my absence to go house-hunting.'

'Did she? It's a thought. We just need to see what's what – if the places we used to love are still the same. It's been a long time since we've been back and things change. Obviously,' added John, 'even if we find somewhere we won't leave you in the lurch till you're sorted too.'

'Thank you, but you've got your own lives. I'm sure I can

find agency staff, or something. Not,' he added quickly, 'that you'll be an easy act to follow.'

'No,' said John.

John and Elspeth were far more than cook and house-keeper, gardener and chauffeur. They also provided companionship, patience, loyalty and occasional advice. They were people who put up with his impatience and they anticipated most of his needs. No... that didn't come with part-time temps.

He arrived at the airport with little time to spare, but with only hand luggage and a business class ticket, he knew he would be able to whisk through to the gate in double quick time.

'Safe journey,' said John.

'Cheers. And good luck with the house-hunting.'

'Thank you. You be sure to let me know what flight you're due back on so I can be here to meet you.'

Two hours later Laurence was in his window seat with a large whisky, trying to work out what the two women in his life were up to. One was easy to work out – his ex was trying to take him for every penny she could get her grasping paws on. But Belinda...? Belinda was being less than up-front about her plans for the future. Why hadn't she told him she was selling? Why hadn't she levelled with him? Because it was none of his business, that's why, he told himself. They'd only just got to know each other, they'd been out together once and her plan for the pub wasn't the most scintillating topic of conversation and certainly not on a first date. Just because almost every other bugger in his life seemed to be trying to screw him, didn't mean she'd joined the queue. In fact, it was completely ridiculous that he'd even thought it.

He finished his scotch, toed off his shoes, reclined his seat and draped himself in a blanket. As he snuggled down, he knew one thing was for certain – he needed to talk to her; he needed to apologise for being a dickhead earlier. Furthermore, he needed to find out if she was planning on staying in Little Woodford if she retired because, he realised as he drifted off to sleep and the plane headed towards the Atlantic, it was important to him that she did.

TWENTY-ONE

'Where's that steak pie?' snapped Belinda.

'Coming right up,' Miles replied, cleaning the edge of the plate with a cloth.

'Good. About time too.'

Ashley and Miles exchanged a look.

'What's needling her?' asked Ashley.

Miles shook his head. 'Search me. She's been a cow for days. She was as happy as Larry on Wednesday, after her new bloke took her to the Flower Pot. She was full of it the next day, told me all about the food, but since then…'

'The Flower Pot?'

'It's a Michelin-starred restaurant, where the bill for two is likely to be about the same as the bill for *everyone* here, all lumped together – on a very busy night.'

'Not cheap then.'

Miles shook his head again. 'That, Ash, is an understatement. Her new bloke must be loaded.'

They both got busy with their next tasks; Miles turning his attention to a couple of steaks on the grill, Ashley to washing up a dozen pots while, in the corner, keeping to himself, Jamie was concentrating on piping cream artistically onto a bunch of puddings.

Everyone worked solidly for the next thirty minutes, filling orders, or keeping the kitchen clean and tidy. Finally there was a definite slackening of the pace – the punters had all had their starters and mains and were busy eating. The next rush would be the puddings, but as they were all pre-prepared, they would be quick to serve. There might be some late arrivals who wanted a meal, but the worst was most definitely over.

All three of them slumped slightly as the pressure came off.

'I've been meaning to ask, but I guess, as you haven't told us… your last audition? How did it go?' said Miles.

'Guess,' Ash responded dejectedly.

'I'm sorry. It seems like it's a tough old business.'

'It wouldn't be so bad,' said Ashley, 'if it didn't cost so much to get told you're rubbish.'

'They're not telling you *you're rubbish* but that you're not right for them.'

'Huh.'

'When's your next one lined up for?'

'When I can save enough money to pay for it.'

Miles sucked his teeth. 'It doesn't seem right.'

'It's the way it works.' Ashley sighed. 'And even if I *do* get a place at a drama school, there's no guarantee I'll get work at the other end of it.'

'Many are called, few are chosen.'

'What?'

'Never mind. What are you going to do if you don't make it to drama school?'

'Uni I suppose – only I haven't applied for this year so I'll have to take a gap year. Or I could sack the whole thing and just get a job.'

'Not having a degree isn't the be-all and end-all. I haven't got one.'

'But you've got a proper profession.'

'You could have one too. I could teach you all sorts about cooking and cheffing and general kitchen work... if you wanted me to?'

Ashley thought about it. 'I suppose. Mum's bloke, Ryan, said I ought to learn to become an electrician – people always need them and I might get a job in the theatre or film as a gaffer.'

'Cooking's the same and I know a guy who runs a catering business for the film industry – goes on location. Hard work and long hours but he gets to meet all sorts of famous people.'

'It's not the same as being on stage or in a film, though, is it?'

'Probably not but I bet it's more financially secure – unless you're Tom Hanks or Colin Firth.'

'And you could teach me stuff?'

'Easily. Come in thirty minutes before you're supposed to and I can get you sorted out with the basics like knife skills and making a béchamel sauce...'

'A what?'

'It's a... never mind. You'll know what it is when I teach you.'

'You're sure?'

Miles stared at Ashley. 'I wouldn't have offered if I didn't mean it. Besides, if my plan comes off for my own place, you'll be more use to me as a sous chef than a kitchen porter.'

'Cool. And thank you.'

'Three apple crumbles, one with custard, two with cream and a raspberry mousse,' said Belinda from the door.

'Back to work,' said Miles and went to collect the desserts from the fridge.

———

A couple of days later, on the Monday morning, Miranda sat across the table from Heather in the vicarage kitchen and tried not to stare at the hideous green tiles. She wondered if she should mention that it was possible to buy tile paint and turning them white was an option. Or maybe Heather liked them that colour… in which case such a suggestion would be insulting to her hostess's taste. Miranda decided not to mention it.

'You were saying about the new sponsors,' prompted Heather.

Miranda dragged her attention away from the tiles. 'Oh, yes. They all want to have a full-page ad in the programme, which of course is included in the deal. And a couple are asking if they can have banners, either on the marquees or on any fences in the grounds.'

'I don't know about the grounds,' said Heather. 'That's quite something to ask Mr McLachlan.'

'He might agree,' said Miranda. 'And, if not, there's the inside and the outside of the marquee – we could get at least four big banners up using both sides of the tent.'

'If the marquee hirers will agree. They might not like us pinning stuff to the fabric. Marquees are expensive bits of kit.'

'True.'

'What will happen if the sponsors don't get their way?'

'I imagine they'll reduce what they've promised to give us.'

'Ouch,' said Heather.'

'They are being very generous. We need to do our best to accommodate them.'

'In which case you need to get hold of Diane and get the details of the marquee people off her. Then ring them to see what you can arrange.'

'Consider it done,' said Miranda. 'Actually, I'll do it right now. Have you got her number?'

Heather leafed through the file in front of her and gave the number to Miranda, who programmed it into her phone before she hit the dial icon.

'Ah, Diane, it's Miranda here. About the fête...' She outlined the problem. 'OK. I look forward to hearing from you,' she said before disconnecting.

'And?' said Heather.

'She hasn't got the details with her at the moment, but she's going to ring the company and get back to me.'

'Excellent. When she does talk to you, could you ask her to email me the bank balances.'

'Of course. They should be pretty healthy – we've had more sponsorship and precious few outgoings just yet.'

'And this year we won't have to hire a generator or a water bowser – all thanks to Laurence. When I next see him, I'll offer to pay for his utilities, although I somehow doubt if he'll take the money.'

'No, but it shows we're not taking him for granted,' said Miranda.

'Indeed. And I need to go to the house fairly soon as I have to do a proper risk assessment. Although it's a perfect setting I do worry that the river is right at the bottom of the garden. We're going to have to find a way of fencing it off securely and, even with a fence in place, we need to tell the insurance company about the change of venue and the presence of the Catte.'

'I don't think a disclaimer would cut much ice with the insurance company, if there is the merest hint of us being lax in the health and safety department.'

'And since you're the one with the legal training, I very much think you may have a point,' said Heather.

'And since I've got a modicum of legal training,' said Miranda, 'I think, when you do the site visit for the risk assessment, I should accompany you.'

Heather gave her a steady stare. 'You just want a gander at the house, don't you?'

'Absolutely not.' But her deep blush completely gave her away.

That evening, Ashley reported for duty at the Talbot kitchen early.

'First lesson – knife skills,' said Miles. He handed a steel and a veg knife to Ashley, picked up the same implements himself and said, 'Watch and learn.' He started slowly, drawing the blade of the knife at an angle down the thick, ridged steel rod then turned his hand so the opposite side of the blade was against it and repeated it. 'Now you do it.'

Ashley had a go.

'Get the blade at a slightly bigger angle.'

'Like this?'

'Much better.' Miles then speeded up his sharpening, his knife flashing at a ridiculous speed for a few seconds. He felt the edge and picked up a tomato. He sliced it in half with no effort at all. 'The most dangerous thing in a kitchen is a blunt knife,' he told Ashley. 'If a knife isn't sharp you need a lot of force to make it cut things. If it slips…' He showed Ashley a white ridge on the palm of his left hand about an inch long. 'That's the result of me trying to cut a beetroot with a blunt knife. It did a lot of damage I can tell you – severed a tendon. My middle finger still doesn't work properly, twenty years on.'

'Ouch,' said Ashley.

He handed his knife to Ashley. 'That's what a sharp knife feels like.'

Gingerly Ashley felt the blade. 'But this could cut you badly, too.'

'Yes, but because you're not pushing hard, it'll give you a nasty nick, but probably won't slice a chunk of you off. Right. Keep practising.' Mike grabbed another few tomatoes and put them on the counter. 'Test out the sharpness on these and when you think you've got it right, bring it to me.'

Ashley got going. It was difficult to keep the edge at the right angle, as he changed the blade from side to side, but after five minutes he felt he'd done enough. He tried slicing the tomato but he could see instantly the difference between his knife and Miles's. The tomato started to squash before the blade bit through the skin. He sighed and picked up the steel.

At the end of half an hour his knife was approaching the standard Miles had demanded – he'd taken thirty minutes to accomplish something Miles had done in thirty seconds, probably less.

As the pub began to fill up and the orders came in, he had to stop practising and get on with his usual duties of washing the pots, loading and unloading the dishwasher, clearing down the surfaces and keeping everything orderly for Jamie and Miles. In the occasional lulls, he'd pick up the steel and his knife, concentrating on his technique, rather than speed. By the end of the evening, he felt he might actually be getting somewhere.

'Tell you what,' said Miles, as they gave the kitchen a final mop-down at the end of service, 'take home the steel and practise on your mum's knives.'

'She's only got a couple and one of those is a bread knife.'

'Well, have a go at sharpening the one that isn't. When can you next come in?'

'I've got two essays to write, so I think it'll be Friday.'

'I'll see you then and I expect you to have mastered this.' He tapped the steel. 'If you have, we'll move on to slicing and dicing.'

Ashley had often watched Miles and Jamie reduce carrots and onions to thin slices in seconds. 'Great,' he said. He wondered if his mum would be impressed if he gained some cookery skills. He suspected that he had a better chance with those under his belt, than if he actually passed an audition and managed to get into drama school. He'd have what she would think of as a proper, useful skill rather than what she called poncing about on a stage.

TWENTY-TWO

Why hadn't Laurence phoned, or even dropped in? were the questions that occupied almost every waking moment of Belinda's days. It had been a week since they'd had that wonderful evening at the Flower Pot, and six days since she'd given him her phone number, followed – almost instantly – by that row. She was feeling distraught and bereft, although she tried not to show it. The punters didn't need to know that inside she was crying her eyes out. Had she been unreasonable when she'd told him she couldn't just light out for dinner at his house? She didn't think she had been but, judging by the way she'd been sent to Coventry, what she'd done was obviously beyond the pale.

Maybe she shouldn't have had such a public go at him, but he'd been an arse himself. Just because he'd taken her out for a swanky meal didn't mean he had the right to assume she was at his beck and call. But apparently he thought it did. In which case, she thought, did she want to be in a relationship with someone so demanding and self-centred? Except that he was desperately attractive... and funny... and kind...

and maybe the row was only a blip. In which case why hadn't he got in touch? She didn't have his number, so she couldn't instigate a thawing of relations.

Because of that, she'd gone down to the Reeve House that morning, ready to eat humble pie. The main gate at the head of the drive was shut and the little pedestrian wicket gate to the side was bolted. There was an entry phone sited discreetly on the gatepost and she'd pressed the buzzer on that but there had been no response. Nothing, zip, nada. Given he had staff, it seemed unlikely that no one was in, so was she being blanked? Was there some sort of swanky security system involving video cameras and his house-keeper had been given orders to have nothing to do with her? Disconsolately she'd turned away and come back to the pub.

As she'd walked home, she remembered Maxine knew him. Maybe Maxine would have his number. But even if she got it, did she dare ring him? Might it irritate him further? Well, so what? Frankly, she thought, she had nothing to lose.

She waited until she was about the reopen the pub for the evening session and rang her friend. Maxine led a busy life, what with her painting and everything, but she was probably winding down by five-thirty and wouldn't mind being interrupted.

'I've got a massive favour to ask,' Belinda told her.

'It depends what it is, but if it's in my power to help you, I will.'

'It's about Laurence McLachlan.'

'Okaaay,' said Maxine, warily. 'Only I know he's very careful about his privacy.'

'It's all right. He told me himself who he is and I haven't breathed a word to anyone else. He even took me out to dinner but... well... we've had a misunderstanding and I want to ring and apologise, but I haven't got his number. Have you?'

'I'm not sure about the ethics of that.'

'He's got mine.' She paused. 'I mean, I could drop round to the Reeve House.' She winced at her own bare-faced twisting of the truth. 'But it'd be easier to phone. Please, Maxine. Please.'

'Put like that…'

Belinda felt her heart lift and grabbed a pencil. She scribbled down the number. 'Cheers, Max, you're a lifesaver. A drink on the house, next time you're in.'

'Daft moo,' said Maxine, kindly. 'Hopefully, I'll see you Saturday lunchtime.'

Belinda stared at her phone. Should she? No – she needed to pluck up some courage first. Breaking all her own rules, she poured herself a tot of brandy.

———

It might have been a Wednesday evening in the UK, but it was morning in LA and Laurence was sitting in his agent's high-rise office. In front of him was his legal team, explaining the various options regarding his divorce. The IRS had been dealt with, but a final settlement still hadn't been reached, and it seemed to him that every time the alternatives were batted back and forth, the bills rose exponentially.

Yes, he agreed, he had been married for the best part of thirty years and yes, he and his wife had had two kids together, but his boys were men now. Logically, they shouldn't enter into the equation but somehow it seemed he owed them a living. And apparently, despite the fact their mother had done absolutely *nothing* to contribute to the family finances and had spent her considerable spare time trying to dispose of as much of his hard-earned money as possible on Rodeo Drive, despite the fact she'd been the one to have a *whole string* of affairs… he *still* owed her a living too. A very comfortable living. Probably a more comfortable one than he was going to enjoy. Once again, he felt his blood pressure zoom up, but this time it was calmed by the knowledge that agreement between both parties was very close. Soon they could take the case to court and then he'd be a free man again.

The phone in his pocket began to buzz and he hauled it out. An unknown number. He hit the button to decline the call.

'Sorry,' he said, switching his phone off, to avoid any more interruptions.

'So,' said Mylo, 'waddya think you'll earn over the next five years?'

'How should I know? You're my agent, you tell me. Anyway, what's that got to do with anything?'

'I'm asking because, when the divorce is finalised, if you perform again, the money'll be all yours.'

'Supposing I don't want to?'

Mylo shrugged. 'Up to you, but apart from what Jessica is costing you, these guys—' he gestured at the three suits sitting across the big conference table in Mylo's fifty-fourth-floor office '—don't come cheap.'

Laurence stared at his team and the phrase *bloodsuckers* flashed into his brain. Everyone was leeching off him. Boom – there went his blood pressure again.

'The thing is,' continued Mylo, 'one of my other clients has just had to go into rehab and there's a residency going in Vegas for three months. I mentioned your name…' He nodded at Laurence. 'They thought you might be a fit.'

'You mean their guests are old enough to remember who I am.'

'If the cap fits... You've hardly been busy, have you? You could perform there as a solo artist.' He and Laurence locked eyes. 'Just think, no touring but a steady income.'

Laurence thought about it. A residency in Vegas was bound to be a pretty lucrative deal. They frequently attracted big-name artists – Elton and Shania came to mind straight off – but Las Vegas...? Just about as far removed from the old and picturesque charms of Little Woodford as one could get. Vegas? Brash, brassy – the urban equivalent of *teeth and tits*. But he'd get to live on site, probably in a top-of-the-range suite, with every creature comfort. He'd perform once a night – maybe a matinee on a Saturday and maybe another midweek. He wouldn't have to travel...

'How much?'

'Half a million.'

Tempting but... 'Nah.'

'A week.'

His mind did such a fast U-turn there was almost a smell of burning rubber in the air. So, he'd have to buy a bunch more clothes including a tux. What the heck.

As he left the meeting, heading for a place to have coffee and have a think, he realised he'd need more than just clothes, if he was going to be out here in the States for months and he was going to have to sort out a whole mass of other stuff. Not least, he'd need to get Elspeth to rescue that beer mat, with Belinda's number, from his fleece pocket, so he could square things off with her. He'd need to get the main bit of the house closed up and to sort things out with the fête committee, so the day wasn't jeopardised by his absence. But right now, his priority was getting Elspeth to rescue that beer mat.

He pushed open the door to the coffee shop and escaped from the torrid heat of the busy street into the cool gloom of a cafe. He liked this place – he always used it when he was visiting Mylo, because it had the shabby-chic air of Central Perk in *Friends* rather than the polished glitz of the more fashionable coffee bars. And they did a great flat white too, which he ordered at the counter before he took a seat in a quiet corner.

He switched on his phone again and rang Elspeth.

'How's things?' he asked.

'Just fine. We had a few days in Scotland and had a good look around the Edinburgh area. My, but there's some big new estates being built. The city hasn't altered though – still beautiful. Oh, and we've said that the vicar's wife and her friend can come around to check out the grounds for their fête – a health and safety inspection, apparently.'

'Great, great.' They chatted on about various things and he told Elspeth that he'd have to delay his return for several months.

'So, would you mind if John and I went up to Scotland again, for a while?'

'Not at all. Why not? I won't need you and there's no point in sitting around your flat twiddling your thumbs all day. I'll be able to get hold of you, if there's a change of plan and, as long as the fête ladies are happy, take as long as you like.'

'Thank you, Laurence, you're a gent.'

'But one other thing; I left my fleece in the kitchen last week. There's a beer mat in the pocket, with a phone number written on it. Can you rescue it for me please and text me the number?'

There was a pause.

'Elspeth?'

'Yes... yes, of course. I'll get it and text you.'

'Cheers. And I'll let you know when I'm likely to come back.'

———

Elspeth disconnected and went into the boot room to find Laurence's green fleece. There it was, hanging by the back door – where she'd put it when she'd finished washing and drying it. She felt in the pockets... There was the beer mat; a crumbling cardboard mess with a brewery logo on one side. She turned it over and could make out some hieroglyphs on the reverse. The biro was almost illegible. She took it over to the boot room window, squinted at the figures and felt a ripple of relief run though her. Still just readable. She picked up her phone and began to text the numbers through to Laurence... 0788... or was that a 9? No, definitely an 8 – 07880 and then she rattled off the rest of the number and pressed send. Done.

———

Belinda switched on a smile and tried to look happy and welcoming for the benefit of her evening customers. Her phone was tucked down her bra, so she would be absolutely sure of feeling it buzz if there was an incoming call. Although her hopes of getting the one she wanted seemed slight, she wasn't going to risk missing his call if he had a miraculous change of heart.

The first time she'd rung, he hadn't answered and after that, it had gone straight to voicemail. Laurence couldn't have made it clearer that he didn't want her calls if he'd sent her a message saying 'sod off', but still she nursed this tiny spark of optimism that he might have a change of heart; he might forgive her...

A voice told her to try again but pride silenced it. She'd given him her number; he'd have known who was calling him and he hadn't wanted to talk. And furthermore, she'd been refused access to his house. She had been blocked, from his phone and his life. She felt irrationally livid.

She might as well delete his number. Angrily, she did.

Bollocks.

———

In LA, Laurence got the text from Elspeth and instantly saved the number before he rang it.

'You are not authorised to access this service,' an electronic voice told him. He wasn't authorised... What the actual fuck? He felt a burst of rage.

Belinda had blocked him. He'd blown it with her. That was that. He might as well delete the number. Angrily, he did.

Bollocks.

TWENTY-THREE

As February morphed into March and then April, Belinda managed to haul herself out of her gloom enough to turn her plans into actions and actually put the pub on the market while, in its kitchen, Miles continued to teach Ashley cookery. His knife skills were coming on apace; he could slice and dice at a reasonable speed and produce even-sized results. From there he'd learned how to make mirepoix and Julienne strips; he learned how fillet fish; bone and roll a leg of lamb and joint a chicken. He could make a roux and now he progressed onto béchamel and mornay sauces; he learned how to make mayonnaise – 'Why, Mum buys it in jars?' which had earned him an eye-roll from Miles – and hollandaise.

In between sessions at the pub, Ashley worked for his A levels, went to a couple more auditions and got more despondent with each rejection. And what was worse, he was now starting to be rejected by the theatre schools he really cared about joining. What if every one of his top ten refused to take him? What then?

He wondered if he'd have stood a better chance if his school had offered drama and theatre studies at A level, but they hadn't. His pals at the Players Theatre had said his experience with them would stand him in just as good stead, but as the rejections rolled in, Ashley wasn't so sure. His exams were hoving up fast, his time in secondary education was coming to an end and, without a place at drama school, his future plans were looking very rocky. He barely had any time to spend with his friends, quite apart from the fact that, because he was treading a different path, he seemed to have less and less in common with them. He was starting to feel increasing different, isolated, fed up and dejected.

'Today is pastry,' said Miles, as Ashley came into the kitchen one Friday evening.

'Great.' His voice was devoid of enthusiasm. He took his apron off the peg and put it on. Was this what the rest of his life might be like… working in a kitchen and acting in low-budget, am-dram productions to thin audiences in his spare time? He had dreamed of so much more than this, but his dreams seemed to be fading fast.

'We'll start with a basic shortcrust.' Miles got out a bowl. 'Rub the fat and flour together using your fingertips, like this,' he said. 'You want it all to look like fine breadcrumbs.' He pushed the bowl back towards Ashley. 'Off you go.'

Ashley looked at the industrial food processor in the corner and thought how much simpler and quicker it would be to use that. Jamie did, but he knew Miles was determined he should learn how to do everything without shortcuts. By the time the pub was ready to open, he'd put a pastry covering on a dozen steak pies. Even he had to admit, they did look pretty good and would look even better when they'd been cooked. Maybe there was something to be said for cooking appetising food for people. He supposed it wasn't so very different from acting – you were putting on a show for the gratification and enjoyment of others.

———

'So, where's lover boy?' asked Bert, coming into the bar the following lunchtime.

'I don't know what you mean,' lied Belinda, starting to pour his pint.

'Yes, you do. That Scots chappie you were mooning over.'

'Oh, him. And I didn't *moon*.' She tried to sound indifferent. 'Anyway, I've no idea. Maybe Little Woodford wasn't to his liking and he's moved on.'

'Really? Because my Joan says he's the guy what owns the Reeve House. Lozza Lachlan. Not,' he continued, 'that kids these days would have heard of him, but I bet you have.'

'No,' lied Belinda again. 'I haven't.'

'He was a big noise in his day,' said Bert.

'Was he now?'

'And you've never heard of him?'

'No.' This conversation was starting to annoy – and upset – her, but the last thing she must do was let on to Bert how much she cared. If he got wind that she minded about Laurence's disappearance, it would be all over the town, before anyone could say *Ninety-nine*. She finished pouring his pint. 'Three-sixty. How come you know all this?'

'My Joan heard it off Mags, who says Amy knows.'

Why wasn't Belinda surprised? 'Maybe he moved here for a quiet life, but that's been blown.' She wondered how Amy had found out.

The pub began to fill steadily with the weekend

lunchtime regulars and after about half an hour, in walked Maxine and Gordon Larkham. They came to the bar to order drinks and pick up a couple of menus.

'Um… Maxine?

'Yes.'

'Do you know what's happened to Laurence? Only he doesn't seem to be around anymore. He hasn't been into the pub for weeks and weeks.'

Perplexed, Maxine shook her head. 'No. Should I? I gave you his number. Why don't you ring him?'

'That's just it, I did and he wouldn't take my call. Calls,' she corrected.

'Oh.' Maxine shrugged and looked uncomfortable. 'In that case I don't think I can help. And he's not at the Reeve House?'

Belinda shook her head.

'Did you try asking Elspeth?'

'I went down there weeks ago and either she's not there, or she's not answering the door. Or she's not answering it to me.'

Maxine looked more edgy.

'Sorry,' said Belinda. 'I seem to be putting you in a difficult position. Forget it. Want to start a tab?'

'Yes. Yes, please.' Maxine and Gordon collected their drinks and their menus and moved off to a corner table. Belinda could tell, from the way Maxine glanced at her now and again, that she and her husband were talking about her. She faintly thought of asking Maxine to ring on her behalf, to find out what was going on, where he'd gone and why he'd suddenly lit out, but she had her pride. No, it would be too demeaning.

———

Ashley was starting to recognise some of his fellow hopefuls. There were quite a number he'd definitely seen more than once and they nodded warily to each other in acknowledgement. It was still a lonely process, with few people talking to one another – after all, they were rivals in a merciless round of auditions and rejections. And, bizarrely, although Ashley was confident that he now knew pretty much what the format of each audition would be, confidence in his ability was waning with each drama school he visited. He was even starting to doubt his choice of audition pieces.

In the waiting room, at yet another theatre school, his stomach rumbled from nerves or hunger. As he hadn't eaten since breakfast, and it was now almost two, it could be either.

'Pullen,' said a scrawny bloke, with a sheaf of papers in his hands.

Ashley stood up. *Let's get it over with,* he thought. The sooner he got told he wasn't wanted, the sooner he could get the train home. He had an English essay to write for Monday morning and the Sunday lunch shift at the pub to get through tomorrow, so his weekend was hardly going to be relaxing.

He went into the rehearsal studio. The panel was sitting in front of a wall of mirrors, so he could see his reflection and the room seemed huge and intimidating. He wondered if it had been done on purpose.

'Off you go,' said the woman in the middle. She sounded bored.

Ashley took a deep breath and began his piece from *The Graduate.* He'd got around halfway through, when the woman put her hand up.

'Stop.'

Was he that bad?

'Do it again. I want you to do it as an old man, as if you are recalling what happened in your youth.'

What? He thought on his feet, tried to internalise how it might feel still to be embarrassed in fifty years' time about something he'd done in his youth. He'd have to change the tense, because it'd need to be in the past. He composed himself for a second, took a breath, lowered the timbre of his voice, and eased himself into the piece. He started to sweat at the effort of changing so much of the original speech on the hoof. The strain of thinking about the next sentence while speaking a different set of words was crazy. He wasn't sure he could keep going.

'That's enough.'

He wasn't sure whether to be grateful or sorry to have been stopped.

'Thank you, Mr Pullen. If you'd like to wait outside.'

That was a first. Feeling faintly hopeful, Ashley went into the corridor and sat on a blue plastic chair. His leg jiggled nervously. The minutes ticked by, then the door opened and the woman put her head around the door. Ashley leaped to his feet.

'Thank you, you can go.' She was about to disappear, but Ashley caught the door and stopped it from swinging shut.

'Sorry, but what was that about?'

'You did well but... Good luck.' She turned her back on him and Ashley let the door close.

Ashley felt as if he'd been kicked. His feelings of hope lay in pieces. How brutal was that?

———

When Maxine got back from the pub she rang the Reeve House.

'Afternoon.'

'Elspeth?'

'Speaking.'

'It's Maxine here. Maxine Larkham.'

'Oh, hello. I'm sorry, but Laurence isn't here at the moment – I am assuming it's him you want.'

'It is. Do you know when he'll be back?'

There was a pause. 'I really have no idea. He's in the States at the moment; has been since February.'

'The States? February?'

'Yes, it was all rather sudden. He left instructions for John and myself to shut up the main bit of the house, so I don't think he's going to be back for a while.'

'But what about the fête?'

'Oh, that's not for a few months. I expect he'll be back by then. In fact, I'm sure he will.'

Maxine sincerely hoped so. She knew, from fête committee meetings, that he'd agreed to be the star turn. People were going to be mightily let down, if he didn't show up.

'But I thought he liked it here,' said Maxine.

'Och, he does that. But... well... he had personal reasons.'

'I'm sorry to hear that.'

'As they say in France – *cherchez la femme.*'

Cherchez... Did Elspeth mean Belinda? But then, who else could it be?

'Oh dear.' She wondered what on earth Belinda could have done that made him put thousands of miles between them and maintain total radio silence. He'd admitted to Maxine that he disliked the intrusiveness of people in LA and liked his anonymity in Little Woodford. Maybe Belinda had overstepped that mark. Whatever the reason, Maxine wasn't going to jeopardise her own relationship with him by getting involved. She regretted giving Belinda his phone number.

TWENTY-FOUR

Heather walked from the vicarage to the community centre, enjoying the June sunshine. The oaks around the cricket pitch were looking luscious, a bright shade of green; Maxine, she thought, would know exactly what colour it was in artistic terms. She breathed in the fresh air and felt happy and calm. Life was good, the fête was on track, her husband was content, their congregation seemed to be untroubled by problems. *Yup, God is in his heaven; all is most definitely right with the world,* she thought cheerfully.

She reached the large wooden structure that served locals as a public meeting room and unlocked the door. As always, it smelt faintly musty and damp, with a lingering whiff of instant coffee. She set about arranging the room, getting out a trestle table and was busy carting chairs out of the store-room when Miranda bowled in.

'Morning, Heather,' she said breezily. 'Lovely day, isn't it?'

'It most certainly is. I get the feeling summer is just around the corner.'

Olivia joined them. 'But it's your day off,' said Heather. 'Surely you've got better things to do with your free time.'

'Possibly, but this is an ideal way of seeing all my friends.'

And then Jacqui arrived, followed by Maxine, who switched on the tea urn and produced a packet of chocolate hobnobs and a pint of milk, before the rest of the fête stalwarts trooped in.

When the meeting and greeting was done and everyone was settled round the table with a mug of tea or coffee Heather opened her notebook and looked around the group.

'Oh… no Diana?'

The others looked around the table too. Apparently not.

'No apology?' asked Maxine.

Heather shook her head. 'Maybe she's been held up. It's not essential she's here, but I'd quite like an update on the bank balance.'

'I think,' said Miranda, who was in charge of sponsorship, 'it should be around fifteen grand. Although she will have had to pay the deposit on the marquee and there will be outgoings soon for a couple of other things – the hire of the tables for the flower and produce show, fencing to secure the river bank and the PA system.'

'But that won't amount to much at this stage. A few hundred,' said Heather. 'So that's good. All very healthy.' She glanced at her agenda and rattled though the preliminaries.

'Right – categories for the flower and produce.' She looked at her fellow committee members before handing out copies of the previous year's programme with its list of the various competitions. 'I suggest, in the interest of simplicity, we leave things as they are.'

'Except,' said Olivia, 'Joan Makepiece always wins the best sponge cake category, Bert usually sweeps the board with his vegetables, and Jacqui's been known to pick up most of the prizes in the pickles and chutney section.'

'So?' said Jacqui defensively.

'*So*, nothing. You're a hard act to beat,' said Olivia, 'but I was wondering about mixing up the classes. Trying to include things for people who might think they haven't a chance, because it's always the same people who get the rosettes.'

'Like?' said Heather.

'Best garden on a plate, best friendship bracelet, best photograph…'

'But we've never had anything like that before,' said Jacqui.

'Precisely,' said Olivia.

'You might have a point,' conceded Heather. Instantly the women around the table began exchanging ideas.

'But we'll still have best pickle, won't we?' said Jacqui, after a few minutes.

'I think,' said Heather, 'now our finances are looking so good, we can afford to have all the existing prizes and add a few new ones. We'll keep the money at ten pounds for a first, a fiver for a second and two quid for third. All in favour?'

All hands were raised.

'Right, so let's decide on the criteria for the new competitions. And we'll keep the entry fee to fifty pence for each category?' The others nodded in agreement.

An hour, and another round of hot drinks later, the decisions had been made and half a dozen new categories had been added to the list.

'We'll have to remember to increase our order for rosettes, too,' said Heather. 'I'll ring the supplier.'

On her return home she put her list of tasks on the dining room table and rang Diane. She got put through to a messaging service.

'Oh... er... this is Heather. I'm just ringing to check you're OK, as you missed the fête committee meeting. Let me know if there's anything I need to know in the finance department and to say you'll be getting some invoices from various companies in the not too distant... Well... er... bye.'

She put the phone down, confident that Diane would ring her back if she needed to tell her anything. Anyway, she'd see her soon enough, when she came round to get the payments countersigned. Just then, she realised she couldn't remember countersigning the cheque for the marquee deposit. Had she? She must have done. Goodness, the things that slipped her mind these days. Old age she supposed – which was why she was an inveterate list-maker.

———

Eight hours later, when it was still midday in Las Vegas, Laurence was busy in his suite at his hotel. The air con was on full blast, as he sat at the piano he'd insisted on as part of his contract. His long fingers ran up and down the keys as he warmed up with a few scales and arpeggios. Not that he needed much by way of rehearsal; he'd been playing the same set for the past months. In fact, it had got to the stage when performing was becoming tedious, although the applause was still warm and it was nice to be fêted. At least every night was slightly different, because each audience brought a different vibe to the room: one night they'd be insatiable for encores; on another, he only got demands for a couple.

But, all in all, he was glad his tenure at the hotel was coming to an end. For a start, he'd be glad to get home to a less screamingly fake environment. Nothing in this city was normal or natural. Although he'd lived in America for far longer than he'd lived in Little Woodford, he missed the quiet beauty of the place, the unpredictable weather, the people… everything.

And Belinda.

Maybe when he got back and he wandered into her pub for a pint of Rabbit Punch, she'd relent. That was, unless she refused to serve him. He had to hope not.

Behind him, a maid was packing his cases. Tonight was his last performance; tomorrow he'd return to LA, where Mylo had him booked into a recording studio. As soon as he'd laid down the tracks for a new solo album, he'd be on the plane back to Blighty. That was the plan. Mylo, of course, was delighted that he'd written some new stuff.

'Leave it with me,' he'd told Laurence. 'I'll make sure you make it big again. All the major radio stations will get downloads. We'll say you're available for any of the chat shows too. How about that?'

'I'm not sure I—' Laurence had started to protest.

'Think of the money. Think of the exposure.'

He knew that it might all come to nothing. The music industry was fickle. If his new album tanked, he'd be free to get back to Little Woodford sooner rather than later. Perversely, he rather hoped it might.

He put the lid of the piano down and picked up his mobile. Eight p.m. in the UK, so Elspeth would be around.

'Laurence. How's it going?'

'Evening , Elspeth. Very well. I'm ringing to say that I'm finishing in Vegas shortly, then I've got business in LA. I'm not sure how long all of that's going to take. Hopefully, just a few weeks, but as soon as I'm done, I'll be flying back to the UK. Whatever happens I'm going to be back for that fête. Can't let Little Woodford down.'

'That's good to hear. If you send me the details of your

flight, I'll make sure John's there to meet you. And I'll open up the main house and give it a good airing.'

'Thank you. Has anyone been asking after me?'

There was a pause, as Elspeth thought. 'The ladies from the fête committee have been round a couple of times – once with a fencing contractor, to see how we can close off access to the river.'

'Anyone else?'

'No – not a soul. Why?'

No, of course not. If Belinda had blocked him on her phone, she wasn't going to hotfoot it down to his house to drop off a letter or leave a message. He'd been clutching at straws. 'No reason.' He sighed. 'Anything else going on?'

'Other than the fête? No. It's all been pretty quiet here, although John and I are still house hunting, so we might have missed out on some excitement. Oh, word has got out around the town as to your real identity.'

Laurence felt strangely sanguine about that – it was bound to happen. 'Let me guess – you heard it in the post office queue.'

'The supermarket, actually, but the same difference.'

'I'll give that town its due, it has a first-class intelligence system. Maybe I should send the CIA over; they might learn a thing or two. And talking of things you've heard… any news on the sale of the pub?' He tried to sound casual.

'Not a dicky bird. Of course, that doesn't mean it's not going to happen. Do you want me to make enquiries?'

'No, no, not at all.'

'As you wish.'

Laurence had no doubt Elspeth would ask around, if only to assuage her own curiosity. He supposed he could ask her to go in to the Talbot, make abject apologies on his behalf, ask Belinda to relent, to ring him… But he had his pride. 'Right, well, looking forward to coming home and seeing you and John again.'

'It'll be lovely to have you back.'

He put his phone back beside the piano and started playing one of his new tunes, one of a dozen or so for the album. Most had been written since his arrival in Vegas – except this one.

'That's lovely,' said the maid, holding a beautifully folded shirt.

Laurence swivelled on the piano stool. He'd forgotten about her. 'Thank you. Glad you like it.'

'What's it called?'

'Belinda.'

———

'Stop writing,' boomed Mr Johnson, the invigilator.

Ashley threw down his pen and stretched. That was it, it was over – that was his last exam and he felt a whoosh of relief. No more revising, no more excruciating nerves before turning over the paper, no more writer's cramp. At the end of some of his other exams, he'd felt worried; had he done as well as he should have done, had he answered the questions correctly, would he pass…? But this time, he didn't care. He was finished. A levels were over. Pass or fail, it was now in the lap of the gods… and the examiners.

Mr Johnson moved between the lines of tables, gathering up the papers, allowing each student to leave. Finally, it was Ashley's turn to escape into the main playground and the bright June sunshine. There the students were milling around, chatting to their friends about their chances.

Someone clapped him on the back. 'How did you get on, Ash?' asked Zac.

Ashley shrugged. 'OK, I think. You?'

Zac shook his head. 'Well, I've got to get a B, if I want to get into my first choice of uni. You're all right though – you don't need the grades.'

'If I don't get into drama school, I might.'

'How many have you tried for?'

'Ten.'

'Ten? And still no joy. I mean… maybe it's not for you.'

'Don't you think I've thought about that?' snapped Ashley.

'OK, keep your hair on.'

'Yeah, well… I wouldn't mind if it was just rejection, but the cost… I must have spent well over a grand, what with fees and travel costs and it's not money I can afford.'

'At least you've got a job. How's it going at the pub?'

Ashley brightened a little. 'Actually, it's good. Miles is teaching me all sorts of stuff. Seriously, if I don't make it to drama school, I'm considering taking a gap year and working in a kitchen full-time. That way I can learn enough about cooking to earn my keep and get a proper job, if acting doesn't pan out.'

'I'd like to take a gap year – maybe earn some money for a few months and then go travelling.'

'Wouldn't it be better to put the money you earn against your student loan?'

Zac looked bemused. 'What? Who cares about student debt? I'm banking on Dad getting me an internship where he works in London, when I finish uni. Unless I cock up massively, that'll be me fast-tracked into a job in the City.' Zac rubbed his fingers and thumb together. 'Loads of money.'

Whoopee, thought Ashley cheerlessly. Lucky old Zac. It was all right for some.

'Anyway, are you coming down the skate park? I've managed to score some booze from Mum's wine rack. I think we should do some celebrating, don't you?'

'What about the girls?' Ashley looked around for Megan and Sophie.

'They won't want to join us. They've still got some exams to go.'

Ashley thought about Zac's offer. He wasn't sure he wanted to celebrate but, on the other hand, he didn't have anything else to do. His mum would be out working, and he didn't have a shift at the pub today. He'd half planned to go and see the drama group – it had been six months since he'd last been there, what with his job and A levels. But he might as well join Zac for the time being.

'Why not?'

They fell into step as they walked out of the school grounds to the skate park. They slid into the space under the half-pipe, where Zac produced a bottle of slightly warm Chardonnay from his bag. He twisted off the cap and passed it over.

'Are you serious about cooking, if you don't make it to drama school?'

Ashley grimaced as he swallowed, wiped the neck of the bottle and passed it back. 'Why not?'

'Fancy yourself as the next Jamie Oliver?'

'What's wrong with that? Besides, it's a useful thing to be able to do.'

Zac glugged the wine. 'Why, when there's Just Eat, Deliveroo, PizzaExpress, Domino's…?'

'For one, it's all fast food and secondly it's much cheaper if you can cook your own. I should know; I see the mark-up at the pub. A basic steak and chips costs about three quid to make and they serve it for around twenty.'

Zac took another slurp. 'Yeah, but they've got to pay you and Miles and there's other overheads.'

'In your own home that doesn't come into the equation.'

Zac shrugged. 'If you say so.' He handed the bottle to Ashley who shook his head.

'Nah, you're all right.'

'You a wine buff as well, now? This stuff not chilled enough for you?'

It wasn't – it was disgusting – but Ashley wasn't going to risk further ridicule. 'Nah, you scored it, it's yours. Besides, I've got stuff to do. I want to check out a couple more drama schools – see when they're holding auditions.'

Zac shook his head. 'You used to be fun but now…'

'Some of us have to sort out everything for ourselves. Some of us don't have *Daddy* giving us a leg up.'

He thought he heard Zac mutter, 'Loser,' as he left. He'd show him. One way or another, he'd make it. He straightened his back and squared his shoulders. He was going to be a *Somebody* one day. He *was*.

TWENTY-FIVE

A couple of weeks later, in downtown LA, Laurence sat at the grand piano in the recording studio, the sound of the final chord dying away, and saw Mylo's pudgy face grinning at him though the soundproof window. Beside Mylo, was the engineer whose job it was to deal with the technical wizardry of the tracks.

'Sounds great,' said Mylo's voice into his headphones. 'I think this might be one of your best yet.'

Laurence took the headphones off, unplugged the jack, stretched before he got up and made his way through the heavy swing door.

'I'm hopeful,' said Mylo, when he joined him. 'I'm definitely getting *interested* vibes from some of the music press and there's a bunch of radio stations who want a couple of downloads.'

'Really?' He knew, of old, how Mylo liked to hype things. 'The last couple of albums didn't do so great.'

'Because they were not as good as this. Trust me. Besides, that spell you did in Vegas didn't do you no harm neither.

People have remembered who you are – how much they like you.'

'I suppose.'

'I don't want you going nowhere for the time being. I've got a bunch of stuff to get fixed – cover art, sleeve notes, running order, and I don't want you disappearing off to where I can't get a hold of you.'

'I'm only going to fly back to the UK.'

'No, you're not. If my plans come off, I'm hoping to get you some slots on the chat shows. You want this to be a success, don't you? You want to make up the money Jessica's taken off you.' Mylo eyeballed his client, before adding, 'Don't you? Come on, it'll only be a few weeks more. Think about your pension plan. Besides, what have you got to go home to?'

Mylo was right... what *did* he have to go home to? And the idea of being applauded, being *appreciated*, for a while longer, here in the States, was quite seductive. Almost as seductive as Belinda, but that was in the past and this album was in the present.

'Yes, OK,' he said, capitulating.

———

A day later in Little Woodford, in hot July sunshine, Heather wandered round the back of the high street to the little yard near the station, where there were half a dozen light industrial units. The yard had once been the sidings for the station, in the days when a couple of branch lines had fed off the mainline to the local area and Little Woodford had been a bit of a railway hub. Of course, all that had gone with the Beeching cuts in the Sixties and the town had thought itself lucky to get away with keeping its station at all. The loss of the sidings had seemed like small price to pay for their continued connection to London.

The third unit down housed the printing company. What with service sheets and the parish newsletter, they got a fair bit of business from the vicar and his wife.

'Hello, Mrs Simmonds,' said young Jake in reception. Young Jake was now heading towards middle age, but Heather had known him since he'd been at school in the town. 'What can I do for you?'

Heather handed over a copy of the entry form for the fête's flower and produce competitions and a second piece of paper, with the rules and requirements for the various categories. With around six weeks to go, it was time to start calling for entries for the various competitions.

'Can you produce two thousand of these – folded A4 to make a little booklet? Entry form on the front, the classes and Ts&Cs on the other three sides?'

'Sure thing,' said Jake. 'Got the draft on a memory stick, or an SD card?'

Heather handed over an SD card in an envelope.

'Great. When for?'

'Later this week.'

'No problem. Are you picking them up, or do you want them delivered? Only, two thousand is quite a heavy package.'

'Will there be a delivery charge?'

'Not if I drop them off on my way home.'

Heather smiled at him. He might have been a bit of a tearaway in his youth, but he'd come good. 'Then I'd like them delivered. Thanks, Jake.'

'I'll email a proof for your approval, as normal, and as soon as it's signed off, we'll get the job sorted.'

'Excellent. Thank you.' She turned to go.

'Just one thing, Mrs Simmonds.'

She turned back. 'Yes?'

'We've got an invoice outstanding.'

'Oh?'

'Since before Christmas.'

'Really?'

'You had some posters done... advertising for people to help with the fête.'

'But that was ages ago. Why didn't you mention it before?'

'You haven't been in.' Jake handed her a copy of the outstanding bill.

'But Brian has.' Heather stuffed the invoice into her handbag.

'That's church stuff. I didn't like to bother him with this.'

'Jake, I'm really, *really* sorry. I'll get onto it straight away. I'm sure it's an oversight.'

'No worries, Mrs Simmonds. It's not a lot and, let's face it, if we can't trust you, who can we trust?'

Heather left the print works, feeling slightly concerned. She thought back, trying to work out how the invoice had been missed. She remembered picking it up with the posters. She'd distributed flyers around the town... and she'd given the invoice to Diane at their first meeting. Diane must have forgotten it; after all, she'd been busy sorting out their accounts and getting them a better rate of interest. There was a simple explanation, she was sure, but Diane needed a nudge. Heather really didn't want a local business to be out of pocket.

———

Heather was getting increasingly desperate. In the past forty-eight hours she'd left several messages for Diane and sent a number of emails, but there was no response. She needed to call round. And then she realised she didn't actually know where the woman lived. In fact, she knew precious little about her, apart from the fact she'd volunteered to run the fête committee finances. So, what else did she know? The realisation began to set like cement in the pit of her stomach. The answer was *absolutely nothing*. She'd not asked for references, she'd not seen her credentials... zilch.

She rang Jacqui and Miranda and asked them both the same question. No, they hadn't signed any cheques, either. All invoices were therefore either unpaid, or had been cleared using just Diane's signature. So what was she doing with the money? Heather put the phone on the counter and sat down, hoping the sick feeling was going to go away, but it worsened. What had she done?

She knocked on the door of Brian's study.

'Are you busy?' she asked.

'Not especially.' Brian took his glasses off and swivelled his chair round to face his wife. 'Is everything all right? You look very pale.'

Heather swallowed. 'I think I've been a bit of a fool.'

'Surely not.'

'It's the fête committee.'

'And?'

'I think I might have a problem.'

Brian smiled. 'What is it? Mutiny in the ranks?'

'That might be preferable.'

Brian's smile faded. 'What is it?'

Heather dragged a chair over to the desk from the corner of the study and sat down. 'Our treasurer...'

'Yes.'

'I can't get hold of her. She won't answer her mobile, I've sent texts, she isn't replying to my emails—'

'So? She's out and about. She's gone away for a couple of days.'

Heather took a deep breath. 'I don't know where she lives. And...' She paused and swallowed. 'I remember, when she joined the committee, she said we needed new bank mandates, because some of the signatories weren't members any longer.'

'And?'

'So she produced a load of papers for me, Miranda and Jacqui to sign. I think she might have changed the bank, too. She said the interest rate wasn't up to much at the old one. I don't even know where the bank account is anymore. And the print firm has just told me there's an unpaid invoice. And...' She could hardly bear to go on.

'And?' prompted Brian.

'And I know there have been... *should* have been other outgoings, deposits mostly, but I don't remember counter-signing any of the cheques.'

'So?'

'So, I've checked with Miranda and Jacqui and they haven't signed anything, either.'

'Maybe it hasn't been necessary, yet. The fête's a couple of months off.'

'But she said she'd paid the marquee deposit – the same company as last year.'

'She can't have if she needs more than one signature.'

'Which means,' said Heather, 'either she's made herself sole signatory, or she's fibbing.'

'Or both.'

Heather stared at him. He'd voiced the conclusion she'd come to. What other explanation was there? She felt weak and sick with worry. 'I think there was around fifteen thousand in the account.'

Brian took a deep breath and exhaled slowly. 'You need to contact the marquee company. If the deposit has been paid, then your fears may be unfounded. But if not...' Brian stared at Heather for a few seconds. 'I think you need to involve Miranda and Jacqui at the very least. They may know something, remember something... have paid more attention to what they were signing. And then I think it might be a police matter.'

'Oh, Brian. Suppose we're right? How can I make amends? We can't afford to pay that sort of money back.'

'It's not your fault.'

Heather raised her voice as she said, 'Whose fault is it? I'm the one who welcomed her with open arms. I should have done some checks. I should have asked for references. I failed on all counts.'

'Get hold of Miranda and Jacqui. You have to talk to them.'

'You're right,' said Heather, more quietly. 'I'll get them to come over as soon as possible. Please God,' she prayed fervently, 'let them know more about this woman than I do. How could I have been so stupid?'

While Heather was waiting for Jacqui and Miranda to come over, she got out her fête file and looked out the details of the previous year's event. She found the letter of confirmation from the marquee company they had hired and dialled their number with trepidation.

No, they hadn't heard anything about this year's event. Did she want to book a marquee?

Heather replaced the handset and shut her eyes. The fuzzy invoice that Diane had shown them was probably Photoshopped from the previous year. Diane had produced it to make them all think arrangements were progressing as normal while, in reality, she was waiting for the sponsorship money, before absconding with it all.

Shock, shame and a feeling of helplessness percolated through Heather, like water through limestone, leaving a similar cold, stony accretion of guilt and remorse. A voice nagged in her head. How could she have been so stupid? So trusting? Such a mug? It repeated itself, over and over.

It got worse, when Jacqui and Miranda admitted to being equally vague about the details.

'We thought *you'd* done all the checks,' said Miranda.

Tears of shame rolled down Heather's cheeks. 'Now what?' she whispered.

'There's a branch of the police that specialises in fraud. We need to report this to them,' said Miranda. She tapped her phone a few times. 'Here we go – Action Fraud.' She rang the number. 'I'm on hold.'

Heather fetched her laptop.

'Is there a website?' she asked.

Miranda nodded and showed her the details. While she continued to listen to holding music, Heather accessed the site and began tapping in the details. 'There,' she said finally.

Miranda disconnected her call. 'No wonder fraudsters are so prolific.' She chucked her phone on to the kitchen table. 'I mean, what's the point?'

'What can we do now?' asked Jacqui.

Heather shook her head. 'I've no idea. I don't even know if Diane's rinsed our bank account. If I knew where the account was, I'd go and ask the branch for details.'

'They wouldn't give them to you, not if you're not a signatory,' Miranda told her. 'I think we have to plan for the worst and hope for the best.'

'In which case, what's the plan?' asked Jacqui.

'We'll have to cancel.' Miranda looked at her two friends. 'What else can we do?'

'We have insurance,' said Heather.

The other two brightened. 'Really?'

'I'm not sure if this is covered, though. It's mainly for public liability, that sort of thing.' She pulled her file towards her and leafed through the folios, till she found what she was looking for. She scanned the pages of small print while the other two sat quietly.

'I'm not sure,' she said eventually.

Miranda glanced at the kitchen clock. 'It's half past four. Ring them now, because I doubt if you'll get an answer from them over the weekend. We may be lucky to get an answer from them this late on a Friday afternoon, anyway.'

Heather rang the number, listened to the options, pressed different numbers on her phone several times…

'Oh, yes. Hello. Yes, I'm ringing about a possible insurance claim.'

The other two sat and listened while Heather explained the facts of the matter.

'OK, OK, thank you for your advice,' she said eventually.

The other two looked at her expectantly.

'It's not looking hopeful. I'll need to get a crime number from the Action Fraud police, but they think that even then we won't be able to claim because of lack of due diligence.' Heather seemed to shrink. 'Lack of due diligence; that's my fault. Everything is ruined. What are we going to tell the sponsors?'

Miranda shook her head. 'I have no idea. But I do know there are going to be quite a few, very awkward conversations.'

'But not till we know definitively what's going on.'

Miranda nodded. 'I agree. For the time being, we carry

on as usual. And let's not tell the rest of the committee yet — just in case we're wrong.'

Jacqui snorted in disbelief.

'I've told Brian,' admitted Heather.

'I think we can trust him to be discreet,' said Jacqui.

Just then the doorbell rang. It was Jake delivering the fête's flower and produce entry forms. And the bill. Another bill they couldn't pay.

TWENTY-SIX

'You can make a start by sharpening these knives,' said Miles, shortly after Ashley had buttoned up his white jacket, ready for the evening shift. 'And then I'm going to teach you how to cook perfect rice.'

'What's wrong with boil in a bag?'

Miles sighed and shook his head. 'I hope you're joking.'

'Might be.' Ashley had the knives done to Miles's standard in about five minutes.

Miles handed him a bag of basmati rice and the scales.

'One and a half times the amount of water to rice, so if you're going to cook four hundred grams of rice, how much water do you need?'

There was a pause as Ashley worked it out. 'Er... six hundred mils.'

'Give that boy a gold star,' said Miles. 'Now then, rinse your rice.'

Ashley did as he was bid and then was taken through the other steps of seasoning, boiling, simmering and finally fluffing it up.

'Easy, isn't it?' said Miles.

'Pretty much.'

'And a lot cheaper than buying boil in a bag. Your mum could save quite a bit, if you show her how simple it is to do it this way. Anyway, cookery lesson over for today. Let's start prepping the veg.' Miles picked up a large box of mushrooms. 'Wipe down all of these and remove the stalks, then trim them; I'll use them for mushroom soup. Caps in this bowl, stalks in this one.' He handed Ashley two large stainless steel bowls.

'Yes, chef.'

'And when you've done that, I want you to produce fat chips like I showed you last week.'

'Yes, chef.'

'Good lad.' Miles clapped his protégé on the shoulder. The lad was coming on nicely. If he didn't make it on the stage, he might make a fine chef one day. If the weekend wasn't too busy, he'd move Ashley's training up a notch – he thought it was time Ashley learned some patisserie skills.

———

On the Monday morning, Amy rang Jacqui Connolly's doorbell, ready to start her cleaning shift.

'Morning, Jacqui.' She headed for the kitchen and started to pick up her cleaning materials from the cupboard under the sink. 'The usual today, is it?'

'Please, Amy. And maybe leave the kitchen till last. I've got work to do from home.'

'Righty-o,' said Amy. 'Not going into the surgery?'

Jacqui's husband was the senior partner in the local practice and she often worked as a receptionist there, or she had, since she'd dried out. She and the doctor had lost their only daughter, shortly after she'd gone to university. She'd been taken ill – more than likely Freshers' Flu they thought – only it hadn't been. It had been meningitis. Jacqui had blamed herself and hit the bottle. It had been several years before she'd managed to take herself in hand and stop.

'Not today. I've got some other stuff to do.' She indicated the pile of papers on the table.

Amy peered at them. 'Oh, the fête. Not so far off now, is it? Did I hear that new bloke, who's living in the Reeve House, is going to let you hold it there? And he's going to open it and all.'

'How did you hear that?' asked Jacqui. 'It's not public knowledge.'

'Oh,' said Amy airily. 'You know what this place is like for gossiping. Not that *I* do, of course, but working in the post office you'd be amazed what I get to hear.'

It took all Jacqui's self-control not to roll her eyes. She was saved from having to comment by the phone ringing. She went to answer it, giving Amy a chance to look at the stuff on the table. A handwritten to-do list was on the top.

1. Ring old bank and ask where fête funds transferred to when DM closed account.
2. Google Diane Maskell + accountant. Previous?
3. Speak town clerk re electoral roll. Address?
4. Ring other orgs – see if they've had dealings with Diane.

A noise in the hall made Amy jump. She grabbed her cleaning things guiltily and dumped them on the counter, before picking up the kettle.

'Cuppa?' she asked as Jacqui came back into the kitchen. She saw Jacqui's eyes stray to the table. 'Yes; lovely.'

When Amy finished filling the kettle and had plugged it in, she saw the note had been turned face down. Something was up, she thought and wished she knew more about this Diane Maskell. She'd ask her mum – maybe she'd come across her. It was a shame Mags had given up her hairdressing salon. In the old days, when she'd done just about everyone's hair in the town, she'd been a mine of information.

But one thing was blindingly obvious, even to Amy; Jacqui and the fête committee were very keen to get hold of Diane Maskell and it had something to do with money. Tomorrow she cleaned for Miranda and on Wednesday she did for Heather; maybe she'd get the opportunity then to dig a little deeper.

———

Miranda put down the phone, feeling drained. In her previous life, as a lawyer, mostly dealing in medical negligence cases, she'd thought of herself as robust. Tough, even. But ringing round the sponsors to tell them what had happened to their generous donations and listening to the accusations of incompetence and even *collusion*, was one of the hardest things she'd ever done. And with each phone call it seemed to get worse.

She ticked the name of the agricultural supplier off her list and made a note that any future approaches would be a waste of the fête committee's time. It had been phrased considerably more strongly than that, but did the actual words matter? The gist was the same.

She was about to tackle another company, when the doorbell rang. An excuse to procrastinate – thank God.

'Heather. Come in.'

'Am I disturbing you?'

'Yes, and I am very glad you are. I'm ringing the sponsors.'

'Oh, Miranda…' Heather's voice was full of guilt and sympathy. 'Is it ghastly?'

'That's one word for it,' said Miranda, as lightly as she could. 'Bloody awful are two more.'

'I should be doing this.'

Miranda stared at her guest – at frail, bird-like Heather, who was all heart and kindness and generosity and who probably wouldn't cope well with being told she was a shitty fraudster or a fucking incompetent, or any of the other choice phrases Miranda had endured that afternoon.

'Perhaps not,' said Miranda. 'Tea? Coffee? I have almond milk, which I think you prefer.'

'Tea, then please.'

Miranda led the way into her beautiful white, light, shiny kitchen.

'I do love your kitchen. So clean and bright.'

Miranda took a teapot from the cupboard, put in several spoonfuls of leaf tea and filled it from the special tap that dispensed boiling water, before she popped a pod into her coffee machine for herself. 'You know,' she said as casually as she could, 'if you wanted to freshen up your kitchen, you can buy some very good paints that work on tiles.'

'Really?'

'It's not quite as good as retiling, but so much cheaper.'

'Thank you, I'll tell Brian. Those green ones in my kitchen have rather passed their sell-by date.'

'A tiny bit passé,' agreed Miranda. Dear God, they were so dated, Mrs Noah wouldn't even have considered them for the ark.

Heather perched on a stool by the counter and saw Miranda's sponsorship list. 'Let me do the rest,' she offered.

Miranda shook her head.

'Because you think I wouldn't cope with the opprobrium?'

'Well...'

'I haven't always lived in a nice parish like this,' said Heather. 'Brian's first living was in London; Tower Hamlets. We had to have metal grills on all our windows and a letter box screwed to the outside wall, to stop local kids smashing the glass, or putting burning rags through the door. Vicar-baiting was the local pastime of choice. Of course, if we remonstrated, we made things worse.' She gave her host a steady stare. 'I'm tougher than I look.'

'Even so...' Miranda removed the list from Heather's hand and put it out of reach. 'Let's sit down.'

'I don't suppose,' said Heather, as she followed Miranda to the big white sofas, 'these companies have a record of the bank account into which their donations were paid or any other information about Diane?'

Miranda shook her head. 'Sadly, no. I'd make contact with the prospective sponsor, then I'd forward the details, by email, to Diane. I assumed it was all being done by BACS transfer, but apparently not. She would contact the sponsor direct, ask for a cheque to be left at, say the front office, or with the shop manager, for her to collect. No paper trail at all.'

Heather sighed. 'I know it's unchristian, but I sincerely hope she gets her comeuppance.'

'Well, if you and Brian can't sort something out, then who can?'

'I'm not supposed to pray for bad things to happen to

people, but, frankly, in Diane's case, I'm prepared to make an exception.'

'Then feel free,' said Miranda. 'I'm thinking about wax effigies and pins, myself. Let's hope something works!'

'I think, as a courtesy, I need to go and see Mr McLachlan. He's been very generous in offering us the use of his garden and promising to make an appearance. He needs to be the first to know about the cancellation.'

'This is the point of no return,' said Miranda.

'I rather think it is. Right then,' said Heather. 'I shall go and see Laurence.'

———

Elspeth answered the door, when Heather rang the bell some fifteen minutes later.

'I can pass on a message,' said Elspeth, in response to Heather's request to speak to Laurence. 'I don't rightly know when he's planning on coming back. I do know,' she added swiftly, 'that he'll be back for the fête. He told me, only last week, he's coming back specially.'

But that was the thing, thought Heather. He needn't make the journey just for that. She had to get hold of him and stop him.

'He didn't expect to be gone this long, but he's been caught up in some unexpected business in the States,' said Elspeth. 'Can I give him a message?'

Could she honestly tell him what had been going on, how *stupid* she had been, via a third party? She thought not. 'When will he be back?'

'Och, that I can't say. It could be a few more weeks, but definitely back for the end of August.'

Oh, Lordy! That was cutting it fine. She really needed to get to him before then.

'I need to speak to him about the arrangements… if you could ask him to ring me. It's quite important.' She smiled. 'He's got my number.'

'Yes, of course.'

Heather made her way back up the drive. It was a phone call she wasn't looking forward to.

TWENTY-SEVEN

'Here,' said Bert, as he leaned on the bar a few days later and watched Belinda pour his pint. 'What's this I hear about you wanting to sell the pub?'

Belinda looked up sharply. 'And who told you that?'

'I dunno. Seems to be common knowledge.'

Belinda sighed. It was bound to be. There mightn't be a shingle outside, but it was on the open market, so someone was bound to spot it sometime. And, she told herself, the whole point of marketing the place was so that people *did* know it was available to buy. She could hardly pretend it was a secret.

'So, who's going to buy it?' continued Bert.

'If I had a crystal ball, I'd tell you. Three-sixty, please,' she added.

'It'd better be someone we like. We don't want no one mucking around with this place. You tell 'em that.' Bert's hand was ferreting around in his trouser pocket, looking for the change.

'I'll do my best.'

'See that you do. And what's this I hear about the fête?' He found a handful of coins and passed them over.

'My, you have been catching up on the local news,' said Belinda. 'And I'm not on the committee, so it's nothing to do with me.'

'My Joan says they've got financial problems.'

Belinda was nonplussed. 'Have they?'

'Seems like someone's emptied the bank account. Nicked the lot. All the sponsorship money and everything.'

Belinda was shocked. 'Who'd do a thing like that? Heather must be beside herself.'

Bert shrugged. 'Not what you expect in a nice town like this.'

'We've had our moments. Remember that shyster Amy dated for a bit.'

'Billy Rogers? He was a wrong 'un.'

Belinda nodded. He certainly had been – thief, drug dealer and all-round nasty piece of work. Probably out of jail again, but he couldn't be in the frame for this crime – if indeed a crime had been committed; she only had Bert's word for it. Billy Rogers probably couldn't even spell the words bank account, let alone empty one.

'You should ask that fancy man you dated if he can help,' said Bert. 'If he's got enough money to take you to the Flower Pot, he's got enough to bail out the fête.'

'How do you…?'

'How do I know about your expensive dinner?' Bert chuckled and tapped his nose.

Belinda gave him a pleading look.

'Well, put it this way, my Joan heard it off of Mags Pullen, when she did her hair last, and Mags heard it off Amy—'

'Who heard it off Ashley,' finished Belinda. She rolled her

eyes. And if Amy and Mags knew, then the whole town did. Why didn't she just drape a banner from the pub sign?

More people came in and Bert moved away to his usual table.

Belinda wondered if Bert's intelligence was genuine. He'd been right about a couple of other things. But the more she thought about it, the more it added up; she'd heard a couple of her regulars wondering when the entry forms for the various classes in the flower and produce competition were going to be available. Well, never, if Bert was right. Poor Heather. Belinda wondered if there was anything she might be able to do to help. She ought to trot down to the vicarage and have a word with her. Quite what she could do, except offer moral support she wasn't sure, but Heather might appreciate the show of solidarity.

Several hours later, between the lunchtime session and the evening one, Belinda stood outside the vicarage.

'Is it true?' she asked, when Heather had invited her in. She didn't, thought Belinda, look entirely well. She was pale and had lost weight – not that there was much of her, to start with.

'About the fête?' said Heather bleakly. She nodded. 'It's awful,' she added, as she filled the kettle and plugged it in. 'Oh, Lordy, I've just realised we still haven't told the rest of the committee about this. And now the word is out. I really must tell them myself before they hear it second hand.' She shook her head. 'How could I have been so remiss?'

'You've had other things on your mind. How much have you lost?'

'A lot. Maybe as much as fifteen grand.'

'Oh, Heather. That's awful.' Belinda sank down on to a kitchen chair. 'I feel there must be something I can do to help.'

Heather shook her head. 'Trust me, if I thought there was, I'd ask you. And we've put the backs up of so many people – all the businesses in town who gave us money... everyone.'

'The businesses will get over it. I bet they write off more than they gave you in sponsorship all the time, on stupid things like staff perks, or people nicking office stationery.'

'Maybe.' She sighed heavily. 'And I've yet to get hold of the star of the show and break the news to him.' The kettle boiled and she made two mugs of tea.

'I'm not with you,' said Belinda.

'Oh... I thought word had got out about our celebrity guest. I thought everyone knew. You know what this place is like.'

'I certainly do,' said Belinda recalling her recent conversation with Bert.

'The guy who moved into the Reeve House—'

'Laurence McLachlan.'

'You knew who bought it?'

Belinda nodded.

'He was going to let us hold the fête in his garden *and* open it for us.' Heather plonked the mugs on the table.

'I didn't know that bit.'

'I need to tell him that his kind and generous offer was wasted. But I left a message with his housekeeper, asking him to ring and he hasn't. I know he's got my number. I imagine he'll ring me when he's got a mo. He's a busy man and I don't want to risk annoying him. I want to tell him in person. To apologise properly for wasting his time. I'm worried he'll come back here, specially for the fête, to find it's a wasted journey.' Heather paused for breath and sipped her drink. 'I suppose I could go back and ask Elspeth for a number but then it looks like I'm checking up on her, and if she has asked Laurence to ring me, and he hasn't, then I'm pestering. Sorry, I'm gabbling on here. It's the worry.'

Belinda smiled sympathetically at her friend. She completely understood. 'I suppose,' she said, 'you might ask Maxine for his number. She's got it. Although she can be a bit cagey about giving it out. I think she feels she ought to protect him from the general public – or maybe I've got the wrong end of the stick. But anyway… in these circumstances…' Belinda shrugged. 'Worth a shot,' she said, wondering if she could possibly ask Heather to relay the number to her – she'd never stopped regretting the moment when she deleted it in anger.

'Maxine! I'd forgotten about her. Of course, she knows him quite well, doesn't she?'

Belinda didn't let on to Heather that, for a short while, she herself might have known Laurence better, but nodded. 'She does.'

'Belinda – you might be a lifesaver. Thank you.'

'Just one thing… when you talk to him, *if* you talk to him, could you tell him that it'd be nice to see him back in the pub. Tell him, Belinda says *hi*.'

———

Maxine shut the front door behind her visitor and pottered back into her kitchen checking the time on the clock as she sat down at the table. She was shocked by the news Heather had just broken, but she understood why Heather wanted to be the one to tell Laurence what had happened; why the fête was getting cancelled.

'Please don't tell him yourself.' Heather had pleaded. 'Just say I need to talk about arrangements, and leave it at that,' she'd said. 'I need to be the one to explain what a fool I've been – it's my penance.'

Maxine promised solemnly not to mention it. She did a rapid calculation and worked out that it would be morning on the west coast of America. Probably not too early to ring. If she didn't get through, she'd text.

Laurence picked up on the third ring.

'Laurence. How are you? Is this a convenient time to call?'

'Lovely to hear from you, Maxine. How's my favourite artist?'

'Pretty good. Enjoying the summer.'

'And how are the courses at the hotel? I hope you're getting better students than I proved to be.'

'Yes, they're going fine. But what about you?'

A heavy sigh swept over from the States. 'Going slowly mad. I came over here to deal with a whole load of fallout from my divorce – which, I am pleased to say has been resolved – but then I got caught up in other stuff. I packed enough for a week, ten days tops, and I've been here since mid-February.'

'That's an age. Which brings me to the reason for my call. I hope you don't mind, but I gave Heather, the vicar's wife, your number. She needs to talk to you about arrangements for the fête.'

'No, that's fine. I had a message from Elspeth to ring her, but when I checked my phone, I found I haven't got her number. I know I did have it – it was on a piece of paper, but I can't have put it in my mobile. Elspeth and John are off again house-hunting, so there's no point asking them to help. I figured that, as it's a few weeks off yet, I could leave it till they get back. After all, it can't be anything urgent. As far as I can see, all they need me to do is turn up and cut a ribbon.'

'Something like that,' said Maxine vaguely, wishing she wasn't bound by her promise. She changed the subject. 'Oh, and on the subject of numbers I hope you're not annoyed that I gave Belinda yours. She said it'd be OK – that you'd taken her out to dinner, but then you wouldn't take her calls. Did I do wrong?' She tailed off and listened to the silence. 'Laurence?'

'You gave her my number? Are you sure? Because she never rang me. I was hoping she might. We had... a misunderstanding.'

'She said.'

'Yeah, well, some things just don't work out. Water under the bridge. Now, if you'll excuse me, Maxine, I've got to go. I'm doing a radio talk show in five minutes. They need to mic me up. Looking forward to seeing you when I'm back. We must do dinner again.'

And the line went dead. Maxine wondered if he really hadn't minded her handing out his mobile number.

————

Heather let herself into the vicarage, fortified herself with a cup of strong tea and took a deep breath, before she dialled Laurence's number. Voicemail. She'd try again later. Instead, as a distraction, she began to pull together what she'd got for the next parish newsletter. She was engrossed in editing a piece about epitaphs on gravestones in the churchyard, when her mobile rang.

'I had a missed call from this number,' said a voice with a faint Scottish accent.

'You did?' Then Heather remembered. 'Mr McLachlan?'

'Laurence, please.'

'It's Heather Simmonds and thank you so much for calling back. I was going to ring later.'

'So, I've saved you the trouble. Sorry I couldn't take your earlier call – I was tied up with a PR thing. Anyway, you don't need to know about that. I gather you want to talk about the fête, right?'

'I do. The thing is…'

'Yes?'

'The thing is… we're going to have to cancel it and I didn't want you flying back specially, when it's not going to happen.'

'Never mind my flight – that's terrible news about the fête! Why on earth?'

'It's a long story, Mr… Laurence and it's all my fault, but we simply can't afford to run it.'

'But surely there must be local business, or well-wishers, who might help?'

'They did… they have… and then…' Heather paused. She could hardly bring herself to admit what was going on. 'We've been the victims of a fraud.' She explained her part in the affair, her stupidity.

'You're kidding me.'

'I only wish I was.'

'But the police… There must be action you can take.'

'If we could, believe me we would.'

'I am so sorry.'

'Yes, well… We are hugely grateful for your offer of help with everything, but you're off the hook.' She tried to sound cheerful, but she could feel tears threatening.

'The offer stands. You've got a promise you can use the grounds next year.'

'There won't be a next year.'

'No *next year*?'

'It's complicated, but no.'

'OK. Gee, I am so sorry. But I appreciate you letting me know. Thank you.'

'No, thank *you*, and goodbye.'

Heather tapped the icon to disconnect and stared at her phone. Damn – she hadn't passed on Belinda's message. Couldn't she do anything right? The threatened tears rolled down her cheeks. She was useless.

TWENTY-EIGHT

'What was all that about?' asked Mylo, as Laurence put the cell phone back in his blazer pocket.

The pair was travelling along a massive freeway between Burbank and Santa Monica, with Mylo at the wheel of a big black Buick; eight lanes of blacktop, shimmering in relentless sunshine, flanked by scrub, occasional billboards and the Los Angeles river, which flowed between its artificial concrete banks. It couldn't have been further removed from Little Woodford. He was thinking about the Reeve House, the river Catte and the weeping willows that shaded it, the nature reserve, the pub, the high street, the leisurely pace... All the things he so loved about the place. All the things he missed. So different from the manic, diesel-fumed, smog-filled sprawl of tarmac and buildings he now inhabited. A conurbation the size of Belgium, he'd been told. Whoop-de-do.

'Sorry? What?'

'That phone call?'

'Oh, a problem at home.'

'Is that all?' Mylo checked his watch. 'OK, so next up is

KCRW. They have half a million listeners a week, they're hot on new music and you're scheduled to talk for about ten minutes, live on air, in about an hour. After that it's back to Burbank for *Ellen*.'

Laurence sighed. This had been his routine for days. He knew it was all part of launching a new album. He appreciated Mylo's efforts, but he hated this whole merry-go-round. In and out of radio studios, TV studios, sound checks – *what did you have for breakfast?* – make-up on, this sofa, that sofa, the same questions, the same faked interest and... why? All to shift a few more records, score a few more downloads. Was it worth it?

His phone buzzed again. What now? It was a text.

Should have said... Belinda asked me to say hi.

Laurence stared at the message. Really? An olive branch? But why now, after all this time? He tapped back:

Tell Belinda thanks xx

If he needed to get hold of Belinda, Heather might help. Get hold of Belinda... he wanted to do that more than anything. And not just via a phone call. He wanted to *really* get hold of her. Soon.

His decision was like an epiphany.

'I'm going home,' he said to Mylo.

'Yeah, sure in a week or so.'

'No. This evening, or as soon as I can get a flight.'

'But we haven't done the east coast yet.'

'The east coast can wait.'

'But...'

'They've got the tracks we're releasing ahead of the album. They don't need me. The music speaks for itself.'

'But Loz.'

'But nothing, Mylo.'

'You cannot be serious.'

'Never more so. I'll do KCRW, I'll do *Ellen*, but that's it. Cancel the rest. Say I'm sorry, say I'm sick. Say anything – I don't care.'

'You sure are sick,' muttered Mylo.

Laurence pulled his phone back out of his pocket and tapped it a few times. From the driver's seat, Mylo could hear the repetitive beep of the dial tone.

'Yes, please,' said Laurence, to whoever had answered it. 'What ticket availability have you got from LA to London tonight...? Business class is fine... One way... Nine thirty-five tonight? That's fine. I'll take it.' He pulled out his wallet and handed over his credit card number before he turned to Mylo. 'Short of you kidnapping me, I'm flying out tonight. While I'm doing the radio show, can you fix for the hotel to pack my stuff and deliver my luggage to the airport? And ring Elspeth. Ask her to get John to meet me – I'll let you have the flight number. If they're not around, check me into Woodford Priors.'

'Where?' Mylo sounded sulky.

'The local hotel in my home town.'

'I thought LA was your home town.'

'Not anymore.'

———

'Are you off out?' asked Elspeth. She switched off the hoover in the big main hall, as Laurence headed past her.

'I thought I'd check out the town. Besides, a ten-hour flight and half a day lost hasn't done my metabolism any good. I couldn't sleep last night, my body clock is all over the place, so I thought a walk and some fresh air might help.'

'Will you be back for lunch?'

Laurence stared at her. She might look all innocent, but she was a shrewd cookie.

'I don't know.'

'Did you get hold of her, when you were in the States?'

'Who?'

Elspeth gave him a hard stare. 'You know very well *who*.'

'No. She blocked my calls.'

'Why would she do that? What on earth did you say to her, the night you lit out?'

'Nothing — I invited her to dinner; she declined…' Elspeth stared hard at him. 'I did… I did get a bit stroppy.'

'Did you now? In front of her customers?'

Laurence sighed. 'I was upset. Disappointed.'

'And stroppy.'

'I think I might have been worse than that.'

'Worse?'

'Probably out of *stroppy* territory and into *arsey*.'

'Arsey? Then best you eat a whole portion of humble pie.'

Laurence nodded.

'And good luck,' added Elspeth, in a softer voice.

Ten minutes later Laurence pushed open the door to the pub. He peered around it nervously as Belinda glanced up. Her face froze. Shock? Anger? Both?

He hesitated before he walked slowly to the bar.

'Am I allowed to drink here?' he asked.

'You want to know if you're barred?'

Laurence nodded.

'I think I've got every good reason to do that.'

'I'm sorry.'

'Really?' Her voice was larded with scepticism. 'You made it about as obvious as was humanly possible that you didn't want anything to do with me.'

'I didn't.'

'You blocked my calls. Every time I phoned, it went straight to voicemail.'

'But you blocked mine.' His voice was getting louder, fuelled by indignation.

Bert, in the corner, was riveted.

'Shhhh,' said Belinda and lowered her own voice. 'How could I block you, when you *never* phoned. Not *once*. It's been almost four months, Laurence. Four months!'

'But I did phone.' His voice went up half an octave, in indignation.

Belinda shook her head. 'Are you calling me a liar? Do you want to check my phone?' She waved it at him.

'I don't understand.'

'Ring it then... go on. I swear I didn't block you so, if you ring mine, I'll get the call, won't I?' She stared at him defiantly.

Laurence looked sheepish. 'I... I can't. I deleted your number. I got angry and... well... But I swear I didn't block you. You ring mine and I'll prove it to you.'

'Ah...' It was Belinda's turn to look uncomfortable.

Laurence stared at her. 'Problem?'

'Umm...'

'You deleted my number too, didn't you?'

'Might have done,' she muttered. 'After getting directed to voicemail every time, I decided you were a lost cause. I mean, after about my fifth attempt to get hold of you, what was the point? I gave up; decided to move on. I knew you had my number so—'

'I... I didn't programme it into my phone the night you gave it to me. I put the beer mat in the pocket of my fleece and had to ring Elspeth to get it, because after I left you, I was summoned to the States by my agent. Maybe Elspeth read the number to me wrong, maybe I had fat-finger syndrome, but I phoned time and time again and all I got was a stupid message saying I wasn't entitled to access this service or some-such. I gave up. I figured you didn't want to talk to me. I'd behaved like a prick – it was understandable.'

'And I shouldn't have shouted at you.'

Laurence was about to agree with her, but changed tack and said, 'I was rude to you, in your own pub. You had every right.'

Belinda nodded. 'Shit, this is like something out of a French farce. What a stupid mess.' She smiled ruefully at him. 'A pint of the usual, sir?'

'I'm still a regular, am I? Yes please.'

From his corner Bert cheered and then said, 'Let's hope she stops behaving like a wet weekend now!'

TWENTY-NINE

Ashley sat on the platform at Little Woodford station, watching the mist rise off the trees in the nature reserve, just visible above the roofs of the town centre. On a weekday, at this time, the platform would be packed with commuters heading up to London for the day job, but being so early and a Saturday morning too, Ashley was on his own. His legs jiggled with nerves and, in his head he went through the lines for his audition, but he'd made his mind up; if he failed this time, he was going to give it a rest, throw in the towel, concentrate on his culinary skills and accept failure. And failure on this occasion seemed highly likely. This time he was heading for a drama school way up there, with the likes of the Royal Academy, the Central School of Speech and Drama, the Old Vic, and the Guildford School. He'd applied to the Euston School almost as a dare to himself and the idea that he had any chance with this audition was almost laughable.

If he failed, well, it was time to face reality. Maybe he was destined to be a chef, not an actor. He hadn't told anyone of his decision. He'd probably still act, because he loved it, but it would only be in local productions. He'd still have to audition for parts, but he wouldn't have the same stress and expense – or the rejections with no explanation, no feedback. Had he chosen the wrong pieces to perform, did he have the wrong accent, did he look wrong, was he just useless…? It was the *not knowing* that was doing his head in. And it was cold comfort that the members of the local theatre company all told him he had real ability and should keep going. They were friends and acquaintances. They would, wouldn't they?

Ashley glanced down the line and saw the distant light of the London train approaching. He stood up, hitched his rucksack, higher on his shoulder and waited for the train to pull in. As the doors swished open he realised that he really wouldn't miss the stress, the strain and the expense of auditioning. In a way it was quite cathartic. At least, with cooking, you knew if you were doing the right thing, and the praise, although rare, was heartfelt. People expected their food to be perfect and he got that. As long as there were no complaints, you were doing OK – probably more than OK.

London was eerily quiet, when he arrived an hour later. It was too early for the West End shops to be open, there were no office workers hurrying along and the pavements, uncluttered by people, were riddled with pigeons, which barely moved out of the way as Ashley headed for his destination. Every now and again, he stopped to check the map on his phone. If the app was to be believed, he was going to be early, but he could grab a coffee, go over his lines again, try to calm his nerves. He didn't quite know why he felt so anxious; he'd made up his mind about his future… In fact, he rather wondered what the hell he was doing. Mightn't he be better off binning the audition and wandering around the capital, taking in the sights instead? But as he thought this, he arrived at his destination.

OK, one last throw of the dice.

———

A middle-aged woman came into the room, where the twenty hopefuls were waiting.

'First of all I'm going to name the people who, I'm afraid, haven't been successful. Thank you for coming and good luck in the future. The rest, please remain seated…'

Ashley picked up his rucksack, gripping it tightly, and prepared to stand up, as the rejected left the room one by one. And then it was just him and a black girl. They stared at each other.

'If you two would like to come with me…'

Ashley could barely stand. His legs were juddering. He tottered out of the room, his heart thundering, his mouth dry. And then he'd remembered the other callback and how that had ended. *Don't get your hopes up*, he told himself.

The woman stopped outside a door. 'Kattie. You're first. Ashley, if you'd like to take a seat and go straight in, when Kattie has finished.'

Ashley muttered, 'Good luck,' to Kattie.

'You too,' she responded, her eyes wide with fear and anticipation.

Ashley plonked himself on the chair, his rucksack clasped on his knees. He strained to hear what was happening on the other side of the door. There was a murmur of voices, then a silence for a bit, maybe several minutes. Then he heard more voices, but nothing distinguishable. Was Kattie performing a dialogue with someone, was she being interviewed…? A couple more minutes ticked past. Finally she came out. She stared at him and shrugged, but she was holding the door open for Ashley to go straight in. Did her body language mean it had gone badly, that she didn't have a clue… What?

Ashley only realised he was still gripping his rucksack, when he got in front of the panel. Self-consciously, he dropped it on the floor and stood there.

'Ashley Pullen,' said a man at the end of the row of three. 'I'm going to give you a short scene to read through, then I'd like you to perform it with Grenville, here.' The man at the other end raised his hand. He handed Ashley a laminated card. Ashley scanned it quickly and with a leap of happiness realised he recognised the script. It was a piece from *Journey's End*, which the theatre group had done the previous year. He'd played Raleigh and now he was going to reprise it, the role of the kid, fresh from public school about to go over the top on the Western Front.

He read it through twice, to make sure he wasn't going trip over any words and then grabbed his rucksack. In the script Osborne tells him to put his pack down − it would be useful to have a prop. From under his eyelashes he saw the female member of the panel nod approvingly.

At the end of the dialogue, which only lasted a couple of minutes, he felt weary. He'd put everything into it.

'Thank you, Ashley. Can we just check we have your email correctly?'

'Nothing's changed,' he said.

'Thank you. We'll let you know.'

Ashley picked up his rucksack again and left. He was rather hoping Kattie would be waiting, so he could exchange notes with her. What had she been asked to perform? What had they said to her? But the corridor was empty.

Ashley made his way back, following the fluorescent yellow 'exit' signs to the door and then went down the steps to the street. There was a bench, which he slumped on. He wasn't sure if he felt elated he'd got a callback, or devastated that he had no idea how he'd done. Was he going to be told the result tomorrow, or in a week? Was it a good thing he'd read from a play he knew, or would he have sounded stale? On balance, he thought, it was almost worse than a straight rejection. At least with a rejection you knew where you stood.

Feeling drained, he tramped back to the station, a rumble of thunder competing with the rumble of traffic on the streets. Ashley reached the station, as the first fat drops plopped on the pavement. He was lucky to have missed the storm. He was lucky to have had a callback. These things went in threes, didn't they? He wondered what the third thing might be. His audition? No, no hope there, he decided. His luck wasn't going that well.

———

At half five, as Ashley reported to Miles in the kitchen for the evening service, Belinda was unlocking the front door and waiting for the thirsty hordes. It wasn't long before the first of the Saturday evening drinkers made an appearance. By six the pub was buzzing, by seven it was rammed and Belinda was rushed off her feet, as she took orders, pulled pints, cleared tables and loaded and emptied the glass washer. At nine o'clock, the diners were starting to finish their meals and there was a lull between the early evening customers and those who liked a later session – maybe coming back from the cinema in Cattebury or just fancying a drink before turning in for the night.

She sensed the presence of another customer at the bar, as she rang up the sale on the till. She turned round with the bill and found herself face to face with Laurence. Her heart rate zoomed – like the rev counter on a Formula 1 racing car when the red lights went out. Ridiculous, she told herself. Behaving like a lovelorn teenager, at her age. She switched her gaze from him, to the customer waiting to pay.

'Nineteen pounds and fifty-six pence,' she said, holding her hand out for the cash.

Act cool, she told herself. Don't let the other customers see the state you're in! She turned to Laurence. 'Yes, sir. Rabbit Punch?'

'Hello, gorgeous.'

'Shhh.'

'I bet they all know. Bert'll have made sure of that.' But he'd lowered his voice. Anyone wanting to eavesdrop now was going to have to make a serious effort, or be a top lip-reader.

'I know but…'

'Are you ashamed of me?'

'God, no.' She opened the beer tap and watched the golden liquid stream into the glass.

'Now, I promise not to get stroppy, as Elspeth would call it, but I need you to put some cover in place, so I can take you out to dinner again. Come up with some dates that work for you.'

'I can do that. And thank you, that'd be lovely. I'll try and get something organised for next week.'

'Please. And what are you doing later?'

'Later? Running the pub, you dipstick.'

'No, I mean *much* later.'

'Collapsing into an exhausted sleep.'

'Oh. Only I was wondering about a nightcap.'

Belinda's insides did a somersault that wouldn't have disgraced a Beth Tweddle floor routine. 'That'd be lovely. Only it might have to be an early-morning-cap, because I'll be shattered. Would that be acceptable? Three-sixty,' she added in a normal voice.

'Very.' He took his drink and handed over the correct money. 'Till later,' he said, as he moved away from the bar and found a spare seat where he could watch her, his eyes smiling.

Belinda spent the next two hours trying not to stare, as she thought about him staying the night. The anticipation was almost unbearable.

THIRTY

'Laurence, I need to get up,' said Belinda, slapping away his hand.

'Don't be a spoilsport,' he murmured in her ear.

'I need to bottle up, to say nothing about cleaning the place, before the customers come in. And Miles will be in shortly, to start the prep for lunch service.' She rolled away from him and swung her legs out of bed.

Laurence sighed and sat up. 'I suppose I need to be patient,' he said.

'Not so very. You can stay again tonight, if you want to.'

'No, I mean for you to stop work. There's a rumour going round town you're selling up.'

Belinda reached for her dressing gown. 'Is there now?'

'Is it true?'

'It might be. Where did you hear it?'

'Elspeth told me a while back. She said she heard it in the Co-Op.'

'Not the post office?'

'It might have been. Why?'

'Because Ashley helps Miles in my kitchen and his mum, Amy, who works part-time at the post office, is the town's biggest gossip.'

'Well, does it matter if your secret is out?'

'I suppose not.'

'Except that it's going to ruffle some feathers. You *are* the pub.'

'The new landlord or landlady will be just fine.'

'But supposing they change things? Turn it into some bog-awful theme pub, or fill it with screens showing Sky Sports. It'll be ruined.'

'In your opinion. There's plenty who might welcome it.'

Laurence gave her a horrified look. 'You're kidding me.'

Belinda shrugged and tugged the tie-belt of her gown tight. 'People are all different. And whoever buys it will be entitled to run it how they want. I mean, I'll advise them against too much change, but it's not enforceable by law. Now, I'm going for my shower and you need to get back, before Elspeth sends out a search party.'

'Entitled to run it how they want, eh?' said Laurence. 'I do hope they don't.'

———

About one o'clock Laurence turned up again.

'The usual?' asked Belinda.

'How I *love* having regular status,' said Laurence. 'The stuff dreams are made of.'

Belinda's mouth twitched. 'And I've got something for you.' Laurence's face brightened. She picked up a piece of paper.

His face fell again. 'Oh. There was me hoping for

another *nightcap*. That'd give the locals something to talk about.'

'Shhh.' Belinda was struggling not to laugh. She lowered her voice. 'It's the dates when we would be able go out.'

Laurence scanned the list. 'Get cover for all of them.'

'What?' she said, louder than she intended. Bert looked at her from the far side of the pub, his ears almost visibly flapping. She whispered, 'Have you any idea what that'll cost me in extra pay?'

'I'll pay.'

Belinda frowned. 'I'm not asking for charity.'

'No, but *I* am asking for your company.'

'I'll sort out cover for *some* of the dates.'

'At least half.'

'I'll see.'

'Please.'

'Half.'

'Excellent.' Laurence looked at the list again. 'This first one… come to dinner at mine.'

'That'd be lovely. Thank you.'

'Not sure if I can wait till Wednesday, but I'll try.'

'Daft man, it's only three days.'

'That's aeons.'

And he sounded as if he meant it. Belinda felt all fuzzy inside.

———

Elspeth had just brought a tray with afternoon tea to Laurence in his study, when his mobile rang. Mylo. What did he want?

'Mylo, what can I do for you? It must be urgent if you're ringing me on a Sunday. What is it in LA? Nine?'

'Eight,' said Mylo. 'I should charge you overtime. I haven't even had breakfast yet.'

Laurence was tempted to say 'Diddums' but restrained himself.

'So, this album of yours…' continued Mylo.

'Yes.'

'It's doing well. *Really* well.'

'Glad to hear it. You must be pleased too. You put a lot of effort into the promo.'

'No, I mean *REALLY* well. Seriously, I don't know if it's because you haven't written anything new for about ten years, or if it was your residency in Vegas, or if it's because you've disappeared from LA, so you're a bit of a mystery man right now, but all of a sudden, you are flavour of the month.'

'I'm glad,' he repeated.

'So, now we need to push in the UK.'

'Mylo, the Brits aren't interested in me. I'm a has-been here. They're not interested in jazz—'

'Then explain Jamie Cullum.'

'He's more of a singer-songwriter. And he's young and good-looking.'

'He didn't write *"Ninety-nine"*.'

Laurence sighed. 'That was years ago.'

'Look, if I can get you a gig at Ronnie Scott's, you'd do it, right?'

'That's a big *if*.'

'But you would,' insisted Mylo.

'Up to town for an evening and then home again… yeah, I'd do it.'

'Good. I'll work on it.'

'Thank you… I think.'

'I'll get back to you about that.'

Well, that was an unexpected turn of events. Laurence couldn't deny he was flattered to hear his album was a success.

'Thanks, Mylo—'

'Before you hang up… one other thing. There's some guy called Graham Norton – a chat show host—'

'I know his show – very successful.'

'Well, he's interested, too. Wants you to do a show for the autumn series – play a track.'

'It's only July, Mylo.'

'October is only a few weeks away. The record company wants to put out a track early, ahead of the UK release date – get a bit of traction. If you do his show it'll be perfect timing for the album.'

It would, but Laurence wasn't going to hold his breath. His last few albums had tanked. 'I'll think about it.'

'Loz, there is nothing to think about. Until a few months ago you were a has-been. Apart from me, your ex-wife and a few die-hard fans, everyone else thought you were dead. And now… you won't get a second chance to make a comeback like this one. It'll set you up for life.'

'Mylo, the residency set me up for life. I don't *need* any more money.'

'Everyone *always* needs money.'

'OK, I'll do *The Graham Norton Show* – *if* they still want me by the time we get to the autumn.'

'You could sound more excited.'

'Mylo, I don't care. I have a grand life here; I go to the pub, I have friends – *good* friends, *real* friends, I potter around in my garden. I'm even thinking of taking up fishing.' He heard Mylo splort. 'No one hassles or stalks me. It's like being a regular human again.'

'Which is overrated. What's wrong with being a star? A household name?'

'Been there, got the T-shirt, got the divorce...'

'It paid for your new house.'

Which was true. 'Let me have the details about the Norton show.'

'Yeah, no sweat, I'll send you everything you need to know.'

'I can't wait.'

Laurence couldn't deny that a bit of him was chuffed by Mylo's news. It had been a long time since he'd had a hit, but was it a Faustian pact – would he be trading a relatively normal life for all the drawbacks of being a household name again?

THIRTY-ONE

This time, when Belinda walked up to the ornate wrought-iron gates of the Reeve House they were standing wide open. Even though she had an invitation to dinner, she was feeling apprehensive. The trees, in full leaf, which lined the drive stopped her seeing what lay ahead. Then she emerged from the tunnel of foliage and saw the beautiful house.

'Wow!' she breathed. By heavens, it put her little flat over the pub in its place. Although she was glad she didn't have to clean it. Just think of the amount of carpet that would need hoovering and as for those leaded panes... It didn't bear contemplating.

She strode up to the front door and tugged the bell pull. It was like being in a Hammer horror movie. She half expected a butler or a vampire to open the door – this was more than surreal, she thought. She stepped back to look at the front of the house, looking gloriously mellow in the evening summer sunshine. Too beautiful for a horror movie – maybe a period drama. In which case, she mused, she ought to be wearing a crinoline and arriving by carriage.

'Belinda.'

'Laurence… hi. Love the house.'

'Come in, come in.'

Laurence stood aside and Belinda stepped over the threshold, into the massive hall with its hammer beams, truly vast fireplace and gallery.

'I'm half expecting Errol Flynn to leap into action, fighting a baddy on the stairs.'

'Swashing his buckle?' said Laurence.

Belinda laughed. 'Is that a euphemism?'

'What… like *nightcap*?'

Belinda hooted. 'Something like that.'

'Anyway, let me get you a drink. What's your poison?' He gestured to the built-in bar in the corner.

'I think a gin and tonic would be nice.'

Laurence deftly mixed her drink and one for himself. 'Now then,' he said as he handed a glass to her, 'let's go into the garden. It's too nice to be stuck indoors.'

He led the way through a small door to the side of the grand staircase, along a corridor and into a massive kitchen.

'This is Elspeth,' he said, introducing her to a woman who was busy rolling out pastry on the massive refectory table, in the middle of the room. Beside her was what looked like a large fillet of beef.

She wiped her hands on her apron. 'And you must be Belinda. I hope you like beef Wellington.'

'I'm sure I will. I don't think I've ever had it. It's not the kind of dish we serve at the pub. We're more steak-and-chips.'

'And nothing wrong with that,' said Elspeth. 'Everyone likes steak and chips.'

Laurence led Belinda through a side door, which opened onto a terrace stretching the width of the house. As Belinda looked to her right, she could see a series of French windows standing open. She wandered along the ancient paving slabs and peeked in to the first of the rooms. There was a desk, several small armchairs around a low table and beautiful, pale lemon soft furnishings.

'The morning room,' said Laurence, behind her. 'And this,' he said, guiding her to the next window, 'is the formal dining room.' Red damask wallpaper and a table to seat twenty gave the room a dramatic feel. 'I'll give you a guided tour, if you'd like.'

Belinda turned to him. 'I think I'd rather see the gardens. It's such a lovely evening. It seems a shame to go back indoors.' She walked across the terrace to the low balustrade, which overlooked a parterre of intricately patterned beds, edged by manicured box hedging. Beyond the formal bedding a large, immaculate lawn sloped gently down to the river, fringed on the far bank by willows and poplars. The view was utterly stunning. Belinda sighed happily, as she sipped her drink.

'This is glorious,' she said.

'That's what I thought when I first saw it. But let me show you John's pride and joy.'

Belinda followed him to the far end of the terrace where there was a high wall and some espaliered fruit trees.

'Peaches,' said Laurence, as he led her down the steps towards a door in the wall.

'Very *Secret Garden*,' observed Belinda.

The door opened on to a large vegetable garden, with about a dozen raised beds, divided by gravel paths and filled with rows and rows of weed-free produce – carrots, asparagus, peas, chard, kale, potatoes, wigwams of beans... The beds around the edges were full of flowers and buzzing with pollinators. A long, low glasshouse ran along one wall.

'Oh, my,' said Belinda. The sheltered garden was a perfect suntrap.

'Good, isn't it?'

'Perfect. But you must produce tons of stuff.'

Laurence nodded. 'John takes what we don't use to the food bank in Cattebury.'

Belinda turned and looked at her host. 'How kind is that!'

'Not really. Elspeth can't stand waste. Trust me, she has got making the most of everything down to an art form. I shall miss her when she goes.'

'Goes?'

'She and John want to retire and go back to Scotland – they have family there. They came with me to the States and have been very loyal, but I need to accept that they have their own lives.'

'But you're Scottish – don't you want to live there too?'

'Me? Hell, no. The midges, the weather... No, I bought this place as my forever home. I just need to find people to help me look after it. Still, there are few problems that can't be solved, if you are willing to throw enough money at them.'

'Well... if you've got the money.'

'Happily, I have.' He stared at Belinda. 'I know, I know, that makes me shallow and venal—'

'And lucky.'

'And I count my blessings every day. Especially since I moved here.' He stared intently at Belinda. The mood shifted as she stared back.

'Och, there you are,' said Elspeth right behind them, making Belinda jump, so her still-full glass slopped over. 'Dinner's nearly ready. I've laid two places in your snug. I hope that's right.'

'Perfect,' said Laurence. He offered Belinda his arm. 'Shall we?'

The re-entered the house via the morning room – Belinda paranoid that her shoes would leave dirty marks on the pale Persian rug – and then walked across the panelled hall to a cosy room with a grand piano and a slew of gold and silver discs adorning the walls.

'Oh, my,' exclaimed Belinda for the second time that evening.

'They remind me that I actually can write a good tune,' said Laurence. 'There are times when I sit in front of a keyboard, without an idea in my head and I wonder if I've just been kidding myself that I am a musician. I think it's called imposter syndrome... that feeling that it's all a bit emperor's-new-clothes and someone, somewhere will call you out for being a total fraud.'

'But you wrote *"Ninety-nine"*. That was a massive hit.'

'No one likes a one-hit wonder. Least of all the record companies.'

'But you've written a load of stuff since.' Belinda gestured at the gold discs.

'Nothing quite so successful. Although, my agent tells me the new album I've got out in the States is doing quite well.'

'Well, then.'

Elspeth came into the room pushing a trolley. 'Scottish smoked salmon to start,' she said, putting the plates down on the small table in the corner of the room. She added a plate of wafer-thin brown bread and some lemon wedges. 'The wine is in the cooler, Laurence. I'll leave you to it. Ring when you want me to bring in the next course.'

'Please,' said Laurence pulling out a chair for Belinda and offering her a damask napkin. 'I take it you'd like some wine?'

'Love some.'

'It's a Sancerre.'

'Delicious,' said Belinda, taking a sip, before she tucked into her food. It was sensational.

They ate in silence for a minute or so, both enjoying the food and the wine.

Then Laurence said, 'Such a shame about the fête.'

Belinda looked up. 'You've heard?'

'Heather rang me in the States. She didn't want me flying back just for that. She said it was something to do with fraud?' Laurence stared at Belinda. 'In a place like this?'

Belinda nodded. 'She told me someone has nicked all the sponsorship money.'

Laurence lowered his knife and fork. 'Who would do a mean thing like that?'

Belinda shrugged. 'Search me.'

'And I was really looking forward to it. It would have been so cool to have a proper old-fashioned village fête on my doorstep. I know Elspeth and John were planning on entering a whole load of the flower and produce competitions. They'll be gutted when they hear.'

'Blimey, that would have put the cat among the pigeons. There are people in this town who win almost everything every year. They're not used to having any proper competition. Bert and his wife always take most of the prizes in the vegetables and best cake sections.'

'Is it... was it rigged?'

'As it's judged by the WI, I think that's unlikely.'

'No, you're right. The ladies of the WI would be above reproach.' Laurence ate another mouthful, before he asked, 'And tell me... do they do cream teas at the fête?'

'They do, although it's always a bunfight – literally.'

Laurence cocked an eyebrow.

'The teas are done in the same tent as the flower and produce, which makes for a bit of a squash; there are never enough tables so there's always a queue with people getting twitchy that the WI's legendary cakes might run out, before they get seated.'

'I can see that might lead to rioting,' said Laurence with a grin.

'Oh, yes.' Belinda put her knife and fork together on her empty plate. 'That was just as good as anything we ate at the Flower Pot. Delicious.'

'Then tell Elspeth. She'll be delighted.'

'She's going to be a hard act to follow. You seem very fond of her and John. You're going to miss them terribly when they go.'

Laurence nodded. 'But I'll find someone, when the time comes. Cometh the hour, cometh the man… or woman… or both. In the meantime, I hope you've got plenty of room for everything else Elspeth has prepared and I hope you don't want me to walk you back to the pub when we've finished. I hope you can stay the night. And—' he held up his hand '—before you say anything, I have a brand-new, spare toothbrush.'

By the end of the meal, Belinda felt absolutely stuffed. As Elspeth came into clear away the tiramisu and to ask if they'd both like coffee, Belinda was glad she'd decided to wear a loose cotton frock and not something with a waistband, for the button would have surely pinged off by now.

'Come and sit on the sofa,' said Laurence.

Gratefully, she tottered over to the big chesterfield and tried to sit down without too much of an 'oof'. As she arranged herself on the squidgy cushions, she wondered if she'd be able to get up again. She was faintly surprised when Laurence didn't join her, but moved across to his piano.

'I wrote this for you,' he said, as his fingers began to caress the keys.

The music was beautiful; lilting, uplifting, happy… Belinda was swept away and almost moved to tears. As the last chord died away, she said, 'You wrote that for me?'

'My muse,' said Laurence, moving to sit beside her.

'I've never had anything so beautiful done for me before.'

'A special tune for a special lady.'

'Thank you.'

THIRTY-TWO

'So what are we actually going to say?' said Heather, as she stared around the little group of women.

Once again the committee stalwarts – Jacqui, Miranda and Olivia – were gathered in her kitchen. This time their meeting wasn't to discuss how the fête was going to progress, but how they were going to wind up everything to do with it. Heather's insistence that she needed to pick up the outstanding bills for the printing had already been shouted down by the others and they had worked out how to divide the costs equally between themselves. It hadn't amounted to a vast sum – well, small change for Miranda, a rather more significant sum for Heather – but they were resolute that Heather was not going to bear the cost alone. That had been an easy problem to sort, but there were other things that still needed to be settled, like what they were going to do with the cash boxes, the signage, the bunting – miles of it – the tombola drum, the lucky dip barrel, the whack-a-mole game…? And they needed to agree the wording of a press release.

'Do we actually need one? The whole town knows,' said Miranda. 'Once I'd told the sponsors, they seemed only too happy to tell everyone – just to make sure we got the blame.'

'Maybe everyone does know,' said Heather, 'but we... *I* have to take responsibility for the mess and put out a letter in the local newspaper.'

'Name the bitch,' said Jacqui with venom. 'Blame *her*.'

'Jacqui!' said Heather and Olivia in unison, shocked.

'I'm sorry, but that's what I think.' She didn't sound sorry at all.

Heather sighed. She felt the same, if she was completely honest with herself, but if she gave in to such feelings where would it end? She knew she ought to forgive Diane, there were probably extenuating circumstances but... no, she couldn't. And that was that.

'I think,' said Miranda, 'we can say what happened, without naming names. Announce that we were victims of a cruel fraud, that all our funds have been embezzled and, as a result, this year's fête has been cancelled and all future ones are in jeopardy. We need to publicly thank the sponsors for their past support and name them all – really make a song and dance about how generous they were. At least we can give them a tiny bit of good publicity – cold comfort, but that's about all we can do.'

Down the hall, the front doorbell rang.

'Brian will get that,' said Heather. 'Bound to be for him, anyway.'

Miranda drew a notepad towards her and got out a biro. '*It is with regret...*' she said slowly as she wrote, '*that due to a criminal act of fraud...*' She looked up. 'Well, it was, wasn't it? I don't think we should mince our words.'

'Excuse me,' said Brian from the door. 'You've got a visitor.'

Heather frowned as she looked up. 'Brian, I'm a bit tied up.'

'I know and I wouldn't usually interrupt but...' He opened the door wider.

'Mr McLachlan.' Heather's eyebrows shot up. 'What... I mean...' She scrambled to her feet. 'Look, I'm so desperately sorry about everything.'

Laurence stepped into the kitchen. 'You and me both.' He smiled at the group. 'Good morning, ladies. I'm sorry to interrupt, but I'm wondering if I can do anything to help. Brian here tells me you're the fête committee, right? I was only expecting to see Heather, but it seems like serendipity, if you're all here.' He smiled at them. 'I'm Lozza Lachlan, by the way, although I prefer Laurence McLachlan these days.' He smiled again. 'I'm here to help.'

'And this is Olivia, Miranda and Jacqui,' said Heather pointing to each of her friends in turn.

'Delighted.'

'And as for help,' said Miranda, 'there's nothing to be done. Our insurance won't pay, the police have recorded the crime, but don't seem to be doing anything further, we're broke, the sponsors are livid—'

'Which is where I come in,' said Laurence.

Heather looked perplexed. 'I don't think there's much you can do.'

'There is. If the event goes ahead, as planned, and they get their perks, or free tickets, or advertising space, or whatever it was you promised in return for their cash.'

'Yes, well...' said Heather. 'But as that isn't going to happen...' She shrugged.

'It will, if I pay for it.'

Four jaws dropped simultaneously.

'You can't...'

'No…'

'It's too much to ask…'

'We couldn't possibly…'

'Shhhh,' said Laurence, holding up his hand.

'It's far too generous,' said Heather. 'We can't, we *won't* accept.'

'Please… indulge me. This way, I get to play at being lord of the manor, the fête goes ahead, the locals are happy, you're off the hook…' He grinned again. 'Win-win.'

'But it's… no,' said Heather. 'Just – no.'

'Give me three good reasons why not.'

'Because it's fifteen thousand pounds,' said Heather.

Laurence looked at her steadily. 'I *know* that is a lot of money. A really *big* chunk of cash, but I have just earned an obscene amount working in the States. I can't take it with me, my ex-wife and my two kids are already very well provided for, and I'd like to do something more useful than stick it in the bank. Helping out the fête seems like a perfect project. So, I ask again… indulge me, please.' He stared intently at each of the women around the table. 'And I'm still waiting for two more reasons.'

The women exchanged glances.

'Well,' said Laurence, rubbing his hands, 'as you can't think of anything else, it looks like I win!'

'But…' began Heather.

'No *buts*. You're going to write a letter to each of the sponsors, telling them their pledges have been made good and they're going to receive exactly whatever the promised deal was. And then you're going to put out a press release saying the fête is going ahead and distribute the entry forms around the town.'

'But we need to explain how it's going to be possible.' said Heather.

'Does it need explanation?'

Heather nodded. 'The sponsors might want to know.'

'A *gift from a well-wisher* would cover it, don't you think? Does it matter, provided no one is out of pocket and the event goes ahead?'

'We may have trouble getting a marquee, at such short notice,' said Jacqui. 'We usually book ours back in the spring.'

'Leave it with me,' said Laurence. 'Tell me how big it needs to be and I promise I'll get one that's suitable. Heather, can you let me have the details?'

Dazed, Heather nodded.

'Right, I think that's everything. I'll leave you ladies to carry on with your meeting.' And with that he breezed out of the house, leaving a stunned silence behind him.

'Crikey,' said Heather, sounding shell-shocked.

Miranda tore the piece of paper she'd been writing on in half and began again. '*It is with delight,*' she said aloud as she wrote, '*the fête committee can announce that this year's event will be taking place after all…*'

———

Ashley, also feeling a bit shell-shocked, stared at the email. He recognised the address and knew this was the result of his last audition.

His finger hovered over the screen. Did he dare tap it and reveal the answer? Involuntarily he shut his eyes, as the tip of his index finger hit the glass.

Dear Mr Pullen,

The Euston School of Dramatic Arts is pleased to inform you that you were successful in your audition…

Ashley didn't read further. He'd done it. He'd only been

and gone and done it. Yessss. He flopped on to his bed in his little room and stared at the ceiling, not knowing whether to laugh or cry, or both. The relief almost outweighed the sheer joy of discovering he wasn't delusional. He really *could* act. He was good. He was good enough for one of the best drama schools in the country – one that he'd thought he didn't have a chance of getting into. The one he'd applied to, almost as a joke. He couldn't wait to tell his mum. She'd be thrilled. She'd be up at Miranda's gaff, this being a Thursday morning. He thought about ringing her, but he wanted to see her face. He checked the clock. He had time to belt up to the top end of the town, before getting back to the pub for the lunch service. Besides, it was a glorious day and the walk would do him good. The trouble with Miles teaching him patisserie, was that he ate too many – especially the ones not quite good enough to be served to the customers.

He leaped off his bed, jigging with excitement and happiness. Life was never going to get much better than this. He ran down the stairs and out on to the street. He had to restrain himself from telling everyone he passed his news. One or two passers-by gave him curious stares but then found themselves grinning back as he smiled joyfully at them.

Panting, breathless but still euphoric, Ashley ran up the gravel drive to Miranda's house and rang the bell. His mum opened the door.

'Ash? What you doing here? And why've you got that stupid grin on your face?'

'I passed, Mum. I got a place!' Ashley took his mother's hands and began to spin her round on the doorstep.

'Leave off,' she said crossly. 'Passed what?'

'My audition. I'm going to drama school.'

'Oh, is that all.'

Ashley crumpled and Amy must have seen his disappointment.

'But you're glad, so that's good,' she added.

Ashley forced a smile back onto his face. 'Yeah. I wanted you to be the first to know.'

'Cheers. I expect your theatre mates will be pleased for you.'

He noticed his mum hadn't said she was. 'Yeah. Well, best I let you get on.' A feeling of dejection swept over him, as he turned and headed back down the drive. Was it so much to ask his mother to realise how much it meant to him? He kicked at a piece of gravel and sent it skittering onto Miranda's lawn. If it got caught in the mower blades, it would ruin them. Sod it, he thought angrily.

'You look like you've lost a fiver and found a sixpence,' said Belinda, when he went in through the back door of the pub and headed for the kitchen.

'A what?'

'A six… never mind. What's up, Ash? Want to tell Aunty Belinda?'

Ashley shook his head. 'It's Mum.'

'Shit, Amy's not ill, is she?'

'No, nothing like that.'

'So?'

'So I've got a place at the Euston School of Dramatic Arts and I told Mum. I might just as well have told her I'd managed to cut my own toenails. Her reaction was, *so what?*'

'Oh, Ash – that's a downer. But massive congrats from me. That's fantastic. Even I've heard of that place. You must be well chuffed. In fact, we'll open a bottle of fizz after the lunch service and we'll have a little celebration. I know Miles and Jamie will be just as thrilled. Just think, we'll be drinking to a star of the future.'

Belinda's obvious happiness at his news went some way to restoring Ashley's own.

'Thanks, Belinda.'

'We're going to miss you here, of course, when you go off to the bright lights.' She stopped and stared at him. 'Fancy that... you're going to be a film star.'

Ashley laughed out loud. 'Hey, a bit early to think that. I may never do more than crappy ads and walk-on parts.'

Belinda shook her head. 'I can feel it in my bones, Ashley lad. I'm never wrong.'

'Wrong about what?' said Miles, coming into the kitchen in his clean chef's whites.

'Our Ash has only got into a top drama school.'

'But that's fantastic... for you,' added Miles. 'We'll really miss you here.'

Ashley's spirits lifted a little more and, by the time Jamie came into the kitchen to add his congratulations, he was almost back to where he'd been an hour earlier.

At two-thirty, when the last of the customers had left, the kitchen had been cleaned down and the tables in the bar cleared and wiped, Belinda popped the cork on a bottle of fizz and invited her staff to toast Ashley.

'To Ashley,' they chorused, while Ashley looked a little embarrassed.

'You'd better get used to being the centre of attention,' said Miles. 'When you are on the red carpet, at all those premieres up in Leicester Square and you're being papped at every place you turn up, as a household name, I hope you remember your old mates.'

'Don't be daft,' said Ash, blushing.

'I bet Colin Firth said that, and all,' said Belinda.

THIRTY-THREE

July drifted into August; news of the fête's reappearance on the town's social calendar was the subject of speculation and gossip for a few days, before it disappeared off the radar again. The entry forms with the terms and conditions, which luckily Heather had forgotten to throw away, were distributed around the town, along with news that the fête was going to be held in the grounds of the Reeve House and would be opened by Lozza Lachlan. That bit of information was greeted with total indifference by the under-forties, but the older generation began to get quite excited at the thought of seeing a real-life celebrity in the flesh.

Along with the arrival of August, came the knowledge that A-level results were on the way. In fact, when Megan, Sophie, Zac and Ashley gathered in the skate park on a Monday in the middle of the month, because it was Ashley's day off, they knew that, by the end of the week, they would learn, one way or another, what the immediate future had in store for them.

'It's all right for you, Ashley,' said Sophie. 'You're sorted.'

Ashley felt like telling them about the crushing disappointment of the failed auditions, but decided they wouldn't understand and, besides, those were all in the past. 'Yeah, I'm lucky like that. But you'll be all right.'

'I've got a nasty feeling I'm not going to get the grades,' said Zac.

'You should have started revising earlier,' said Megan.

'Don't you have a go; you sound like my mum.'

Megan gave him a steady stare. 'So what happens if you're right?'

'I've got a cunning plan.'

'Oh, really,' said Sophie.

'Yeah, I'm going to take a gap year and reapply next year. That way, I can see which courses will fit my grades and I can tell Mum and Dad I've got my first choice.'

'Don't you think that's a bit like lying?' said Ashley.

'Who cares? Anything for a quiet life, I say.'

The other three looked at each other, all a little worried, but none of them quite having the guts to call Zac out.

'Anyway, you're not the only one thinking of a gap year,' said Ashley. 'I need to get some serious savings put together, before I head off to drama school – living in London ain't going to be cheap. The cheapest room I can find so far is around a hundred and fifty a week but then there's the cost of food and travel on top… And Mum can't help.'

'No,' said Megan. 'That's a lot of money.'

'Frankly, I'll be pushed to earn enough, even if I work full-time. I think I've got to make some serious cash first and save it all, to keep me going while I study.'

'That's why I'm staying local,' said Sophie. 'Quite apart from looking after Mum, rents around here are almost as bad as London, so at least I won't have *that* expense on top of my student loan. The bus fare into Cattebury will cost a bit, but a lot less than it would to rent a flat.'

'I sometimes wonder if this further education thing is worth it,' said Megan. 'Maybe we'd be better off just getting a job.'

'But who'll employ us without a degree?' said Sophie.

'Miles gave me a chance,' said Ashley.

'Doing cookery,' sneered Zac.

'Shut up, Zac,' they all yelled.

Ashley looked at his phone to check the time. 'Talking of cookery, I need to get going.'

'But I thought this was your day off,' protested Megan.

'It is, but there's something I want to do.'

'Such as?' Megan persisted.

Ashley looked at his friends. 'Promise you won't laugh.'

The three looked at each other and then back at Ash.

'Promise,' they said.

'I'm entering the flower and produce competition. I need to practise my traybakes.'

Zac guffawed. 'Your what!? Traybake? How sad is that?' he whooped.

'Shut up, Zac,' said Megan and Sophie together.

'What are you making?' added Sophie.

'Chocolate fudge and a coconut and lime drizzle.'

'They sound well lush,' said Megan. 'If you want someone to test them…' she added, hopefully.

'You are so talented,' said Sophie.

'Miles says he's a natural,' said Megan.

'Cooking's still a girl's job,' said Zac.

'Don't be such a sexist twat,' said Megan.

Zac coloured at the put-down, but Ashley ignored the jibe; he was more interested in what Megan had said.

'Miles said what?' he asked.

'He says you're a natural. He says you could really make a career as a chef, if the acting doesn't work out. He said he only ever has to tell you what to do once and you just get on with it. And you've got a really light hand with pastry.'

'Oh, puh-lease,' said Zac.

The two girls shot him a filthy look.

'Your dad is hardly a role model for the male sex, is he?' said Megan. 'So I don't think you've got any right to criticise Ashley. And frankly, it's absolutely brilliant having a stepdad who can cook and Mum thinks so too.'

Zac opened his mouth and shut it again and Ashley jogged off back to the council estate, feeling ridiculously chuffed. All of a sudden life was looking pretty good. Of course, there was still the worry of how he was going to afford to live in London, but that was a bridge he'd cross later.

———

'We've made on offer on a place near Edinburgh,' said Elspeth to Laurence, a couple of days later as she came into his snug with some coffee.

Laurence regarded her from his position at the piano. He closed the lid and stood up.

'I won't say I'm not gutted to be losing you but I suppose it gives credence to the old saying about *if you love something you must let it go.*'

'We're not going for a bit. It'll be well into the autumn before we can think about moving.'

'Even so…'

'We'll be here to help with the fête and John will make sure everything is made good after. There's bound to be some clearing up to do – your lawn is going to take a hit.'

'It's only grass; it'll grow again.'

'And do I take it you've got hold of a marquee?'

'One? I've got three.'

'Three – why on earth?'

'One for the flower and produce, one for the tea tent and one as a concert venue for the evening.'

'But…'

Laurence raised his eyebrows. 'But?'

'Have you told the committee? They only wanted one.'

'I'm off to see Heather shortly. I thought I'd give it another hour – don't want to arrive on her doorstep too early. I can't see there's a problem – they're not incurring the extra expense and a little bird told me the tea tent and the flower and produce have usually been humped in together, which isn't satisfactory.'

'And the tent for the concert?'

'Why not? I thought I'd ask Belinda if she'd set up a temporary bar, while the locals chill to some music from yours truly.'

'And she's agreed?'

'I'm sure she will, if she can get cover at the pub for the evening.'

'And if she can't?'

'Then I'll invite people to bring their own drinks – have a picnic. Don't worry, it'll all be fine, trust me.'

———

The next day, Megan's whoops of joy at her grades might have been heard across the county.

'What about you?' she asked Sophie, who was still clutching her envelope.

'I daren't,' said her friend.

'Do you want me to open it?'

Sophie took a deep breath, shook her head and ripped it open; her hand was visibly trembling as she pulled the sheet of paper out. 'Three Bs.' She sagged. 'That'll do me!' She grinned broadly and hugged Megan. 'We've done it. We've only been and gone and done it.'

'No need to ask how you two have done,' said Ashley, joining them. 'You look well pleased.'

'It's the relief,' said Megan. 'How about you?'

'Two Bs and a C. Not that it matters, but I'm quite pleased. Not bad for a council estate kid. Mum's chuffed too, although now she wants me to go to uni, not drama school.'

'But you got into the Euston... I mean, that's the acting equivalent of Oxbridge,' said Sophie. 'Mum was *so* impressed when I told her.'

Ashley shrugged. 'Yeah, well, poncing about on the stage isn't a proper career according to my mum.'

'She'll change her tune when you're a film star.'

Ashley gave Sophie a friendly push. 'Give over,' he said. 'Don't talk daft.' He spotted Zac across the school hall, where the students had gathered after picking up their envelopes. He raised his voice and shouted over the hubbub. 'Zac. Zac!'

Zac pushed his way through the groups of teenagers who were sharing congratulations and commiserations.

'How did you do?' asked Ashley.

'Looks like it's plan B,' said Zac.

'What about clearing?' asked Megan.

'I think even clearing will struggle with a D and two Es.'

Sophie's eyes widened. 'You're joking.'

'Nope.' Zac produced his results and showed them.

'Oh, Zac,' said Megan. 'I don't know what to say. What are you going to do?'

'I'm going to tell my folks a monumental fib, tell them I

got an A and two Bs, say that in order to fund my gap year I need a job, ask my dad to give me an internship so I can get a decent reference and then hit the world of work. Hopefully, by the time they realise I haven't left the country or gone to uni, my results will be a thing of the past and no one will care.'

His three friends exchanged doubtful glances.

'It'll work,' said Zac. Then he added, 'It's got to.'

THIRTY-FOUR

On the Friday, Belinda got a call from the estate agent handling the sale of the pub. As she put down the phone, she knew she needed to pass on the news to Miles as soon as possible. She glanced at her watch. Only ten – it was still a while before he was due in to start lunch service and besides, he'd be busy with the prep then. Better to see him in the peace and quiet of his home. Making up her mind, she let herself out of the side door, trotted the twenty yards or so to the Beeches' and rang the bell. A few seconds later, Bex opened the door, looking frazzled and a crescendo of noise blew out into the garden, like a shaken-up fizzy drink having its cap released. Peace and quiet?

'Belinda, how lovely. What can I do for you?'

'Is Miles around?'

'Sure. Come in, if you can stand the chaos.'

Belinda peered over Bex's shoulder and saw the toy-strewn hall and four small boys throwing Lego bricks at each other.

'Lewis and Alfie had a sleepover last night,' explained Bex. 'It's bedlam.'

Belinda could tell.

'Boys, *boys*,' shouted Bex. '*BOYS!*' She clapped her hands. 'Go and play outside, please. Mummy's got a visitor. Why not play in your den?'

The whooping and shrieking faded as the pack of small boys charged across the hall, through the kitchen and out of the back door.

'I'll get Miles,' said Bex. 'He's upstairs, fixing a shelf. Make yourself at home in the kitchen. The tea in the pot is fresh.'

Belinda wandered into the lovely kitchen, with its range and the boys' pictures Blu-Tacked to the fronts of the units, the plants on the windowsill, the smell of fresh baking. Sitting quietly at the table, oblivious to the recent tsunami of small boys that had swept past, was Emily, rolling out some leftover dough with a miniature rolling pin and looking as if she was making pretend cakes or scones. The dough, rather grey in colour, had obviously been played with for some time.

'Have a biscuit,' lisped Emily.

'Oh, yummy,' said Belinda, taking the proffered lump of sticky pastry and pretending to eat it.

'You mustn't eat it,' said Emily solemnly. 'Mummy says you'll get a poorly tummy.'

Belinda didn't doubt it.

'Morning, Belinda,' said Miles, bouncing into the kitchen with a cordless drill in one hand. 'Tea?' He put the drill down and grabbed some mugs off their hooks.

'Please.'

'What brings you here?'

'We've had an offer on the pub.'

Miles put the mugs down on the table and lowered himself onto a chair. 'Oh.'

'The full asking price.'

'Oh.' He stared at Belinda. 'I can't think why this is a bit of a shock. I mean we put the place on the market, with the aim of selling it. But now it's happening…'

'You having a change of heart?'

'No. It's just that the *end of an era feeling* is stronger than I expected it to be.'

Belinda nodded. 'So I need to find a new home and you need to find somewhere you can carry on feeding the five thousand.'

Miles nodded. 'All of a sudden it's getting urgent.'

'What is?' asked Bex coming into the kitchen. She got the milk out of the fridge and the biscuit tin off the shelf and began to pour the tea.

Belinda told her.

'Oh,' said Bex, as she distributed the mugs. 'So when will the pub change hands?'

'No idea, not yet,' said Belinda. 'But I imagine it'll be sooner rather than later.'

'If you need somewhere to stay, while you look for a new home, you'd be welcome here,' offered Bex. 'I mean, you probably would rather poke pins in your eyes, but we have plenty of space and the guest bedroom does have its own bathroom, so you wouldn't have to share with the kids.' She took the lid off the tin and pushed it into the middle of the table.

'That's very kind.' Belinda felt touched by the offer. The unexpected generosity, coupled with the realisation that Miles was right – it *was* the end of an era – knocked her off balance emotionally. She sipped her tea and helped herself to some home-made shortbread, till she regained control. 'But what about you, Miles?'

'I thought I'd try and get a sort of retro French bistro going… checked tablecloths, set menu, steak frites, moules-frites, onion soup, pâtés, cheeses… cheap and cheerful. Probably only a lunch service to start with, but you get the idea.'

'Love it. I'll patronise it.'

'Just need to find the right place. The trouble is that places rarely come up in Little Woodford.'

'Which is good in a way – no one wants a high street of boarded-up shops.'

'But it's a bugger, when you need somewhere for yourself. And then I'll need planning, for change of use.'

'The council will allow it though, won't they?'

'It's not a given. And, of course, I was rather hoping to take Ashley with me, but that's not going to happen. Not with him being accepted by the drama school.'

'Is this about your plan to start up your own place?' asked Megan, wandering into the kitchen, in her pyjamas. She looked a bit peaky. She'd been out till late, celebrating with friends – 'And why not?' Bex had said.

Miles nodded.

'Well, you might get him for a bit,' said Megan. 'He's talking about taking a gap year to fund his studies.'

'Really?' asked Miles.

'It's what he said a couple of days ago – ask him.'

'And do I gather from Miles that congratulations are in order?' said Belinda.

Megan beamed despite her nagging headache. 'Yes, got what I need for the next step. I can't tell you how relieved I am.'

'I'm so pleased for you.'

'Cheers.' Megan took a biscuit and wandered out of the kitchen again.

'OK,' said Miles. 'That means I've got a plan and so has Ashley, which leaves Jamie. If Ashley doesn't want to work with me, I could ask Jamie. Or he might want to take his chances with the new people. Or he may want to try elsewhere.'

'Oh, he'll be OK,' said Bex. 'When you first mentioned selling the pub, I spoke to Olivia about their staff turnover – mainly to see if there might be a place for you. It seems it's quite high in the kitchens. They train the staff up and then they take their skills and go. Olivia said it was quite flattering to think their staff are so sought after, but also irritating. So, I bet Woodford Priors will give him a place and, if they don't, there's plenty of openings in Cattebury.'

Belinda nodded. 'He's young, he'll get a glowing reference from us and he doesn't have any dependents – I'm sure he'll be fine. And this is supposing the new people don't want to keep him on because, if they've got any sense, they will.'

'Anyway,' said Miles, 'do we know who's made the offer?'

'Not a clue. The agent wasn't giving anything away.'

'Not that it matters – it's just I've got a fondness for the place and I wouldn't want to see it mucked about with.'

'Sadly, once we've let it go, it's a possibility,' said Belinda. 'And we're going to accept… yes?'

'Yes. And cross our fingers the new people don't give it *too* much of a make-over.'

'The locals won't be happy if they do. Can you imagine the reaction of Bert and Harry and the rest?'

And Laurence, thought Belinda. He'd be properly miffed.

'A pint of the usual,' said Laurence, when he came in at lunchtime.

'Morning, Laurence,' said Belinda. 'And a bap, or are you going home for your lunch?'

'I'm going home. I need to make the most of my staff, while I've still got them.'

Belinda looked up from pouring the pint. 'Oh?'

'You mean the bush telegraph hasn't broadcast the news?'

Belinda shook her head and finished the pint. 'No – or should I say, not yet.'

'Elspeth and John are moving back to Edinburgh.'

'But you knew they were going to.'

'They've made an offer on a house.'

'Oh. Three-sixty, please.'

'So it's all a bit urgent now. A bit real.' Laurence handed over the cash.

'I'll tell you what else is also a bit urgent and real,' said Belinda. She cast a glance around the pub to make sure the other occupants were all busy chatting away, but lowered her voice all the same. 'Miles and I have had an offer for this place.'

'No!'

'Sorry, but yes.'

'Who's buying?'

Belinda shrugged. 'No idea.'

'The locals won't like that.'

'They'll get used to it. And I doubt if the new people will do much to change things – if it ain't broke, don't fix it, and all that.'

'Even so.' Laurence hitched himself onto a barstool. 'So what's happening to the staff – Miles and Ashley and the other guy?'

Belinda told him what she knew. 'And talking of plans

and the future,' she added. 'What's this I hear about the fête having three marquees this year?'

'OK,' said Laurence, looking slightly bewildered, 'I was wrong about the bush telegraph – it was too busy broadcasting *that* piece of intelligence to bother with stuff from my personal life. How…?'

'You went to see Heather on Wednesday.'

Laurence now looked completely at sea. 'Yes, but…'

'Amy cleans for Heather on a Wednesday—'

'And Ashley's her son and works here,' finished Laurence. 'My God, if you want to keep a secret, don't live in a small town.'

'I think it's rather endearing,' said Belinda. 'It's because we all care about the place and each other.'

'That's one point of view. The other, of course, is that you're all insatiable nosy parkers.'

'Busted,' said Belinda, with a grin.

'Anyhow, we can talk about the fête and your future when you come over to mine for supper tomorrow.'

'I'm looking forward to it.'

'Good, so am I. And I'll admit to being very surprised the town isn't talking about why you have so many evenings off.'

Bert shuffled up to the bar. 'If you can tear yourself away from lover boy, I'd like a pint of best, please.'

'Of course, Bert. And for your information, Laurence and I are just good friends.'

'Oh yeah. Is that why you're always flitting down to the Reeve House of an evening, 'cos that's what the folks hereabouts are saying. Practically moved in, I've heard.'

Laurence rolled his eyes and shook his head.

THIRTY-FIVE

'Hey, Loz, it's Mylo here.'

'Hi, Mylo. What can I do for you?'

'I got another request for an interview on your side of the pond.'

'Oh, yes. Who and when?'

'Some station called Radio Two.'

'OK,' said Laurence.

'You heard of them?' asked Mylo.

'Certainly have.'

'Any good?'

'Probably the most popular music station in the country.'

'Ain't that nice. Anyway they want you to do an interview. Apparently, you don't have to go to Broadcasting House – wherever that is. They've got a studio near you, you can use.'

'Cool,' said Laurence. 'Let me know the details and I can pitch up. By the way, have you heard any more about *The Graham Norton Show*?'

'They'll start recording in October. They're still thinking about the line-up.'

'Whatever,' said Laurence. 'Let me know if it comes off. And let the BBC have my cell number – easier all round than them having to go through you what with the time difference and everything.'

'Good.'

He rubbed his hands together; an appearance on Radio 2 wasn't to be sniffed at, especially as his album was due to be released in the UK in the autumn. But before that, was the fête and the concert he'd promised for the townsfolk. He was looking forward to it.

───────

Heather, and the ladies of the WI not involved with the flower and produce judging, were completely rushed off their feet in the tea tent. They had expected a good turnout, given the venue, but nothing like this. The grounds and the marquees were packed. It helped that, unusually for August Bank Holiday, the weather was warm and sunny. The crowds might have been less inclined to turn out in wind and rain.

'Thank God for Laurence's generosity in providing a separate marquee,' said Heather, with feeling, as she ferried a tray stacked with dirty cups and plates over to the washing-up station.

Olivia took her hands out of the soapy water, dried them on her pinny, then took the tray of crockery off her friend and dumped it on the trestle table next to her. 'No need to ask how it's going,' she remarked. 'We should be on for record takings.'

'All thanks to Laurence.'

'I know. We are *so* lucky the way things turned out. Despite that woman's best efforts to ruin everything.' Olivia piled another load of dirty cups and saucers into the hot water and began soaping them vigorously.

'Have you seen him yet?' asked Heather.

'Only when he made his speech. I've been in here since. Miranda is coming to take over from me in about ten minutes, so I can have a look around the stalls. Why do you ask?'

'I caught a glimpse of him in the flower and produce tent – looked like he was in his element.'

'Well, he's a showman, isn't he? Being the centre of attention is his natural habitat.'

Heather gestured at their surroundings. 'And what a habitat. It's very tricky not to feel a tiny bit envious.'

Olivia looked at Heather. 'I think we're entitled to be a teeny bit jealous.'

'Maybe,' said Heather. 'I'll console myself with the thought that the heating bills must be phenomenal.'

'I will too.'

'Right,' said Miranda, bustling up, marigolds already on and apron strings tied. 'You get off, Olivia. Go and enjoy yourself for a bit.' She plunged her hands into the water, while Heather went back to the main body of the tent to serve yet more cakes and scones.

Olivia wasn't inclined to loiter over the bookstall or the nearly new or any of the other sales tables, but headed instead for the flower and produce competition. She'd entered a number of categories herself – more in hope than expectation. But the introduction of new categories might have levelled the playing field a little and she hoped her 'garden on a plate', with its miniature water feature might do well. She walked along the yards of trestle tables, looking at who had won the longest bean, the heaviest marrow, the best gladioli, the best traybake… Ashley Pullen? There was a surprise! And he'd taken second place in the overall category, as well. Considering Bex had won last year, and the previous one too, this was a turn-up for the books. *And* Ashley had won the best savoury tart. She'd heard from an incredulous Zac that Ashley was taking his cookery seriously. What a talented lad he was turning out to be.

Part of her wished her son was more like his friend, but at least he was showing an interest in his father's profession. They'd been surprised when Zac had asked if there was anything going, *anything* at all at Nigel's office.

'I'll work hard, I won't disappoint you,' he'd promised. 'Teaboy, dogsbody... you name it. I think I need to get some work experience in – looks good on a CV. And if I do OK, you can pay me so I can fund a bit of a gap-year experience.'

Olivia and Nigel had exchanged puzzled looks, but Nigel had offered Zac a two-week trial and a season ticket to the City. And so far, so good. Maybe he wasn't all bad.

———

Belinda and Laurence were strolling around the flower and produce tent, trying unsuccessfully not to look like a couple.

'Let them gossip,' said Laurence, noticing some of the locals smiling at them. 'It isn't as if it's a secret. Not after what Bert said, the other day.'

'I know but... It just feels all a bit surreal. Me, here, with you...'

'I feel the same,' said Laurence. 'Me, here, with you...'

'Daft bugger,' said Belinda.

Belinda returned her attention to the entries on display. 'Goodness,' she said. 'Will you look here.' She pointed to the red card beside the best savoury tart. 'That's Ashley from the pub,' she said with pride. 'First prize. I am so pleased for him.

I mean, Miles said he's got potential but I thought he was working for the money, not because he really enjoyed it.'

'Well, if he's done this in his spare time, he obviously does enjoy it.'

Just then Ashley bowled up.

'It *is* true,' he said. 'I thought it was a wind-up, when Olivia told me I'd won.'

'Congratulations,' said Belinda. 'But acting's gain is going to be cookery's loss.'

'Not for a year, it isn't,' said Ashley.

'So Miles said. I think you're right to take a gap year and earn some proper money to keep you going. Mind, with your skills you'll easily find a full-time place.'

Laurence butted in. 'Ashley, if I may...?' He grinned at Belinda's protégé. 'We've not met, but I'm Laurence.'

'The tuna bap guy, yes? Mr McLachlan?'

'One and the same. Anyway, as you know, Belinda has sold the pub. I know Miles has offered you a position, when he starts up his bistro, but that may be some months down the line. In the meantime, I am in desperate need of a cook.' He smiled again at Ashley. 'There's a flat that goes with the job. Does it sound like something you might consider?'

Ashley looked shell-shocked. 'Me... cook for you...? Just you?'

'Well, and any visitors I might have.'

'And live here?'

Laurence nodded. 'You don't have to, but it's a bit of an early start if you're going to be here to make my breakfast. You'll get time off during the day, of course and paid holidays. Think about it.'

Dumbly Ashley nodded, as Laurence and Belinda left him to mull the offer over.

'You're full of surprises,' said Belinda. 'Fancy giving Ashley a chance like that.'

'He mightn't like the idea. It can be long hours. But I've got another surprise.'

'Ooh, what is it?'

'You'll have to wait till this evening – I'm going to tell people at the concert; make it public then.'

'You can*not* do that! I'll be trying to guess what it is for the rest of the day. Go on, tell me. I can keep a secret.'

'A secret… in this town? Fat chance.'

THIRTY-SIX

The tea tent was empty, the stalls had packed up and gone, the grass was bruised by hundreds of pairs of feet, the sun was setting behind the house, and the third marquee was now lit by thousands of fairy lights. The sides of the tent had been rolled up so there was an unimpeded view from the surrounding lawns of the low stage and Laurence's grand piano.

'Moving *that* in cost me almost as much as the tent,' Laurence had complained to Belinda.

At the back of the marquee Belinda and a couple of her regular helpers were serving drinks. The pub had been left in the capable hands of Bex who used to work behind the bar, while Megan babysat the children. Megan had laughed at the idea that she might like to go to the concert herself.

'It's old-people music,' she'd said. 'Music to die *to*, not to die *for*.'

Bex thought it best if she didn't tell Belinda or Laurence that.

Dotted on the grass and spaced out in the tent, were

picnic chairs and rugs where people of all ages were enjoying the balmy evening.

At eight sharp, Laurence made his appearance to whistles, whoops and cheers from the crowd. He picked up a mic from the top of the piano.

'Thank you, ladies and gentlemen, thank you very much for coming here tonight and for welcoming me into your wonderful community. I was thrilled when I was asked to host today's fête. I haven't had so much fun in years. And I thought, as a way of repaying the favour, I'd play a few tunes, some of which you might recognise and a few you almost certainly won't, but which I hope you may like anyway. But, before I do that I want to share some news with you…'

He paused and gazed around, his eyes finally coming to rest on Belinda, at the back. 'I know from my short time here, just what an integral part of Little Woodford your pub is; how much the community loves it and values it. So when I heard it was on the market I couldn't bear the thought that it might fall into the hands of strangers who might want to do things like put in slot machines, or a sports TV facility. So I bought it myself and I'm going to put in a management team who will have strict instructions to leave it exactly as it is.'

The last bit of the sentence was drowned out by cheers and applause. Laurence beamed at everyone.

'Well, that seems to have met with approval.' He glanced back to Belinda, who was staring at him with an open mouth. 'I hope that's all OK with you, Belinda?'

Dumbly she nodded.

'That's good,' said Laurence.

'Right, now… back to the music. I recently spent some months in America, where I had a certain amount of free time. I used it to write a new album and this piece I am about to play is a track from it. I hope you like it. It's called *"Belinda".'*

He didn't look at her, as he took his seat on the piano stool and started to play, but half the audience craned round to watch her reaction, as the first haunting, beautiful chords rippled through the still evening air. Belinda looked spellbound. Her two helpers nudged and whispered to each other as she fumbled in her handbag for a tissue. Before, she'd heard it at a private recital – now Laurence was playing it to an audience, and the music assumed even more emotional intensity. It was like a public declaration of his feelings.

When the music died away, there was a momentary silence before the audience burst into applause and Belinda blew her nose vigorously.

'I'm glad you liked that,' said Laurence. 'It's piece I'm really proud of. Now then, here's another new one…'

After an hour and a half, he finished with *"Ninety-nine"* and closed the piano lid, to prolonged applause.

'It's OK for you guys,' said Laurence, 'You've been able to have a drink – it's my turn now,' and with that he jumped off the stage and headed for Belinda's bar.

'Hey, gorgeous,' he said. 'I hope you haven't run out of Rabbit Punch.'

'As if,' said Belinda. 'And thank you,' she added, as she pulled the pump handle.

'What for?'

'For buying the pub, for the music, for everything.'

'Aw… shucks.'

She handed the pint over. 'On the house.'

'So profligate with the profits. That'll have to stop, now I'm in charge!' Laurence grinned.

'You're not yet,' said Belinda. 'We haven't exchanged.'

'Details, details.'

It was gone ten, before the last of the visitors had traipsed up the drive and John could shut the gates.

'And we can leave the rest of the clearing up till tomorrow,' said Laurence. 'I don't know about you, but I'm bushed.'

'It's been a long day,' agreed Belinda. 'But worth it; Heather told me that they made a record amount for local charities, and a couple of the sponsorship companies have already said they' re prepared to forget this year's unfortunate events and help out next year.'

'That's excellent news. Now then… a nightcap? And I mean a proper one, a drink.'

'Why not?'

'Right answer.'

Elspeth met them in the hall. 'Anything else for tonight, Laurence?' she asked.

'No, you get off to bed. Thanks for everything.'

'Och, it was a pleasure. And the locals loved your concert. You might have to do it all again next year.'

Laurence shrugged. 'It was fun.'

'And a young lad called Ashley quizzed me about what it's like to work for you?'

'I hope you said all the right things.'

Elspeth folded her arms. 'Of course. I told him you were a tyrant, that the hours were awful…' She grinned. 'He said he suspected as much.'

'With friends like these…' muttered Laurence.

'I think he's quite keen to take you up on your offer.'

'Good, I just need to find a gardener now, then you and John can scoot off to the frozen north. But that's a problem for tomorrow, I think. Night, Elspeth.'

Laurence led Belinda across to the sofa. 'Brandy?'

'Do you know, that sounds like a great idea.'

'Good.'

Laurence went over to the bar and poured the drinks, while Belinda sat down, slipped off her sandals and shut her eyes.

'Belinda?'

'I was miles away,' she admitted, opening them again. 'What are you doing down there?' Laurence was kneeling by her bare feet.

'Belinda?'

'Yes.'

He offered her a little box. 'I did think about doing this at the concert, but I was afraid you might say *no*.'

'Are you…? Is this…?' Belinda stared at the box.

'Will you marry me?'

'Yes, oh yes. *YES!*'

Laurence took the emerald and diamond ring out of the box and slipped it on her finger. 'You just made an old man very happy.'

Belinda stopped gazing at the beautiful ring and said. 'Maybe later tonight I can make a happy man very old.'

Laurence grinned. 'Go for it!'

———

Six weeks later, Laurence was wearing headphones already plugged into a jack in a tiny BBC studio with a table , a basic office chair and a soundproof door.

'Thank you for coming in, today, Mr Lachlan,' said a female voice in his ears. 'Ken will be coming to you as soon as this next record has finished.'

'That's fine,' said Laurence.

'And if I can just test the levels… what did you have—'

But Laurence was an old hand and interrupted.

'I had an excellent scrambled egg on toast, cooked just the way I like it.'

'Thanks – perfect.' And then the sound of *"Belinda"* came through the cans.

'And that was the beautiful new track from my guest today, Lozza Lachlan,' said the Scottish voice of Ken Bruce. 'Morning, Lozza.'

'Good morning, Ken, thank you for inviting me on your show.'

'My pleasure. And the good news is that that track is riding high in the downloads chart.'

'It's great. I'm thrilled.'

'Now then, a little bird tells me that the lady in question – Belinda – is a real person. In fact, more than that, she's your fiancée.'

'She most certainly is and we're getting married in just a few weeks.'

'Is it true she used to run your local pub?'

'My – you have been doing your research, and the answer is yes, she did.'

'Sounds like it was a bit of a fairy-tale romance.'

'It certainly was – although I am no Prince Charming; far too long in the tooth.'

'Now then, let's talk about your new album – which I am sure you know has been picked as Radio 2's Album of the Week.'

And with that the conversation veered back to real reason for Laurence getting the slot, which was to promote his record.

———

'How did it go?' asked Belinda, when he got back to the Reeve House.

'Yeah, ticked all the boxes, I think.'

'It sounded good. And they played two tracks.'

'Mylo will be pleased,' said Laurence. 'Now then, how about getting a bite of lunch in the pub? I want to check out the new team.'

'Will that be OK with Ashley?'

'I gave him the day off. He's made us a lasagne for supper, which I think we'll be able to heat up without too much problem.'

'I imagine one of us can manage the microwave.'

'Good. Now then, get your coat; it's time we headed for the pub. I had a call from Maxine on the way back from the studio, saying how much she enjoyed the interview. I invited her and Gordon to lunch too.'

'That'll be nice. I haven't seen her for a while.'

'Well, she's a busy lady – teaching, painting, helping with the fête... Not a lady of leisure like you.'

'And I *love* being a lady of leisure. No bottling up, no brewery deliveries first thing in the morning. There's a lot to be said for retirement.'

'I may try it one day.'

'You'd be bored to sobs. You'll still be writing music when the undertakers are trying to measure you up.'

Maxine and Gordon were already at the pub, when Laurence and Belinda arrived.

'This is so weird,' said Belinda, as she crossed the floor to where her friends were sitting.

'What is?' asked Laurence.

'Being a customer.' But she looked around with approval. 'Still, they've been as good as their word and not changed anything.'

'That was a condition of employment,' said Laurence. 'Hi, Max; hi, Gordon,' he said when they reached the table. He kissed Maxine on the cheek and shook Gordon's hand. 'Lovely to see you two again.' He pulled a chair out for Belinda.

'So,' said Maxine after they'd settled themselves and ordered drinks, 'I need to understand why you two fell out and how you got reconciled.'

So Belinda gave her a potted version of the story; the mistyped numbers, the misunderstanding, the too-hasty deletion of details...

Maxine turned to Laurence. 'So why did Elspeth tell me you'd gone to the States because of woman trouble.'

'Woman trouble?' Laurence was perplexed.

'Yes, she said *cherchez la femme*.'

'And you thought she was talking about me?' said Belinda. 'You thought Laurence had flown all that distance to avoid me?'

Maxine coloured. 'Well...'

'The *femme*,' said Laurence, 'was my ex-wife, who was playing dirty over the divorce settlement. I got the chance to recoup some of my losses by playing in Vegas for a few months.'

'So no wonder you were so twitchy, when I asked if you knew what Laurence was up to,' said Belinda. 'Did you think I was some sort of mad stalker?'

Maxine nodded. 'I did wonder, a bit.'

Belinda, seeing the funny side, roared with laughter. 'Just as well fate took a hand and got us back together again.'

'I would have stepped in,' said Max, 'when I heard that tune he wrote for you. Just fancy,' she sighed, 'having someone do something like that for you.'

Gordon looked affronted. 'If you want some sort of

grand gesture from me, you're going to have a very long wait.'

Maxine patted his hand. 'No, it's not your style is it? What was it you said on our wedding anniversary? *"I hope you're not expecting flowers. Why would I buy you something you're going to watch die?"* Changing the subject, have you carried on with your painting, Laurence?'

Laurence raised an eyebrow. 'What do you think? Music I can do – painting I can't. And not even your teaching skills,' and saying this he turned to Belinda, 'and, believe me, they were brilliant, could make me improve from being bottom of the class. No – if I want art, I'll buy it, not try to create it.'

'That's a shame,' said Maxine. 'The first of next year's watercolour courses is scheduled for March. It's still got a couple of vacancies.'

'But you'll fill those, won't you?' asked Belinda.

'The others have been fully booked but I was wondering if you might like first refusal.'

Laurence shook his head.

'I suppose…' said Belinda. 'I mean, now I'm a lady of leisure. You wouldn't mind, Laurence, would you?'

'Why the hell…? You're hardly going to be away for weeks – just a few hours each day. Do it. I had a ball, despite being hopeless.'

'You weren't,' demurred Maxine.

Laurence's eyebrow shot upwards again and he shook his head, again. 'Bless you, Maxine, I love you to bits but you need a reality check… or glasses.'

The group laughed.

'Now then,' said Laurence, 'I think they'll want us to order soon.' He picked up a menu and began to read it. 'I suppose I should be more adventurous than the tuna bap.'

'You certainly should,' said Maxine. 'The food here is awfully good – even now.'

'I'm pleased to hear it,' said Belinda. 'I still feel kind of responsible for this place. I suppose it's like having a kid – even when it's grown up and left home I imagine you still worry about it.'

'It never stops,' admitted Maxine. 'But it does ease off.'

'Then I shall look forward to that day.'

THIRTY-SEVEN

On a dank, dreary day in November, Heather and Brian were enjoying a leisurely breakfast. Heather was reading the local paper and Brian was immersed in the *Times*.

'Oh dear,' he said.

'What is it?' asked Heather looking over the top of the *Cattebury Chronicle*.

'It seems someone else has been diddling local charities out of hard-earned funds.'

'Really?'

'*"Willing volunteer takes charities for thousands"*,' read Brian.

Heather sighed. 'Let me see.'

Brian handed over the paper and Heather scanned the report.

'That is *so* like what happened to us,' she said after a couple of minutes. 'Except it's a different woman.'

'What was your – ahem – treasurer called?'

'Diane Maskell.'

'And this woman is…'

'Deirdre Masters. And she was operating in Somerset, not around here.'

'Don't you think it's a bit of a coincidence she's got the same initials? And as for her location... She can hardly stay in the same place – people would soon wise up to her,' said Brian.

'Maybe,' said Heather. She skim-read the rest of the story. 'Anyway, she's been sent down for four years. *"She exercised a gross breach of trust, and was a cynical criminal who preyed on dozens of local charities up and down the country",*' read Heather. 'Well, not just Somerset, then. And it seems she targeted half a dozen charities at a time.' She looked up at Brian. 'She must have made thousands.'

Brian nodded. 'Some of them almost certainly from you.'

'You could be right. It certainly all adds up. I shan't pray for her. I'm not even sorry she's going to jail,' said Heather defiantly. 'The judge didn't mention any extenuating circumstances so it was probably just greed. I hope her conscience troubles her for the rest of her life.'

Brian looked unconvinced. 'I don't think her sort even have a conscience, so I shall pray that she develops one. I think I'm allowed to do that.'

'Sounds like a plan.'

———

Bex and Miles had worried that early December wasn't the most propitious time to open a new café, but judging by the number of people who turned up for the launch party, they might have got that wrong. Their bistro and wine bar was in a courtyard off a side street near the town hall and their clever decor had given it a truly French pavement café feel; bent cane chairs and tables, jolly umbrellas, checked tablecloths, clever lighting and the likes of Charles Aznavour, Maurice Chevalier or Charles Trenet playing softly in the background. Of course, they admitted later, the presence of the local celeb might have done something to help, but there was no denying the café and the courtyard were rammed to bursting point.

Jamie, who had wanted to stay with Miles and take his chances with the new venture, was busy in the kitchen producing trays and trays of canapés, while Bex and Miles were run off their feet ferrying the food around and keeping glasses topped up. They had thought of bringing the children along for the evening, but when Sophie offered to babysit the three youngest so that Megan could be there, it seemed a no-brainer. Finally, at around nine o'clock, the crowds of friends, well-wishers, the curious, the hangers-on and freeloaders began to drift away, until it was just their inner circle of friends.

'I've got a favour to ask,' said Belinda.

'Ask away,' said Bex, mellowed by wine.

'Laurence and I are getting married just after Christmas. It's not going to be a grand affair, but we'll be inviting our best friends to the register office and back to the Reeve House for a bit of a knees-up after, although the reception will be bigger – lots of locals will be invited to that.'

'Sounds lovely,' said Bex.

'Obviously, you and Miles and the kids are top of our guest list for both bits.'

'Awww… thanks.'

'But would you mind terribly, if we borrowed Jamie for the day to help Ashley out with the food? It'd probably mean shutting the bistro, but we'd pay you compensation.'

'Don't be ridiculous,' said Bex. 'Call it our wedding present to you.'

Belinda gave Bex a lopsided grin. 'We can discuss that nearer the time. But I've got an even bigger favour... I know it's only a register office do and it's not like a church, but I would be SO grateful if you'd lend me Miles for the ceremony – to kind of walk me down the aisle.'

'Of course. I am sure he'd be thrilled. You'll have to ask him yourself – just to make sure – but I think he'd be honoured.'

'Just one other thing... Mylo – Laurence's agent – has got us a deal with *Hello!*'

'Really?' squeaked Bex.

'I know, it's all completely bonkers. Laurence say's it'll be a nine-day wonder. I do hope so – this limelight stuff is all a bit overwhelming.'

'I saw you in the audience on *The Graham Norton Show*.'

Belinda grinned. 'God, that was so much fun. The party in the green room after...' She sighed happily at the memory. 'Anyway, the *Hello!* thing means you might get some spin-off publicity for your bistro.'

'Which won't do any harm.' Bex stood up and gave Belinda a hug. 'That's for being a brilliant friend. Thank you. My turn ask you a favour... can I make the cake?'

———

The day of the wedding was cold, wet and windy but the atmosphere at the reception at the Reeve House, after the short ceremony, couldn't have been warmer.

All the great and the good from Little Woodford were there, along with some of Belinda's staunchest regulars – Bert and Joan, Harry, and Ryan and Amy (who was convinced it was a wind-up so didn't mention her invitation for several days to anyone). The novelty of being 'papped' by the *Hello!* photographer soon wore off for most people – Amy excluded, who tried to photobomb as many shots as she could – and the guests were all rather glad when they finally left.

However, everyone agreed that the bride and groom were impossibly glamorous, the food was a triumph and Ashley and Jamie were toasted for providing a sensational spread, Bex's cake was a masterpiece and the speeches were short and funny.

'It's the best wedding I've been to in a very long while,' announced Heather. 'And, let's face it, as a vicar's wife I've probably been to more than most. In fact,' she added, 'the best wedding, following on from the best fête. I think Laurence McLachlan is a definite asset to Little Woodford. A really good guy.'

Belinda nodded. 'He's one in a hundred. Ninety-nine times better than all the rest.'

If you enjoyed Fates and Fortunes at Little Woodford, then you will LOVE the first in the series, Secrets and Scandals in Little Woodford!

ABOUT THE AUTHOR

CATHERINE JONES lives in Thame, where she is an independent Councillor. She is the author of eighteen novels, including the Soldiers' Wives series, which she wrote under the pseudonym Fiona Field.

Hello from Aria

We hope you enjoyed this book! If you did, let us know, we'd love to hear from you.

We are Aria, a dynamic fiction imprint from award-winning publishers Head of Zeus. At heart, we're committed to publishing fantastic commercial fiction – from romance to sagas to historical fiction. Visit us online and discover a community of like minded fiction fans

You can find us at:

www.ariafiction.com

🐦 @ariafiction

📘 @Aria_Fiction

📷 @ariafiction